Don't Look Back

by

Barbara Anne Machin

Grosvenor House
Publishing Limited

This book is published by
Grosvenor House Publishing Ltd
Link House
140 The Broadway, Tolworth, Surrey, KT6 7HT.
www.grosvenorhousepublishing.co.uk

A CIP record for this book
is available from the British Library

ISBN 978-1-83975-065-6

DEDICATION

I would like to dedicate this book to my sister Rita Ivey Myatt for looking after me so well as a little girl.

INTRODUCTION

Maisie meets a young man at a hospital dance, he was charming and attentive at 22 years old she thought that marriage to Hugh Grainger was all she needed out of life. However, after courting and marrying within six months, she soon knew what the phrase, marry in haste repent at leisure meant. Looking back Maisie realised that she had been in love, with love.

We all experience love and romance in life and sometimes hurt. But for some, it can be a more sinister experience of manipulation and physical abuse, this is a story of a young woman who did unfortunately experience this. Blaming herself and feeling worthless until she was too frightened to speak out. This story depicts such a marriage and how she found the strength to fight back and reclaim her life; good versus evil. Just another twist in the rich tapestry of life we weave, as we move through life.

CHAPTER ONE
THE MEETING

Maisie made her way down the street after work with her friend Dianne, they were excitedly talking about the night out they were both going to have tomorrow, at the local hospital dance. Dianne's brother and sister in law were to give them a lift, he was a junior doctor at the hospital and this was the first time he had got dance tickets for them. So, Dianne and Maisie had decided to do a little shopping on the way home, there was a large department store that stayed open until 8 o'clock and it was only just 5 o'clock so they could have a bite to eat when they got home. They had decided to see if they could find a new outfit. although Maisie's mum had grumbled that you couldn't get into her room now for clothes so why buy more?

'Oh! Mum everyone needs something new now and again, don't be an old grouch.'

Maisie and Dianne went straight to the ladies department, they both looked through the rails of dresses and Maisie came across a dark green silk fitted dress, it moulded to her figure perfectly and the colour suited her too, she had always liked green and she could wear some of her grandmother's emeralds with it. She was quite excited at her find. She set to work to help

Dianne who ended up buying a maroon silk dress, a little like Maisie's but with a cross-over bodice, both Maisie and Dianne were really pleased with their choice of outfit. They stopped for a cup of coffee and when they finished it made their way out arm in arm, excitedly chatting about their coveted finds. Making their way back to the car loaded with the spoils of the trip, Maisie then prepared to drop Dianne off at her home, making arrangements for Dianne and her brother to pick them up at her home the next day, pulling up outside of Dianne's house saying, 'see you tomorrow then Di,' and with a wave of her hand she put her car into gear to make her way home.

Maisie let herself into the hallway calling, 'I'm home mum!'

'There, you are love,' Maisie's mum declared. 'I've saved you some tea, so go and park all them parcels and come and have your tea'.

Maisie realised, yes, she could eat something, but nothing too heavy after traipsing to the shops, she was tired.

'Has Gwen gone out mum?' she asked, a little disappointed that her sister was not in, they were both very close and would help each other to choose their dresses when getting ready to go out. They would also always check each other's clothes and appearance to make sure nothing was creased or that they had no run's in their tights, making sure their appearance was impeccable.

'Yes, she's gone to the pictures with Janice'.

'Okay mum I will just have to show her my purchases tomorrow, because after I have my tea, I think I'll have a shower and have an early night.'

'That's sensible because you will have a late night tomorrow. Now come and have some casserole'

Maisie took off her coat, put her parcels at the bottom of the stairs, and went and washed her hands in the downstairs cloaks. Maisie realised now that she shouldn't skip meals, she was getting hungrier by the minute. The smell of the casserole was wafting through the house, 'Mum you are great I only hope I can live up to you if I ever get married'.

Her mum smiled 'You will love, you will'

After she had finished eating it was almost 9 o'clock.

'Right mum, I'm going up, where's Dad?'

'He's just around next-door, John has got the football match on, it makes sense then if I want, I can watch the telly for an hour myself, football is definitely not my cup of tea. He won't be long before he is back. Maisie love you go on up and have your shower, then if you want you can get into bed'.

'Okay mum I'll see Gwen in the morning,' then quickly giving her mum a kiss she gathered her parcels and made her way upstairs. Going into her bedroom she took her dress out of the bag shook it out and hung it up, that way any creases from being in the bag would come out quickly. After grabbing some clean nightwear, undressing and slipping on a dressing gown she went into the shower she was soon back in her bedroom and snuggling down in bed.

Maisie was almost asleep before her head touched the pillow, she had worked over one or two nights that week, she worked in an accounts office and it was the end of the year and there had been lots of figures and files to be updated, invoices checked and returned to their clients; still she liked the work. Both her and

Dianne had worked there since leaving school and they could easily plan their outings as they saw each other every day.

The next day Maisie was up bright and early putting out her clothes ready for tonight, she just would take a shower before getting ready, she wished that Gwen was coming as well. They very often went out together Dianne and Janice as well. But Dianne's brother had only got two spare tickets. Still they were all going to a musical next week together. Going downstairs in her pale blue dressing gown she sat at the table beside Gwen. Putting some cereal in her dish she excitedly said, 'wait until you see my new dress Gwen, it was in the sale half price'.

'How is it Mum when I want something new, I always have to pay full price, you always do drop on a bargain, you! lucky mare'.

Maisie laughed, 'you shop at the wrong time, when sales are on is the right time'.

Gwen smiled 'I'll come up and have a look after breakfast I'm not doing much today'.

'Good then you can see that I'm turned out correctly.' Maisie said smiling back at Gwen.

'So, I come in handy now and again,' Gwen laughingly replied.

The next day arrived and Dianne, her brother, and his wife picked Maisie up from her home and they were soon excitedly chatting away about the night in front of them.

Dianne and Maisie were soon sitting at a table near to the dance floor. They had just finished their first drink when Maisie offered to replenish their drinks, because they had attended the hospital dance themselves. Apart from having a lift off Dianne's brother, with a promise he would find them when it was time to go home, so they had to go to the bar and fetch their own drinks obviously Dianne's brother and wife wanted a little space to mix with their friends.

'My turn,' Maisie had said with a laugh, standing up to go to the bar. Once served she was returning to the table with two glasses of wine when a young man turned quickly and knocked into her making her spill them all over the floor'

I'm so sorry,' he apologised.' I'll get someone to clean it up and then I'll get you another drink. My name is Hugh, Hugh Grainger and you are? he asked as he smiled at her.

'My Name's Maisie, it was my fault as well I should have been looking where I was going'.

'Not at all Maisie, you just stand here so that no one slips and I'll be back in a moment with someone to clean this mess up, now don't move I will be back,' he said placing his drink on the table the two girls were sitting at, and once more giving her a beguiling smile.

True to his word he was back with a young man who quickly cleaned the spillage up and then dried the place where the drink had spilt with a dry mop so that no one could slip.

'Now Maisie what was it that you and your friend were drinking?'

Maisie looked into his eyes and whispered. 'white wine please'.

'I will be back in two seconds, or more whichever the case maybe,' he smiled down at her holding her green eyes with his dark chocolate brown eyes.

He was so charming and quite good looking. His hair was a dark brown and he had dark chocolate coloured eyes his smile appeared to be just for her. he was of average height and very presentable, she felt drawn to him immediately. When Hugh Grainger came back with the wine he sat down at their table and never left Maisie's side, he danced with both girls but mostly with Maisie. The night came to an end when Hugh asked how they were getting home.

Dianne replied for both of them, 'my brother is here somewhere with his wife, they will be escorting us home.'

'Well in that case Maisie, would you think it presumptuous of me if I asked for your phone number we could perhaps go to the theatre or a film one night if you would be okay with that?'

'I would love to,' she replied scribbling down her phone number. She had an excited feeling inside, she really liked Hugh Grainger and she was really happy that he appeared to like her. As Dianne's brother appeared with his wife, Hugh Grainger stood and said, 'until next week Maisie.'

'Yes,' Maisie replied in a whisper.

As Hugh walked away Dianne said, 'is he a doctor William?'

'I don't think so, I've got a feeling he works in the research department'.

'He seems attracted to Maisie,' Dianne replied.

William just smiled at his younger sister, 'Come on you two let's get you home,' and with that the four of them left to go home. The next day Hugh rang her and asked her to go to see a film and then perhaps they could go for a drink after, Maisie excitedly accepted.

They had been seeing each other for three months when Hugh dropped his bombshell that he was going to work in America, and she was even more astounded when he got down on one knee and proposed to her. But then again after thinking about it, she was not too surprised that he had, because they had shared some very passionate moments when Hugh made it obvious that he wanted to take her to bed, and at one point she was very near to giving in. But her mother's words always came to the fore and stopped her just in time, she thought that she might have put him off by not giving in to him, but it seemed that he was in love with her as she was with him. It was quite wonderful that he would wait he was kind and so attentive, It took all of Maisie's will power to say no. Her mother had always instilled into her and Gwen, no sex before marriage or else he will end up not respecting you.

What she didn't know was this frustrated Hugh, because no one had ever said no to him, smiling to himself he thought of the phrase he charmed the pants of them, this was quite true with any other girl he had propositioned. Yes no one ever said no. Smiling to himself he knew he had to have Maisie and even if it meant marriage, he would have her. He was quite aware he had a huge sexual appetite and would never turn extra sex down. Maisie appeared to be the type of girl who would be faithful and keep house well, besides up until now he had taken his washing to his mum's, so it would be good to have someone to wash and clean for him. After all he would be in a strange country and it would take time to get to know people. To have someone at home to do the washing and ironing would be great, sex on tap for when he didn't have a friend, smirking to himself he never really went short of extra friends with benefits. Maisie's mum tried to convince Maisie it would be better to wait a little longer but Maisie was having none of that.

CHAPTER TWO
THE WEDDING

The girl staring back at her in the mirror didn't look like her, the green eyes that were smiling back at her were large and sparkling full of happiness, in just one hour she would become Mrs Hugh Grainger and she would be on the way to America. Her blond hair had been piled high on her head and a tiara of seed pearls and small yellow roses held her veil in place. At that moment her sister Gwen said, 'Maisie stand up so I can check that your dress and veil are looking straight, now where is your bouquet?'

Gwen began to smooth down the cream lace veil, Maisie had chosen a cream lace and tulle short dress that fell just below the knee and the neckline plunged into a vee at the front with long sleeves. Maisie was not beautiful, however she was very pretty but looked the typical girl next door with a fresh honest look about her.

'Come on slow coach, you can't stay here day dreaming the car will be here soon to take you to the church. You know I'll miss you Maisie.' Gwen said, the two girls hugged, 'are you ready?'

Maisie nodded her head in answer, nothing could spoil her happiness today. When she had met Hugh at the hospital dance, he stayed by her side attentive and interesting. Maisie had hung on to his every word, the next day when he rang her and asked her out that was just six months ago. Soon she would not have to leave him and go back home to her mum and dad's. When they had been together she had wanted to give in to him but she knew she could not disappoint her mum and dad, They had steered them on the right path, but it had been so hard to leave him and go home when all she wanted to do was let him love her.

Then things had moved fast, he had been offered a position in a research department in a large medical centre in New York and had not wanted to go without her. At 22 years of age she was quite certain that all she wanted out of life was to become Mrs Hugh Grainger, she wanted to be held close and made love to, it had taken a lot of willpower on her behalf not to give in to him, now after today she wouldn't have to. Despite her parent's concerns about the short time that she and Hugh had known each other, they had spent time trying to insist that both Hugh and herself needed to give it more time, after all if he went to America, then perhaps after another six months if they still felt the same, he could have flown back to England and they could have married then. At least they would have tested their relationship.

Masie would have none of this, 'no Mum I'm going with him I can't see any reason not to, I love him. Please don't spoil it for me'.

'Of cause not Maisie, we just thought that if you had given it a little more time you would be doubly sure that it is what you want, but you know best love'.

At that moment the door opened, and their dad asked, 'are you two kittens ready now, the cars are here?'

'Yes dad,' they both said together.

The two were so much alike you would quite easily mistake them for twins. Both had blond curly hair and green almond shaped eyes, their dad had always called them his little kittens. Now Maisie would be four hundred miles away and her mother did worry that she had made her mind up so quickly, but you have to let them find out by their own mistakes, hopefully it wouldn't be a mistake. Maisie and Gwen looked a picture, he so loved them both. Maisie in her cream wedding dress and Gwen in her delicate peach tulle dress, the bride's bouquet was in yellow and bronze coloured roses. Gwen had a posy of the same colour, he was proud of his little kittens. He too was a little worried about Maisie, but she seemed sure that this was what she wanted. Looking at Gwen and Maisie they reminded him so much of their mother when he had met her, young and fresh. And he couldn't blame Hugh for wanting to take her with him, he would have been the same, had he been faced with the same thing when he met her.

'Come on you two then, time waits for no one,' and they made their way to the car, their father helped them both in carefully, making sure their dresses did not get caught in the door. He looked at Maisie and realised he was handing her over into Hugh Grainger's care and he felt that he hadn't known Hugh long enough to assess his personality, he hoped with all his heart he would be gentle with his daughter as he himself would not be there to watch over her. His little kittens would at some time flee the nest, he had to get rid of this feeling that it was too soon, he just had this little niggling doubt, still Maisie was of age he had to let go.

The car pulled up outside the church and Maisie, Gwen, and her Dad got out of the car, 'before we go in remember we will always be here if you need us love, don't be scared of asking us for help if you need it, promise me you will ask?'

'I will, but we'll be fine Dad, and we will come back home on holiday to see you all, as soon as we can spare the time I promise'.

The service seemed to pass in a dream. Masie felt as if she was walking on air as the vicar pronounced them man and wife. She couldn't help but keep looking at her hand and admiring the thick gold wedding band that Hugh had slipped onto her finger. The cake had been cut, all the speeches done, photographs taken, it was now time for Maisie to change into her going away outfit. Funny, until now she had not thought about the fact that it would be quite a while before she would see Mum, Dad and Gwen, they had always been there. This thought brought a lump to her throat, she couldn't get upset now, she needed to be strong as she had a whole new life before her. She could not help wishing that they weren't going to America and that she would be here to share her life with her sister, they had always been so close.

Standing there by the car that was to take Hugh and herself to the airport she hugged her mum and dad and Gwen in turn.

'Come back soon my little kitten,' her dad said with a hint of tears in his eyes.

Smiling her answer, she turned and threw her bouquet over her shoulder.

'Why the hell does he call you that?' Hugh asked once the car began to move, 'you're not a baby'.

'I know Hugh it's just his pet name for Gwen and I. Don't be angry Hugh, he will always see us as his little girls', Maisie bit her lip, somehow with that one comment he had spoilt the day for her, she had never heard him criticise her family and it hurt.

'I'm sorry Maisie I didn't mean to upset you but now you are married you will have to grow up, after all it's the start of a new life and I have an important career in front of me'.

'I know Hugh and I will live up to your expectations I promise,' she said smiling into his eyes, 'but they are my family Hugh and I won't see them for a while'.

'They were your family but you answer to me now Maisie, don't forget it'.

Maisie looked at him totally confused, when you get married you still have your family, they were important to everyone's life. She felt that Hugh had just chastised her and she hadn't liked it, still it was her wedding day she would let it lie, he perhaps had not thought of what he had just said. So, Maisie forced a smile on her face and said, 'of course Hugh'.

CHAPTER THREE
THEIR NEW HOME

They arrived in New York around four hours after getting on the plane, Hugh waved a taxi down as he pushed the luggage trolley out of the airport and he quickly gave the driver the address to their new home, crawling through the streets Hugh asked him if he had any addresses for clubs or eating houses in the local area, or any that were accessible by short trips. The taxi driver at once obligingly handed Hugh a handful of cards before stopping outside a large apartment block. Hugh paid the driver who helped him inside with the luggage. Once in Hugh walked over to the porter and gave him his name.

'Welcome to America Mr Grainger,' he said, 'here are your keys. I'll help you on to the lift with your luggage,' he said as he picked up two of the cases and Hugh picked up another two. Turning to Maisie Hugh said, 'come on Maisie, don't just stand there you can manage them two, you're not made of china.'

Maisie was taken aback, Hugh sounded quite sarcastic, they had only been married a few hours. Perhaps he was joking, she thought struggling with the two cases as she picked them up, whilst still hanging on to her vanity case and handbag. Once they got out of the lift and had their cases at the apartment door Maisie breathed a sigh of relief, of course Hugh had not realised that they had been quite heavy.

Maisie looked around her new home. It was an apartment a short ride from the hospital that Hugh would be working at, the curtains to the windows were a deep pink the walls a pale silver grey whilst the floors throughout the apartment were all covered with a slightly darker grey carpet. Modern and uncluttered her mother would have said. There appeared to be no warmth reaching out to her, she was so used to having familiar things around her, her own personal affects, still she could remedy that in time. The apartment itself was spacious, it had three bedrooms, but again the grey and pink dominated them with a grey tiled bathroom and a white suite. It was what her mother would have called a house not a home. And because it was only rented, she would have to make the best of it until they managed to buy something, she hoped they would move back to England she had no Idea how long Hugh was prepared to work here or if it was just a short contract.

'This is excellent,' Hugh enthused, 'great for entertaining'.

His good humour had returned on entering the apartment, his temper was much better than on the flight over. He now had a week off before he was to begin his research work at the hospital.

'So,' he said, 'shall we go out for a meal tonight, Maisie? He asked.

Maisie looked at him, 'would you not prefer to have a shower and relax after the flight? We could unpack and perhaps tomorrow explore the area and find our bearings and go out tomorrow night'.

'If you want,' was his short reply. 'However, we're not in our dotage yet, life is for living we're young yet'.

'Now what have I done?' she thought.

Hugh looked like a spoilt child, Maisie had not seen this side of him before he had always appeared to try to please her. Never mind she would not like to spoil her wedding night. It could be the fact that he was a little stressed about taking up his appointment at the new hospital next week.

'Perhaps you are right Hugh we could go out for a meal if you like'.

'Oh good! Go and put something pretty on, and I'll get changed, we can ask a taxi driver to take us somewhere close'. Hugh had changed in a flash, the long flight had been tiring, and she would have preferred more to have stayed in, and had a romantic night. But if they were only going out to eat then they would soon be back, after all they both needed to give and take.

Changing into a pair of camel coloured slacks and a camel coloured blouse she slipped on a pair of tan coloured flat shoes and placed her matching handbag and a rust coloured cardigan on the chair ready to go. She began to put on her makeup, Maisie never really used a lot of makeup, just cream and lipstick and a spray of perfume and she was ready.

Hugh joined Maisie in the bedroom selecting a pair of black slacks and a white short sleeved shirt and also collecting a black vee necked sweater.

'Are you not going to, put your hair into a chignon, or perhaps a French pleat Maisie?' he suggested glancing at her unruly curls?

'I'm sorry Hugh I thought you liked my hair down?'

'I do. but if you put it up you look more sophisticated and that's the look you need to aim for now if I'm to get anywhere in life my wife must be impeccable'.

'All right it won't take a moment to put it up.' she said with a smile.

She wanted to please him, but Maisie sensed he was different, perhaps she was being too anxious it would be her wedding night tonight and she was already exhausted with the flight from London. She would have really liked to kick her shoes off and relax, but never mind perhaps tomorrow. They probably wouldn't be out too long if she relaxed over her meal, she would be less tired when they got back, she felt a thrill of excitement as she thought of the night ahead. She hoped that she wouldn't disappoint him as she had no experience in the act of love, but she was sure he would coax her to respond.

Making their way to the entrance of the apartments Hugh flagged a taxi down, 'you will enjoy it when we get there Maisie, Rudy's bar and grill please driver,' he instructed.

The music was loud and Maisie felt as if she was falling asleep, the meal in front of her was just too large and Hugh did not seem to notice that jetlag had taken over, she would dearly love to go back to the apartment. However, Hugh seemed to be full of energy, and he seemed to have a huge appetite for drink tonight. He appeared to be talking with all the other couples, he mixed in well, whereas Maisie was so tired and the fact that she was a more reserved person by nature, she was quieter. As the other couples slowly started to disperse and leave, once more they were on their own, he at last looked at his watch, it was quarter past two in the morning '

'I suppose we had better go back,' he said, 'or we won't feel like going anywhere tomorrow,' he said smiling at her.

Hugh was now relishing the night a head, he had waited long enough he thought. 'Now next time we go out Maisie try and get involved in the conversation, because if you don't you will look pretty dumb and uninteresting'.

Maisie was stung by his thoughtless words, why was he acting this way? Surely, he wasn't worried about having sex tonight. If he was, they would be learning together, Maisie smiled at this yes perhaps that was it, all men did not sleep around.

All Maisie wanted to do was sleep, and she now didn't look forward to the rest of the night. Hugh was smiling at her and she was in no doubt what he was thinking. He would want to seal their marriage tonight and she would have to find the energy from somewhere. However, he seemed as if he was being quite judgemental of her. She knew she had to make friends but they were complete strangers and she was after all really tired. It was early days yet, she had lots of time to find and make friends. Getting in the taxi Maisie could not help noticing that Hugh's speech was strange and he was now unsteady on his feet.

Back at their apartment Maisie kicked of her shoes and made to go into the bathroom, when Hugh grabbed her hand and dragged her towards the bedroom, 'please Hugh I need a shower'.

'That can wait, I can't,' he said with a suggestive smile, 'I've waited long enough, I would have had any other women long ago, why I've had to wait so long I don't know'.

Pulling her down beside him he immediately began to pull her clothes off as if he couldn't be bothered to be gentle. and commenced to make love to her, she was half undressed.

'Hugh, you are creasing my clothes,' she objected. 'Please Hugh, you are hurting me,' she protested, as he forced himself inside her making her gasp in pain trying to push him away to make herself more comfortable.

'Lighten up you prude, what do you think I married you for? One more word out of your mouth and you'll get the back of my hand, a prostitute could do better'.

'Please Hugh don't be so rough and stop being so uncouth'.

This only seemed to excite him more, as she gave up, he was far stronger than her so she had to endure his rough lovemaking. Once he had finished with her, he pushed her away, he rolled over saying; 'you better learn to do better than that, or I'll have to show you how it's done. Perhaps I could get someone in to demonstrate, now that would be fun,' he gave an excited laugh. Making himself comfortable on his side he soon began to snore.

Maisie lay looking at the opposite wall, her mum had told her the first time would be the worst and then it would be more enjoyable, she was slightly shocked he had hurt her and had become aggressive. She felt totally abused, but he had drunk far more than she had ever seen him do before, yes that must be the reason for his comments. At once she began to make excuses for his attitude, perhaps tomorrow would be different and perhaps they could talk about it so it didn't happen again. Once he was asleep, she quietly got out of bed and went for a shower, putting here night clothes on she tried to sleep, she could see bruising appearing on her arms where he had forced her to endure his rough behaviour, but the rough way he had taken her kept buzzing around in her head, it definitely had not been how she imagined. He had not been gentle with her, she had never been with a man, but through talking to her friends she had expected him to be gentle and coax her a little until he had taken her virginity. And no way had she expected the harsh comments he had made, in fact thinking back he had been quite crude.

The next week was a whirlwind of getting up in the morning and leaving the apartment, to see all of the sights and landmarks that were well-known. They visited the Empire State building, and also the Rock Observatory. They had lunch of spicy chicken sandwiches at The Commodore. Then in the evening they went on to a jazz club, arriving home in the early hours of the morning. Hugh seemed to have boundless energy, she thought, thank goodness he will be back at work in a couple of days. The thought ran through her mind perhaps she would get a little rest and recharge her batteries, Hugh made love to her every night in a rough fashion, however he no longer hurt her as much. only when he gripped her to hard in the height of what she thought must be his passion.

Perhaps I'm a little too held back, she thought, I must try harder to please him. However, she was not sure she liked some of the things he said in the act of love. These words he said seemed to excite him. He would dig his *fingers* into her and if she complained he would laugh and call her a whinging baby.

'I would do better having a prostitute, at least they know what to do'.

Maisie was now aware that Hugh had a different side to him, as well as the one he had shown her when she met him. She tried hard to understand and thought it was herself that was lacking because she had no experience in sex. She vowed she would try harder. But how would she know what to do if he didn't coax her and be gentle? Surely, he could explain gently so that she could try, it became that she hated bedtime coming around and more often than not it was more than once, more any time the fancy took him and if she said anything, he became abusive and aggressive. Will I ever get used to this life? The disappointment she felt in the bedroom only made her worry how she could make it more enjoyable for Hugh, what was it that she needed to do to improve what she did for Hugh. Maisie was completely at a loss.

If Maisie was under the impression that Hugh would be too tired to go out when he went back to work, she had got it completely wrong, his enthusiasm for enjoying himself, drinking and late nights seemed to give him energy. All Maisie wanted to do was to settle down into a more orderly pattern to life, she was sure her mum and dad had never acted this way at any time in their life, Hugh seemed to live on one huge merry go round. And what surprised her was he still had a huge sexual appetite. Maisie noticed that it didn't matter what she tried, he never seemed satisfied unless he criticized her and was quite spiteful, he always seemed to mark her arms as if he wanted to hurt her. She wished that she could get the same enjoyment out of there sex life as he did, Hugh seemed as if he enjoyed being rough, Maisie longed for romantic encounters and Hugh left her feeling as if something was missing, something that she could not put her finger on, but perhaps it was all in her imagination. Maisie knew that having sex was part of being a good wife, but she couldn't help but think that a good husband should show a little consideration and make her feel that it was because he loved her, not because he thought he owned her.

Maisie also wanted to ask about housekeeping money until she found a job and then she could contribute to their life while she could, who knows they could have children. When she did ask Hugh, his answer was, 'there's no need, we can shop together and I'll pay with my card. You have a little money in your account don't you Maisie to pay for your clothes and any little things you need through the day, after all we'll be eating out most nights?

'We will?' she answered raising her eyebrows. 'But Hugh will we be able to afford to, I know I have some savings of my own, but I thought we could work a budget out to add to the ten thousand pounds that Dad and Mum gave me to start our house fund'.

'Yes of course we will, but there will be plenty of time to start that Maisie we have only just got married we need to have some fun first, 'he answered, and that money he thought will soon have to be put into my account why should you sit on that.

'But Hugh...', she started to say, when he broke in with a scowl on his face.

'For god's sake shut up whining I said. No buts! Maisie we are young yet,' he said with his scowling face close to hers, and suddenly with that he changed and a little of the Hugh from two weeks ago came back as he reached for her and held her close, 'trust me sweetheart I know best' and he began to kiss her face and neck, Maisie responded to his lovemaking pressing her body to his.

She had missed the feeling of being close over the last week and rebuked herself in her mind for having any doubts. Taking her hand, he guided her to the bedroom this time he was more loving. Maisie thought once more they could climb Mount Everest as long as they had each other. It had felt more enjoyable this time, there had been no rough pushing and forcing, he hadn't been as uncouth as he had on previous occasions, perhaps this is how it should be, why did he have these bouts of aggression, when he, knew how to act. Still when he showed his aggressive side she was learning not to answer back.

When they came back into the lounge, he said,' yes, we will have to talk soon. I'm sure your father meant you to give me the money he passed over, so that I would take care of it until we buy a house. But there's plenty of time'.

Maisie tried to turn the conversation to her advantage, 'I can leave that where it is and get a job and we can then open a joint account and both put the same in to pay for the deposit and you could work out what to give me for housekeeping'.

Hugh suddenly scowled, 'I decide what we are going to do, he growled. I need you here to wash and clean up and the rest of the time be on your back, you do what I say. Understand?' Once more he pushed his face into hers, at the same time grabbing a handful of her hair whilst gripping her throat, 'Understand?'

Not letting go until she whispered, 'yes Hugh'.

The next couple of weeks passed in the same way. Maisie trying to pin him down to the important conversation of managing a budget, his body language would suddenly change and she would feel threatened, this would be followed with little spats and disagreements and then his attitude would change in a flash, this was when Hugh would show his strong side, and press on with, This is what we will do because I say so'.

All though Maisie could not stop worrying about the money he was spending and what he was spending it on, life could not just be about going out and enjoying yourself. Besides to her, they were married and their conversations on decision-making should be, a two-way street, and then their problems could be sorted jointly.

Chapter Four
Returning to Work

When Hugh had returned to work, he had reported to the large hospital twenty minutes away from his apartment, despite being a little weary after the late night of the day before. He managed to take in who was who and what research he would be working on. The day passed quickly, having been introduced to all his new colleagues, and taking lunch with the group. Amongst the group was a girl who appeared to be very sophisticated, her long dark hair fell below her shoulders, it was obvious to him she was attracted to him, and at once began to flirt with him. Hugh had always been a good mixer and he was quite charming when he wanted to be. He certainly was not going to pass on this one. But on the other side of the coin was the fact that he had always wanted his own way, however he fitted in quite well. He soon settled into his new position despite still wanting to go out every night. Maisie was still more than a little worried about the amount of money they were spending on going out. As the weeks went by, Hugh began to get closer to the girl with dark hair. Her name was Jodie, and he was aware that he would at the right time be having an illicit affair with her, the prospect of which was quite exciting him. And he was relishing the thought of it, she knew he was married but he could tell she was well up for it, so soon he would be doing what he found exciting, two women, one who would clean and cook and the other to excite him. Maisie was okay when there was no one else between the sheets, but he needed a little more than that, he needed a no holds barred and he could tell that Jodie would be up for any type of sex. Maisie would not try any of the rough sex that he liked; he was getting bored, even when he hurt her it was not exciting him in the way he wanted.

A month passed and Maisie had to broach the subject with Hugh of money, especially as he had asked her that morning if she could slip and pay the month's rent on the flat, the company had found the flat for them however the rent was up to them.

'Yes of course I can, are you giving me cash or a cheque.' she asked?

'Well if you pay with your card, I'll transfer it to your account,' he answered, giving her one of his engaging smiles which she did not see very often these days, 'perhaps we can stay in for tonight, pick something up from the deli and a bottle of wine'.

'Wait,' Maisie said. 'How much will the rent be?'

Two thousand dollars sweet,' he said and quickly gave her a kiss as he went through the door.

Maisie stood and quickly did a mental sum with the exchange rate, that was roughly a thousand pounds, she had got more than enough in her current account, but it would leave a hole in what was there. Never mind Hugh had said he would transfer the money back. Going to her vanity case she took out her cheque book and looked at the stub running total, knowing that she was moving to America she had left her money in her account so that she had enough to manage on until she had got herself a job or arranged housekeeping money with Hugh. She had thought she might have to pay the accounts but with money that Hugh would give her, as she was not working and Hugh was. Still he had said he would transfer it back and she had no reason not to believe him.

Taking out her other papers she looked at what she had got, as well as the money her mum and dad had given her along with money that had been given as wedding presents , she had a saving bond that her grandfather on mother's side had placed in for her fourteenth birthday which had been in for seven years now and had accumulated to £5,316, her dad's parents had died and had left a third of their estate that she had placed in a building society and there was thirty thousand in that so all together she had a good £45,000, plus any interest to go in and her mum and dad had always impressed on her to save a little for a rainy day ,so she also had a little in an ISA account and a small amount in a building society that she had opened herself. When they did buy a house, she wanted to be able to pay cash for her furniture and still keep some back for emergency's that might crop up. Maisie desperately wanted to see them start budgeting for their life together. Spending money without accounting for it, you couldn't possibly know how much you had. So, she intended not to break into these accounts. And for some reason would not give into his suggestion of putting her money in his hands.

The ISA and building society book held another £8,000 this was where she had planned to put any money she could save from her housekeeping if she ever got it sorted, still she was sure with a little persuasion and a little talk at the right time they could sort it, and if she got a job it would soon mount up if they saved her salary. If Maisie had a job, she was more than willing to contribute to their life. As it was, the only time she went out of the apartment was at night time and the most of that time Hugh spent talking to other women, so she just seemed to make the numbers up. It would be good if she did get a little job. Hugh might find her a little more interesting if she had some little antidotes to relate that had happened at work or they had talked about as friends. She hadn't realised how she missed real people's company, people that would go out once or twice a week who were married the same as them, not women who flocked around Hugh when they were out.

Feeling a little better she placed her cheque book and her card in her bag, dressing in a white short sleeved blouse and a pair of white jeans, a short navy jacked and navy pumps. She had brushed her blond curls into submission and applied a little lipstick. She was unaware how attractive she looked fresh and pretty. And didn't notice the admiring looks that people gave her.

Once she was satisfied with her appearance she had made her way down to the reception desk and asked to settle up the first month's rent, on an impulse she paid another two months in advance that would help and Hugh could transfer it to her each month and they would not have to run down there every five minutes to pay it. Deciding that she would take a taxi to the nearest supermarket she decided she would stock the fridge with food, and purchase a couple of bottles of wine, perhaps he would enjoy tonight enough to stay in a little more. Strolling first along the road to do a little window shopping it made a change from staying in through the day on her own. She needed to get a job not just for the money but for her own sanity.

Once she arrived at the supermarket she walked around and obtained a couple of fillet steak's, salad, crusty bread, fresh fruit and some cheese biscuits, and cheese, along with two good bottles of wine. She also bought some fresh Danish pastries for breakfast. Because her shopping was a little heavy, she decided again to take a yellow cab back to the apartments. She made a mental note to stock up and then she would not have the expense of taking a cab that was money she could save.

Hugh came home around 6.30, he seemed a lot quieter, he must be tired. She had already set the table and prepared the salad she had the cheese board with biscuits and grapes ready for afters.

'I'll put the steaks under Hugh. just relax for a few minutes.

'I'll have a glass of wine while I'm waiting'.

'Red or white,' Maisie asked?

'Red,' he replied.

Picking up a glass she filled it with red wine, she then busied herself with getting his steak just right. Glancing at him as she worked on their meal, he looked deep in thought, placing his food in front of him, she sat down opposite him, noticing that he had poured himself another large glass of wine.

Once sitting at the table, she asked, 'is it cooked how you like it?'

'Fine,' he answered quietly.

His mood had changed since this morning, perhaps he was tired, so she decided now was not the time to bring up a plan for their finances. She decided to shelve the conversation until he was not so tired. Maisie realised that once more she was taking the easy way out and that was because she wanted to avoid one of his aggressive moods.

'I was thinking I would look at getting a job Hugh, it would give me something to do in the day'.

'You have a job I've told you, so shut up,' he said in a menacing way.

Maisie backed off at once.

But it was a conversation she still needed to have, someone had to take control of making sure they knew where they were with their money. Maisie did not like having to wait to talk about money with him but he perhaps was still coming to grips with his new employment. She realised she was making excuses for him, but it always seemed the easier way out. And if she went to work it would be far easier.

After they had watched the television for a short while, he decided they may as well go to bed so he would be fresh in the morning. After she showered, returning to the bedroom she came back to find that Hugh was fast asleep, but what Maisie was not aware of was that Hugh had come home after having sex with Jodie in her car. They had driven on to a quiet car park and he would have enjoyed longer so he was trying to work out how he could manage it. But unlike Hugh, Maisie lay awake her mind going over the day. At no point in their short courtship had she realised how complex he was, they had only been married for six short weeks and he seemed to change his personality on a daily basis. She knew it was very stressful to start a new job, never mind change his home and country, however they were a partnership they needed to share their thoughts and feelings to make their life a success and she needed him to start being kind. She could not understand why he had changed. And of course, everyone had success and failures, surely it would help discussing them with each other. Maisie still worried about how he was settling in at work and still didn't like to probe too much. It was a good job that she wasn't a wife who on an impulse would go and meet her husband from work as a surprise, or it would have been her that would have been surprised.

CHAPTER FIVE
SIX MONTHS LATER

Hugh and Maisie had now been married for seven and a half months, Maisie tried to analyse what was wrong, she felt as if she needed to find a job but every time she had broached the subject with Hugh he had said you have plenty of time, I prefer you to stay at home and take care of me and the apartment, what he really meant he did not want her to be out and about and see him lunching with Jodie; she liked the expensive eating places even for lunch. Hugh wanted Masie where he knew where she was, that way there would be no complications.

Saying I'll see you tonight, he left for work. He could by just a look or shouting keep her under control, but she wasn't giving into his demands to put her money into his account, he found himself stumbling from one payday to another, never having much left over. He needed that money at the moment he was trying hard not to be so aggressive once he lost his temper, he wasn't in control of himself. He felt he might cajole her into coughing it up.

Maisie was still worried about money, for seven months she had paid most of the rent on the apartment. Hugh had only transferred two months money. Hugh had already gone to work so picking up the paper she began to read through it until she came to the situations vacant, there was lots of positions for personal aids and PA's, really that was just being a secretary and that was her job in England. Looking at the phone number she decided to ring to see if she could get an interview, it was at a large department store, Hugh would just have to get used to the idea of her being back at work. She didn't want to run her savings down anymore, and the feeling that she hadn't a life persisted to frustrate her. Picking the phone up she rang the number and was greeted by a friendly voice, so telling the young lady what she was ringing about and, once she had finished was rewarded with. 'Just let me have a word, to see that the position hasn't been filled yet, the last day for an interview is tomorrow so I think you might be in luck'.

'I will just list your qualifications', once the young lady on the phone had written down the details and checked them back with Maisie, she said 'just hold the line I'll find out if It's been filled'. Coming back to the telephone she said you're in luck we can fit you in'.

After what seemed a life time the young lady was back on the line saying, 'can you make 12.30 today?'

'Yes of course I can'.

'And you have your certificates to bring with you?'

'Yes, I do'.

'That's great, make sure you are on time, he hates people being late'.

'I'll make sure I am there on time,' scribbling down the address, she knew she had plenty of time to get ready. She would get a yellow cab. Looking around the grey kitchen, she realised she had time to clear the dishes and then go for a quick shower anything else she needed to do she could do when she got back. Choosing a navy suit and a white blouse, a navy bag and court shoes, Masie then went for her shower, once she had completed getting herself ready, she stood in front of the mirror checking her appearance. She couldn't help wishing that Gwen was with her, she would have checked her appearance with a fine toothcomb until she was immaculate, this had been a habit over the years as teenagers how she missed Gwen, and come to think of it her mum and dad as well. She really needed to ring them more often, but it seemed to irritate Hugh, he would say for goodness sake can't you stop worrying about phone calls we have a life here, and he would again press home that she was no longer a child. Very often he would grip her arms digging into the flesh as he made his statements, leaving the flesh on her arms bruised, but then he would say them magic words, 'I'm sorry sweetheart and that meant he wanted something, because she had come to realise he didn't have a conscience, I didn't mean that. But the look on his face belied his regret.

For some reason Maisie began to get the impression that it excited him to hurt her, whether it was mentally or physical. Then she would silently reprove herself for being critical, perhaps if she tried a little harder to please him. The way he made love to her definitely did not excite her, perhaps if she could show a little excitement, he might act better, but how could you if she couldn't enjoy what he was doing to her? Every woman wants to be made to feel special, what Hugh was doing was just one sided. Never mind, if she could get this job it would perhaps make a difference, she would relax more if she was earning some money and perhaps, she could save a little. He hadn't made so many demands on her body quite as much just lately, so perhaps he was worrying about money as well. She had not thought about it before that when he became so aggressive at times it could be because he was worrying about money too.

Hugh was working later these days, he said they had an awful lot of work to do on the research programme, so not to get any tea for him as he would grab something to eat in the Bistro at the hospital. Maisie was getting a little bored of staying in on her own, she hoped he would not be late tonight. Just for once she had a positive feeling. She needed to start this conversation sooner or later and the rate he was going it would be never. So, she had every intention of bringing it up tonight. She would just have to stand up to him if he got abusive.

Taking a cab to the department store she realised it was not far away. If she did get the position, she would easily be able to walk there and back. Walking into the entrance she made her way to the desk as she had been advised to by the lady on the phone.

'Oh yes, you are the 12.30 Mrs Grainger. I'll take you to Mr Johnson's secretary and when they are ready for you Mrs Grainger, they will call you in'.

The time between her arriving and being called in for her interview was short. After being called in it seemed to have gone very quickly, afterwards she was asked to wait outside and have a coffee.

Although to Maisie, the interview itself seemed to have gone quickly she was very surprised when she realised that it had taken just over one hour and a quarter, and that was quite a long interview a good sign. She sat waiting in reception because they had said they would be able to give her a decision to save wasting any time. As she sat there waiting, they called in another young lady who had arrived after her. The other young lady's interview only lasted around, thirty minutes. As Maisie sat sipping a coffee that the friendly receptionist had brought to her, she had a really positive feeling, however the other young lady was not asked to wait. Dare she hope that she had a chance? She hoped so as they all seemed to be so nice. She refused to think in her mind that Hugh would be angry with her, she would have to cross that bridge when she came to it.

Maisie was called back in and spent a further thirty minutes answering a few more questions, after being asked to wait outside a little longer she was called back in and offered the position, spending another thirty minutes talking terms she was over the moon, the salary was $7,500 dollars a month after paying state taxes and making allowances for transport if she wanted to take a taxi home, she would have around $5,750 dollars left. She could pay the rent if she had to and still save a little to put back what she had spent. Mr Johnson to whom she would be PA shook her hand and said welcome aboard. He was an older man with a grey hair and kind eyes,

'Thank you,' Maisie answered with a huge smile. 'I won't let you down'.

She was to start work the following Monday eight thirty until five. This would give her plenty of time to get Hugh's tea, although he was working later and later just lately, so she would always be in before him.

Walking around the shops and picking up a couple of bottles of wine, she decided to walk back. Humming a little tune to herself, she realised she would actually be working in one week's time, perhaps now she wouldn't be so bored. Surely, he would be pleased at that, she would try and make tonight special. Yes! She felt quite positive about the future now, a nice meal and he loved his wine with a meal, he would then perhaps be mellow enough to talk budgets. Maisie walked along feeling as if she was walking on air, if only he would listen to her they would soon have everything sorted to their advantage and they could save enough to either buy a house here or back home. Maisie realised that she had married him knowing that he was going to America to work, so she might find that he would want to continue to live and work here, but she could not help hoping that he might at some time want to return home. Maisie dared not tell Hugh how much she missed her family, she needed at some time to try and get him to think of a trip home to see his mum and dad as well as her family. But she would have to tread very carefully to do that.

Taking off her suit when she returned to the apartment she then set too and did her housework. once this was done, she prepared some salad, she could make an omelette with it if Hugh came home a little early, but around seven thirty the phone rang it was Hugh. '

I'll be quite late tonight Maisie so don't wait up for me I'll get something to eat here'.

Hearing a women snigger, she asked. Is there someone with you Hugh I thought I heard a giggle?'

'It's only Jodie she is laughing at John, he's working late too he's quite a joker. I'll see you later,' he said.

Maisie spent the rest of the night watching television, disappointed that Hugh had not come home and when she got fed up with her own company, she retired to bed early. Just when she felt strong enough to bring up the conversation of budget's and her going back to work. Hugh now was working late and they wouldn't be able to have a much needed, conversation, once again it would have to be shelved. Maisie's brain was overactive, she had planned in her mind how she would approach the conversation and here she was once more unable to approach it.

Waking early in the morning, she realised that Hugh had not come to bed, so making her way to the lounge she found he was asleep on the settee. Going to the kitchen she went and put the coffee on, she would wake him when it was made and then he could go for a shower while she got his breakfast. He must be dog tired she thought, it was too bad of them expecting him to keep working late every night. Carrying the coffee mugs in she gently shook him.

'Why did you not come to bed,' she asked him?

'I didn't want to disturb you it was so late'.

'I wouldn't have minded Hugh, you would have been more comfortable. And you've spent the night in your clothes, here drink this coffee and then you can have a shower and we can talk over breakfast, as she bent over him to give him his coffee, she realised he smelt heavily of drink. A little later after he had showered and got dressed they were sitting at the breakfast bar having their breakfast, Maisie racked her brain on how to start, her mind was going around in circles however reluctant she was to upset him she realised she needed to have this conversation, and there was no time like the present. She thought of her mother's old saying don't put off until tomorrow what you can do today. Plucking up some courage and gulping she watched him place his cup down it was now or never.

Looking at him she just blurted out. 'Hugh, I need to tell you something,' for a brief second Hugh's face changed, however relief seemed to show as she continued talking, 'I went and got a job yesterday'.

His reaction was not what she had expected.

'That's good,' he said, 'now I will be able to save some money if you continue to pay the rent, and going out to work you won't be so lonely on your own while I'm working late'.

'I suppose I can continue paying the rent, but we need to talk budget's so that we have an Idea how much we need of our combined salary each month and what we can save jointly, and how long do you think this extra work will last for? I see next to nothing of you just lately'.

'I know you miss me Maisie, but this could be the making of us'. Standing up he gave her a small smile and reached for her hand and led her to the bedroom 'I have five minutes then I can take another shower,' he said and pulled her on to the bed'.

After making love to her he went to the shower and Maisie could hear him singing to himself. Once again it had been better, he had been more careful and loving, which he rarely was, but now Maisie had learnt not to take him for granted, he could change so quickly what you saw was not always what you got.

If only she could have read his mind, he needed to keep her sweet for a little longer, for one awful moment he had thought she was going to tell him she was pregnant, and that would not fit in with his and Jodie's plans, the fact that she wasn't had made him more amenable. After eating his breakfast, he kissed her on the cheek and said, 'don't wait up for me I'm not sure how late I will be tonight as well, but we can perhaps make up for it in the morning'.

With a smug look on his face he quickly made his way out of the apartment, this was getting better still, he thought, Maisie could pay the rest of the utility bills when they came in, his could be for fun. As long as he kept her satisfied in the bedroom, perhaps she would stop moaning about budgets. Granted he had not wanted her to go to work but he hadn't realised his money would not go far, eating out was costing quite a lot and he always paid, he knew sooner or later Jodie would have to pay a little, but at the moment he was making himself indispensable. That way he could manipulate her into being his meal ticket much like Maisie was at the moment.

CHAPTER SIX
JODIE

Hugh left the apartment and walked the short distance to the next block, he approached a car, sitting in it was the young woman who resembled Cleopatra, with her dark almond shaped eyes and long dark hair. Her dark hair was cut straight and hung below her shoulders with a full fringe, she was very striking and had started an affair with Hugh almost as soon as he started to work at the hospital. It was with her that he was spending his evening's when he was supposed to be working late. He had always had an eye for the ladies and Jodie had a huge appetite for sex and that suited Hugh, he liked going out and having fun. The short while he had courted Maisie and they had gone out together if he had raised the subject of sex, she would have none of it. He had been intrigued because none of his former girlfriends had said no to him. Because the only time's he had tried to get around sex she had steered him right away from the conversation and he had always been one who wanted what he couldn't have. Also, she became more attractive when he realised, she had a little money, and he was finding that he spent his salary almost as soon as he got it. Hence why he was reluctant to pay money into Maisie's bank for the rent and he knew because he had gone through her vanity case and seen the books one day when she was in the shower. He had known about the £10,000 her dad had given her he had been looking for ready cash thinking she might have some in one of her bags. At the moment Jodie was more exciting than Maisie.

Leaning over and kissing Jodie full on the lips, 'it's a pity we have to go to work he said'.

'We are not far from my flat we can spare half an hour,' she said feeling the crotch of his trousers.

'What are you waiting for?' he asked as leaned over and kissed her, pushing her lips apart to let his tongue tease her.

Later after making love they showered ready to go to work, 'they will never notice that we are late, besides it will only be 15 minutes,' she said as they both showered.

'No time for any more,' he laughed, 'we will continue tonight, after we come from the jazz club'.

'Make sure you do,' she commented. 'I don't intend to go short'.

'It's Maisie that will have to do that. You're not still sleeping with her, are you?' she asked. 'Of course! I'm not, who would want Maisie when they have you'.

'Good make sure you keep it that way,' she answered. 'We better get going or we will be in trouble and a great deal later than fifteen minutes, come on,' Hugh said as his hands once more ran over her curvy figure.

As Maisie was preparing for work a week later Hugh said, 'I'm sorry love I will be working late again tonight'.

'But Hugh you have hardly spent a night in for week's'.

'I know, but I promise you it will be over soon when we come to the end of the project. Then I can have a week's holiday and we can stay in bed all day,' he said with a smile.

'And you go out much earlier than when you first started at the hospital'.

'Please stop moaning Maisie, it's hardly fair that I have to go work worrying about you is it' he sounded irritated.' I'll see you later, don't wait up for me'.

Don't wait up for me, that phrase had burnt itself into her brain. Would her married life ever be like her mum and dad's? No, she knew the answer without having to think about it, it looked as if this was destined to be her life.

Maisie settled into her working life, the months flew by, she was enjoying her job and had made friends, they kept asking her to go on a girlies night out but she always said no because if Hugh came home early she wanted to be there when he arrived home to make him some food, it was wishful thinking however she longed for the closeness they had before they were married. Somehow, she knew in her heart she would never recapture that feeling. She wanted to experience that, white hot feeling they talked about in books, when your loved one touched your skin. Perhaps that was it, and it only happened in books, but she knew it didn't, remembering the looks her dad would give her mum, the quick hugs and smiles, yes, she knew her mum and dad's marriage was quite different.

Plating some salad and making herself an omelette she settled down to watch the television. What have I done wrong, she silently asked herself? Maisie thought that marrying Hugh would have been the start of a new life, but instead she could only describe her life as different. When she had been at home yes, she had gone to work and she had gone out at the weekends, but everything in moderation. There had been nights of enjoyment, nights of rest to recharge your batteries, and family time, that had been a good mix. Maisie's life was now work and home, she was beginning to feel a bit fed up, why had Hugh to work late so much? It didn't seem fair or natural, how had he got the stamina for so much work.

Getting ready for bed Maisie felt no better, in fact she felt a little sick it must have been the omelette, she had been having omelettes most nights she would have to start varying her diet more. She felt more tired than usual, in fact she could not stay awake and was soon sound asleep.

Both Maisie and Hugh were quiet the next morning whilst getting ready for work until Hugh said, 'I'm going now'.

'I know,' she said, 'don't wait up for me'.

'No, I was going to say I'll be back for tea tonight so make sure you bring something home with you'.

Maisie did not know if she should cry or laugh, he would be home for tea, the first time in months. She wondered if he realised it would be their wedding anniversary in a couple of weeks. She had been toying with the idea of asking him if they could go home for visit. But even as the thought crossed her mind, she knew it would be met with aggressive comments, so she chose not to bring it up. Maisie just needed that reassurance she knew she would get off her mum and dad. She knew if she rang them that perhaps she would break down and no way did she want her mum and dad to worry about her. This had been her choice, her mum and dad had tried to counsel her to take her time, but she had been to strong headed.

As Hugh left to meet Jodie a couple of blocks away, he thought tonight and tomorrow he would be home for tea, and that would buy him a little time. Jodie was going to a wedding near her parent's home, and she had been pushing Hugh to tell Maisie about her and that he was leaving her because their marriage wasn't working. He could have done with a little more time, he was toying with the idea of trying to prise some of Maisie's money out of her again, he was now aware she had more money than the £10,000 that her dad had given her, now if he could get control of all or some of her money he would have a little more collateral to move in with Jodie. He now had to work out how to obtain it, this was the one area that however he tried to bully her or threaten she was determined to hang on to her money. He had a couple of days before Jodie came back, he could perhaps think of some way to manipulate Maisie.

Although he would have liked to carry on as he was, he found that Jodie was more exciting and unpredictable. And that she would not be the mistress for too long, quite obviously she didn't like playing second fiddle, however Hugh didn't seem to realise that the only one playing second fiddle was Maisie, even though she didn't know it. He liked juggling the two women, he knew that if he showed his cruel streak to Jodie, she would not tolerate it, she didn't mind the rough sex however, that excited them both. So, he got his other kicks out of hurting Maisie, then acting as if he was sorry and hadn't meant to hurt her. He liked to see her struggling to make excuses for what he had done, knowing that he was getting away with it and the more he did it the more it gave him a rush of power, he controlled her and it made him feel good. Yes, he thought it was time he spiced his sex with Maisie up a little, she wasn't someone who was adventures when making love, compared to Jodie she was a waste of space. Still while Jodie was away, she would have to do.

When Maisie got to work, she suddenly felt sick, going down to the toilets she went into a cubicle and was sick. I hope I'm not sickening for something I could do with enjoying my night with Hugh tonight and make him see what he is missing by working all the time. They both needed to sit down and have a good talk she was sick of telling her family that he wasn't in whenever they called and explaining that he was working on an important project, As the day wore on, she felt a little better, still tired but not as sick. At lunchtime she made sure she had something more substantial than salad she even fancied some chocolate, something that she would not very often eat. As she made her way home Maisie made sure she purchased everything she needed to prepare a nice supper for herself and Hugh. After she purchased some lamb steaks, new potatoes, and fresh garden peas, crab for the starter, and some lemon lush pie, she made her way to the off licence and purchased three bottles of wine, and for some reason she picked up some chocolate that was at the point of sale by the till. After all it would be a special night tonight, and she thought it must be at least two to three months since he had made love to her, perhaps tonight would be special. She still missed the closeness that should be there. Maisie felt that it was her fault that Hugh did not seem to care about her, and then at once made excuses for him he must be tired with all the hour's he was doing. Perhaps if she could get him to sit down and talk to her he would see that less working they could cut back and have some sort of life.

Hugh arrived home around seven by which time Maisie had everything prepared all she had to do was grill the lamb steaks when they were ready for their main. Pouring him a glass of wine she asked, 'have you had a good day'.

'Yes, I'll be home for the next couple of nights before we have a last push at finishing the project'

'That will be fantastic I've missed having you at home at night'

Hugh twirled his glass in his hand studying the golden wine in his glass'.

'What have you missed about it?'

Maisie gazed into his eyes. 'You and me being close,' she replied.

Hugh liked having power over his women but he also needed sex and that was the first thing him and Jodie thought of when they reached her flat. 'We can get close later, let's eat first,' he said, 'and we can see where that leads'.

Even though Jodie was more exciting he may as well enjoy what was on offer. Jodie wasn't to know while the cats away he thought. Thinking he could work his meal off on Maisie after eating.

Hugh felt in a good mood he was enjoying the best of both worlds, he helped Maisie to clear the table and load the dishwasher.

'I'll just have a shower. then you can have a shower and get yourself ready for bed,' he said, giving one his most charming smiles.

Maisie heart skipped a beat perhaps life was going to get better after all. The night went as expected and Maisie slept well, waking up early she found that Hugh was already up, she could hear a buzz of conversation she could not hear what was being said.

As she walked into the room he said, 'I'll have to go now see you later'.

'Who was that?' Maisie asked with an enquiring look.

Oh! it was only John from work, he was checking on what we were going to try today'

'He worries about our research and likes to get a feel for what we are going to attempt before we get there.'

'Oh!' She replied, still none the wiser as to why John would need to call before going to work. Hugh was relieved he had slipped out of bed to give Jodie a quick call, he was lucky that Maisie had not heard the conversation, he would not risk ringing her from the apartment again. Because their conversation could not be misconstrued it was of a sexual nature and quite explicit.

Maisie went into the kitchen to prepare breakfast, Hugh followed her and sat at the kitchen island and helping himself to a Danish pastry he picked up the *New York Times* and he began to eat. Maisie poured him some coffee. Looking down at her plate she pushed it away, suddenly she felt a little sick. Getting up and going into the bathroom she stood until the feeling passed, Hugh had not even noticed she had left the room. Going to the sink she filled a glass of water, she wouldn't risk coffee. If she still felt like this tomorrow, she would visit the doctor, she had been neglecting herself just lately, perhaps she needed a tonic. Most definitely she needed to go to the doctors, she wasn't normally a sickly person, being on her own so much at night she perhaps was guilty of not eating well, and not having enough fresh air. She would have to change her habits if Hugh continued to work late, She could perhaps take a little more time walking home and make sure that she ate a better selection of food, she needed to vary her diet.

'Right I'm off make sure you get my tea tonight I'll be home'.

'Of course, I'm looking forward to it,' answered Maisie. 'It's good to have you home'.

Once he had left Maisie washed the dishes and looked around the kitchen, it still looked impersonal with no character at all, to her there was still no real feeling of warmth, it wasn't homely. She didn't feel that she would ever think of it as home. Oh well she thought she would have to make do for now. Slipping into the bedroom to collect her suit jacket from the wardrobe she reached for a scarf and there sitting on the shelf was a packet of her monthly products. Dam! She said to herself why did she not think about it how long was it since she had had a monthly period, she now felt shaky sinking on to the side of the bed she tried to analyse her feelings how would they manage if she was pregnant. Maisie had seen precious little of Hugh's wages in the last twelve months and if she didn't work, she would not be able to help out with the monthly bills. And if she had to rely on what money she had it would soon run out. Maisie decided not to tell Hugh yet, she would wait until she saw a doctor, she was glad now that she had taken out health insurance when they arrived, that would see her through her pregnancy. That is if she was pregnant, thinking to herself she couldn't see it being anything else though. She didn't quite know how she felt and she certainly didn't know how Hugh would feel, she wasn't at all confident that he would be happy about it. It was scary to think she might have a little life growing inside of her. She knew that whatever happened, the baby would be loved by her, but she was unsure how Hugh would feel. He had planted the baby in her so he would have to get used to it.

It was Maisie that was quiet when Hugh arrived home for his dinner, she had already popped a chicken casserole into the oven.

'Dinner not ready yet he asked?'

'No, it will be around another thirty minutes yet'.

'Okay, have we any wine'? he asked.

Maisie said, 'no I completely forgot to get any'.

'I'll nip out and get a couple of bottles,' he said.

'But couldn't we manage for once, it's money we could save'.

'There you go again,' he said with touch of anger. 'Why save money when we don't have to, we should be living our life now'.

'But Hugh we need to plan for the future, what if we have children, we will need extra money because I wouldn't be able to work'.

'No, my dear wife,' he said pushing his face close to Maisie's, 'you can forget about that, we won't have children yet, so I for one am looking forward to having wine with my meal and that's the end of it'. Picking up his phone he grabbed his jacket and going through the door he slammed it angrily after him. Maisie bit her lip, what if she was pregnant, and she was pretty sure that she was he definitely wouldn't be pleased about that?

When she went to the doctor to confirm it, she would have to pick her time in telling him. One thing she realised was that she could not go on juggling the accounts with just her money, he had a responsibility as well as her and whether he liked it or not they would have to talk about it. He needed to understand that everything shouldn't be left to her. And what's more babies cost money, and if she went back to work there would be baby care money to find. Maisie was on pins she hoped when he got back with his wine he would be in a better mood, however she very much thought he wouldn't be.

The night wouldn't get any better, there would be more recriminations when she would have to refuse a glass of wine, he would think she was sulking. She dare not tell him that she might be pregnant, that was the reason she didn't dare to drink wine, so not saying anything about it would be the best way to get around it. If he was angry about having no wine in, she could only imagine what he would be like when she had to tell him; no, it was better to be sure first.

Maisie turned the casserole off, Hugh had been gone a good hour and a half, if she left the oven on it would be ruined. Maisie had just about had enough for one night she went to bed about 11.30pm she knew that if she did stay up there would only be another row, and she wanted to avoid that, being reasonable might help matters more than rowing.

What was upsetting her was that Hugh had never acted this way before she married him, she perhaps should have given it a little more time before she married him. But it was easy to say that after the deed was done, looking back she realised she had been in love with love.

And had she perhaps waited she might have realised that he wasn't for her. He could, if he had married some-one else, have been completely different, she was trying to fight it but she was beginning to dislike this man that was her husband, surely, he must realise what he was like and know that what he was doing was wrong. Maisie realised that she could always smell drink on him, perhaps that was it, if he controlled his drinking, he could perhaps be a different person.

Sleep alluded her and she heard him come in in the early hours of the morning, he undressed in the dark and she could hear him stumbling about, Hugh got into bed and pulled her on her back and forced himself on her, despite her pleading with him to leave her alone, To restrain her he even held her hands together with one hand and his arm across her neck with the other. She felt as if she was choking as he as he pushed away to achieve his satisfaction. When he had finished, he dragged her from the bed kicking her in the back and said, 'you can sleep in the other room, you useless cow,' as she turned to face him he hit her with such force in the chest, then pushing her with such strength that it caused her to fall against the dressing table banging her stomach.

Maisie fled from the room, whatever had come over him she felt completely shocked at what had just happened. Yes, she was getting used to his nasty little jibes and ways but how could she understand what it was he wanted of her, if she knew she could at least try to understand. He had never been so cruel when she first met him, so why now? She could at least try to put it right if it was possible, what was she lacking. She tried to be a good wife but unless he talked to her and explained how could she put it right? Holding her middle, she felt terrified and really alone, her family were miles away in England, she was so upset at what he had done that she dreaded seeing him in the morning.

It was obvious that he had been drinking heavily, the pain where she had banged her stomach was unbearable, she lay shivering on the bed her knees pulled upwards clutching and hugging herself as the waves of pain came and went. Maisie hardly had any sleep that night, because of the pain and the thought that he could do this again, what then? One thing was certain, this type of anger had to stop, she knew if she was pregnant his behaviour would be dangerous for their baby and no way could she let that happen. Yes, she would strive to keep her marriage together but all the respect she had for him had gone. There was no way she could stay with him if this type of behaviour continued, she had felt frightened of him before; now she was terrified, no way could she carry on in this way, something had to change.

CHAPTER SEVEN
A LOVE LOST

The next morning Maisie made her way to the kitchen, wary of what Hugh would be like if he was up. He wasn't in the kitchen, so she placed the coffee pot on and went to have a shower, her clothes were in the bedroom that Hugh had slept in and she was reluctant to disturb him she didn't fancy a repetition of last night. She couldn't believe it had happened. She sat at the kitchen island drinking her coffee and thinking about her mum and dad's words; was she sure she was doing the right thing? Why oh why had she not listened to them? She realised that she had promised for better or worse but the last months of marriage had definitely been worse. When Maisie had showered, she was bruised from just under her breast right down to her thigh the force of hitting the dressing table had marked her more than she thought. Realising the fragile love that she felt for Hugh had disappeared and any feeling for him was lost, she would try to continue to make her marriage work herself, she would have to for the sake of the baby she might be carrying. How she was going to manage it, she for one certainly didn't know, one thing was certain she would work to keep her marriage alive, however it had to alter it could not go on in the same way as the last year.

She was suddenly aware that she could hear the shower running. Slowly she got up, it hurt her to walk, putting the coffee back on she placed some cereal and Danish pastries on the work surface of the kitchen island. Hugh loved to have Danish pastries for breakfast.

'You look pale Maisie,' were his first words, 'and why are you holding your side'.

'You ask why I am holding my side? I fell when you dragged me out of bed last night, I fell and banged myself on the dressing table, I don't know what has got into you, it was obvious to me that you were drunk'.

'Where did you go Hugh? Can you tell me that? You went for wine and just didn't come back, why?'

'I'm a man, your husband,' he glowered at her. 'I can go out without having to explain, is that clear? You should know that I wouldn't hurt you bodily,' his stance changed slightly to being more amenable, I wouldn't hurt you.

'I'm sure you know I wouldn't do that Maisie you must have imagined it'.

'I don't think so Hugh, would I imagine this?' she said, pulling her dressing gown open to show her side that was blue from the top of her breast to her thigh.

'I'm sorry,' he said, 'if it was me, I didn't intend for that to happen you must have just slipped. Please forgive me,' he said placing his arm around her.

I'm not well enough to go to work Hugh I will ring in sick, but no way can I let this happen again you should not have forced me, it should be my choice how and when, not just yours, I didn't marry you to be treated this way, something has to change and now'.

'I'm sorry but you are my wife,' he said with an aggressive look, 'and as such you will when I want'. Looking at her his mood seemed to change again. 'I can only say again how sorry I am,' he said turning the charm on.

'Okay we won't say any more about it,' Maisie replied.

'Right is that it,' he said looking at her through narrowed eyes, 'so, I'll bring in a takeaway and you can rest, you don't have to cook tonight we will have a quiet night in'. Quickly he kissed her on the cheek, leaving Maisie more confused than ever the way he looked at her made her quite sure he had no intention of trying to work at their marriage. It was just word's they had no meaning when he uttered them. She felt sure he must have a split personality, but would not mention it. His demeanour changed too quickly and she did not want to spark his short fuse she would have to choose her words carefully.

As Hugh left, he thought I must keep control of myself, the last time he lost his temper with a lady he ended up in court, he only just missed being locked up. He didn't need another complaint, even if it was his wife, he had been told by the judge if he ever came back to court for the same type of offence he would go to prison, as his other offence would be taken into account. He knew he could not survive in prison and it didn't matter that they were in America, if something like this came to court, they would check for transgressions committed in England. No there was no way he wanted to get caught and be charged again for causing bodily harm, he liked having control and being rough, but he was a coward when it became a threat to himself.

Besides he was sure there would be some quite tough convicts in the American jail, and they wouldn't pick and choose where they put him just because he was English. No he was not going to be caught out again, he promised himself he would watch his step. Until he had left her to live with Jodie, where his fists were concerned, he would have to control his feelings.

CHAPTER EIGHT
GOING TO THE DOCTORS

Maisie rang the medical centre and asked to see a doctor, they fitted her in at 11.30am, after that she rang work and told them that she was unwell and had made an appointment with the doctor. Getting herself ready, she put on a pale green dress and put on her short jacket, She thought a dress was better if she needed to be examined, however she did not know how she was going to explain the bruising on her body. She would have to be careful what she said, she did not want it to get back to Hugh in case he thought she had been complaining about him and that would never do.

She was sitting opposite the doctor, who had just confirmed that she was four months pregnant, he had also done a scan and confirmed that the baby was a little girl. The doctor said the child was small and in light of the bruising he did not think she had done any damage to the child. He wasn't happy with the bruising on her body, he was concerned about how it had come about. Leaving out most of what happened she said she had tripped and fell onto the dressing table. Giving her a sick note for work he told her to take a few days off and rest until the pain from the bruising stopped. He also advised her to put her feet up and rest for the day and in future she needed to be careful, another such fall could damage her baby, 'do you understand me Mrs Grainger?'

'Yes,' she answered, but she was sure the doctor had not believed what she had said. Leaving the doctors, she was relieved he had questioned her carefully and appeared not to quite believe her explanation to how the bruising had come about. She hoped that she did not have to go back to him on the appointments he had set up, if Hugh repeated what happened last night, she was sure that he wouldn't believe a second time.

Going home she had no idea how she was going to tell Hugh she was aware now that he didn't want children yet. But it was done now and he would have to step up to the plate, whether he liked it or not. Maisie felt it was time that she became stronger and stopped pandering to his whims.

Hugh arrived back home at 7.00pm he carried a paper bag holding rice, beef in black bean sauce, lemon chicken and French fries, plus two bottles of wine. He had been sure that if they wanted a sweet that Maisie would have something in the fridge, he was quite happy tonight, Jodie was back tomorrow and he could go back to having a good time, he had missed the sensual sex that he was enjoying with Jodie. Although he had enjoyed taking Maisie last night against her will she had fought him and had never done that before. There was something about women trying to say no and fighting him off that gave him a thrill. And being rough with them made it all the more exciting, it made him feel that he was in charge, and that gave him more sexual satisfaction. Forcing a woman had never bothered him what he wanted he was sure he would get, with this attitude he quite often sailed close to the wind, sometimes too close, and that was when he lost control. He would have to control himself a little more, until he was more certain of what Jodie expected of him and how it would work out, no doubt I will tire of her but at the moment I'm having too much fun. He was relishing the thought of tomorrow night when he would be making love to someone on the same wavelength as him; they both liked to be rough and adventurous.

When Hugh had come in from work Maisie waited for him to freshen up, she had already set the table and they sat down to eat, she let him have his meal and enjoy a couple of glasses of wine. She didn't eat much herself at all she felt a little sick and it was perhaps the fact that she had to broach the subject of being pregnant.

'Hugh, I have something to tell you'.

He looked up from his glass of wine he had just been thinking of what Jodie would do for him tomorrow night. The look on her face suddenly made him wary.

'I've been to the doctors today and he confirmed that I am four months pregnant, you are going to be a father'.

He just stared at her.

'Well say something Hugh are you happy?' she asked in a whisper. The answer was there in his face. 'How could you let this happen you know I didn't want children yet'.

'Why did you not take precautions?

'What do you mean, wasn't that up to you?'

'Its's been you that's done the deed, now we just have to get used to the idea of being parent's'.

'Do you want it?' he asked.

'Hugh how could you ask that, of course I do, it's our child, we have made it. We are married Hugh there is no shame in having a baby'.

'What about an abortion or perhaps you can get rid of it, we can have children when we are better fixed and have saved a little more money?'

'No! no way,' Maisie spat out, 'this is our baby Hugh'.

'Are you sure Maisie?' looking at her he knew she would not change her mind and then he realised that he could perhaps use this to his advantage, it had suddenly entered his mind he could use this as a delaying tactic he could tell Maisie he needed to do the overtime at work more than ever now to make sure they had the money to feed another mouth. And he could convince Jodie that he needed just to see Maisie through this pregnancy and when the baby was born, he would then move in with her. He must save the much needed money somehow, or at least get at the money that Maisie was hanging on to, she paid all the bills out of her money at the moment, if he moved in with Jodie, she was a different cup of tea, he wasn't sure she would be gullible enough to maintain his habits. If he had a little saved, he could pay some. After all he had never been a man who could stick with one woman, he could look out for another distraction, there was plenty of rich women in New York. He just hadn't met anyone with more money than Jodie, he had just found out her father was a very rich man and what Jodie wanted Jodie could have, but she had to get it off her dad and the stumbling block was that Hugh was already married and he needed to extract himself from this marriage without Jodie's father finding out.

There could be no scandal attached for her father to find out about. Marrying Maisie had been one sacrifice too many, to get what he wanted he had seen a virgin and he needed to have her before anyone else did. He was quite sure that if she had given in before they were married, he would have dumped her before he went to America and then he might have had a choice of women as well as Jodie. But if he hadn't married Maisie, he would have had to maintain the apartment himself and that would have left him short of cash to enjoy himself. He would have to think of a plan to get Maisie's money out of her control and into his, with a few lies here and there he could perhaps have the best of both worlds.

'Okay Maisie we will have to make the most of the situation,' his mood seemed to change again. 'I will have to continue working late to make more money and you will have to work as long as you can so that you can continue paying the bills and I will do the saving. No more recriminations about being out late at work and you will have to be more careful with yourself'. 'No more accidents Maisie'.

She could not believe her ears, here he was putting all the blame on her and although she made excuse's for his behaviour, she knew what had happened and it was not just her fault, but at least they were making headway and she hoped this would be a lesson to both of them, yes they both needed to try harder not just her.

'Now you are always on about budgeting, we will have to look at putting your money in with mine, then I can have a better idea on what we have'.

'We don't have to do that Hugh, you will still have your savings and you can save in one of your banks, and when we look at moving you can perhaps sort out a house and I can look at buying the furniture. After all, when the baby is born, I will see if I can go back to work, then we could have a joint account for paying the bills.

'Maisie if we keep this baby,' he snarled, 'you will do as your told, is that clear?' and he leant menacing towards her. He had changed in a flash he seemed as if he was two people, and at the moment she was seeing the black side of him. Not wanting to argue or upset him more she decided to back off for the moment, after all she had got the worst over, but something told her not to hand over her money, if she did that, she would be completely dependent.

'We'll see,' was her answer, inside she knew she had no intention of just handing over her savings, he must have some money put to one side, she had been paying everything that she could, holding on to her cash would serve them well for a rainy day, no one knew what would happen in the future. No, it would be too big a step for her to give up her security, she might need that in the future for her baby, there was no way she wanted to be penniless and with a child, she didn't quite trust Hugh, it was just a feeling, he was too complex. She wondered if she was doing the right thing staying with him, but her nature told her she must try.

Chapter Nine
Life Being Pregnant

As Maisie had thought Hugh did forget their wedding anniversary, she would have understood if they had been married for years, people did as they got older but how could he forget the first anniversary. She could in no way remind him and now had got quite used to her life of spending every night at home on her own. Time dragged and she was aware that she would have to finish work soon on pregnancy leave, however she was quite unhappy with the situation with Hugh, her opinion was that with a little tweak here and a little tweak there they should be able to have a life together and Hugh blocked them all the time with his attitude. He just was not interested in compromising and how he worked from early morning to late night she could not comprehend. If she tried to engage him in conversation in the morning, to try and make a plan on what they spent he would get quite aggressive and all the time she kept backing off.

Hugh had got her where he wanted her, under his thumb. This had gone on too long, nothing would change unless she faced it head on. Yes, he always frightened her when he got aggressive however she needed to stand up to him. His stock answer was always, that's enough and he appeared to snarl at her, 'it's you that wants to keep the brat'.

'Hugh, don't call our child that please'.

There was no way she could carry on like this when their baby was born. In fact, he seemed to go to work earlier than ever and he gave her no explanation why. But tonight, she had decided to stay up and try and have it out with him, there would never be any family life for her and her child, she needed to sort this relationship out. The sooner the better, she didn't feel well but he seemed not to notice how tired she looked. She had to hand it to him, he always seemed to have lots of stamina for the long working day he put in. It seemed that because of her condition and the extra weight she had gained she felt tired all the time and it was an effort to do things. Everyone one at work had been understanding and kind, and Maisie really appreciated it. If she had never got a job her life would be empty. Yes! Going to work gave her little company but not the company she craved. She needed to ask him why he was acting like this, if it was something, she had done she would try to put it right, but no way for the life of her could she understand what.

Thinking of her life before she met Hugh, she could not understand how she had let him change it so much. Hugh had asked her for some money only yesterday and she had refused, she could not understand why he needed money, his excuse was he had paid too much into their savings, and he still kept banging on about her saving's, and this on its own put her on her guard, she was not ready give up the money she had saved without seeing some commitment from him. He'd started as soon as he had got up, and now she had had enough of his bullying ways, she needed to know that he would try to change and understand that commitment is a two way street, as is communication, you need to talk and plan, she couldn't do it on her own. He needed to give her a valid reason why he needed money from her. Otherwise she could see no future in them staying together.

And for some reason she had still refused and said well draw some back out of the savings, I already pay my way. He had bunched his fist as if he was going to hit out, Maisie had backed away but he grabbed his jacket and phone and slammed the door after him. Maisie let her breath out in relief, convincing herself she must have imagined he was going to hit her, but she had backed away. After Maisie had got dressed, she stood for at least another fifteen minutes staring out of the window looking across at all the skyscraper's and her heart longed for the English fields of home, she didn't feel that this would ever be home to her. How she longed to talk to her mum or dad, they would advise what to do, but she knew she couldn't involve them they would be so worried for her and that would be another stick for Hugh to beat her with. One of the things she did not like was the fact that he said she didn't need a mobile phone, and when the account for the landline came in, he checked it to make sure she had not rung to speak to her mum and dad. This over her short marriage had caused quite a few arguments he did not see the need for her to speak to her parents. Saying you are always banging on about money, this is one way we can cut down.

Meanwhile Hugh was lying with Jodie on the bed in her apartment after having a long sexual encounter. 'Hugh how much longer are you going to put off telling Maisie about us, I don't see what difference it will make leaving her now or after she's had the baby, you are here more than at the apartment with her?

'I've told you be patient it will only be another couple of months, I promise as soon as the baby is born, I will tell her and then we will be together for good. And as soon as I get divorced, we can get married quietly and tell your family after'.

Both him and Jodie continued to drink, steadily between making love and the conversation around leaving Maisie was shelved while they engaged once more in what they enjoyed best, rough sex, rolling over once more Jodie began to moan again about him still being with Maisie, she was another individual who liked her own way and God help anyone who tried to stop her. At that moment she was busy trying to get Hugh to change his plans, as ever, she was putting herself first.

'Hugh just think, we could have sex whenever we want and enjoy every minute together, so why Hugh, we could give her a little money to keep her if she hasn't enough, you should be here now'.

'Be patient, Jodie it won't be long now. You keep saying that. But I want you here at night with me I forgave you for getting her pregnant, didn't I?

'Yes, but that was just once, I've no wish to make love to anyone but you and I will be with you always soon. We already sleep in different rooms now, Maisie knows that I'm not happy with her so just try and be patient a little longer, the baby will soon be here, and when it is, I will leave her, she will go back to England to her parents. The baby with her I promise. I'm only there to see her through the pregnancy and as soon as it over I will be here. I don't love her I love you, but the least I can do is help her until she can travel home, she is in a strange country'.

'Just two more months then, nine weeks and if you aren't here full-time that's the end and I will tell her as well, then you won't have me or her, understand! 'And then where will you go for your enjoyment?'

'I'll be right here with you my darling, nothing will stop me being with you, haven't I proved that, every night all these months, think what we have been doing'.

Looking at Jodie he realised her mouth was set in a hard line, there was going to be no compromise. He needed to take her mind of Maisie and the baby, he would make Maisie transfer her money he would be home and dry then he needed to be firmer with her, in his mind he was the patient one it was his right to have her money.

'Jodie please I've told you. I promise, who in their right mind would choose Maisie over you?' he said slowly caressing her breast, and bending to kiss it, he started to try and take her attention from him and Maisie. 'No promise that you will tell her, do you understand,' she reiterated.

'Of course, I will tell her, it would be like making love to a cold piece of wood, so why should I not tell her. You and I are good together Jodie, we are two of a kind we can make our bodies sing when we come together, forget Maisie. I have you, and you are the only one I think about even when I'm there, it's only you in my mind and what we can do together, you must admit it's good and when I live here with you it will be even better. Just be patient a little longer, then everything will come together'. 'Now don't let's waste time on her, let's have a more interesting time.' he said bending to kiss her. 'And I don't need to understand, I will tell her in two months when the baby is born, I promise love', leaning over he started to fondle her neck and stroke her thighs, his hand slipped down to grip her breast causing her gasp in pain, grabbing for him, Jodie quickly pulled him to her.

'I just can't get enough of you,' she said as he took her once more.

Around two thirty he thought it was time he made his way home after all they both had work the next day. Letting himself into the apartment he was taken by surprise that Maisie had waited up for him.

'You're in late, you have never been working until this time of the night?' Maisie said. 'So, I went for a few drinks that's not a crime is it?'

'Don't you ever think of me being here on my own night after night, I thought we got married to be together'

Hugh suddenly lost his temper he wasn't in the mood for any more moaning from women, 'don't question me I don't have to account for my movements to you. So Shut, up nagging, you, fat ugly bag, just looking at you makes me feel sick, who would want to stay in with you, have you looked in the mirror just lately?'

'Don't talk to me like that Hugh, I don't deserve this treatment whatever has got into you?'

He walked over to her and pushed his face close to hers, 'are you going to shut up or do I have shut you up?' he growled at her putting his hand up to grip her face in a punishing hold.

'Don't Hugh you are frightening me'.

Grabbing her by the throat he said, 'haven't I told you to shut up?' and he lost it, headbutting her in the face. She fell to the floor with a thud, and in one angry movement he grabbed her by her hair with such force lifting her head off the floor, he smashed his fist into the side of her face letting go and then giving her a vicious kick, then he stamped on her thigh before he left her there on the floor, swearing under his breath he made his way to the bedroom this was the result of both him and Jodie drinking steadily since finishing work, but the bloody cow had asked for it questioning him. What right had she, he had held his temper with Jodie but he hadn't managed it with Maisie, anyway she needed her to toe the line, he called the shots and she had better understand, it had started yesterday when she had said no to giving him some money out of her savings. He was overdrawn at the bank and it was a week before his salary went into his account, he would have to put the brakes on him and Jodie eating out, Jodie always expected him to pay. But he'd make sure he got that money, it belonged to both of them now and it would tide him over, he would tell her it had to go in the bank that he was saving in as it would get more interest. Just let her try and keep it in her bank, that money would help him to sway Jodie, just let the bitch try and keep it to herself. If she tried that again she would get more of what he had just given her. He wasn't used to being told no, up until now he had been quite controlled but her stubborn refusal was getting his back up, so she had better start changing her attitude and if that beating didn't change her a little, more of it soon would, his good intentions of controlling himself gone. He no longer thought of the consequences of his actions, come what may he intended to have his own way; besides she would be too scared to do anything about it, too scared and embarrassed.

Waking up sometime later Maisie was aware of a terrific pain she needed to get help, dragging herself up she slowly made her way to the bedroom making as little noise as she could. Quietly opening the door, she could see Hugh was fast asleep on his stomach, the light was shining into the room making it possible for her to see without making any noise. For he hadn't closed the curtains. She could see too slowly inch her way towards the wardrobe keeping her eyes fixed on him she had to get a change of clothes and the important documents of her own that she would need.

Gently she opened the door finding a small weekend bag and pushing in a few clothes, she reached for some loose trousers, sweater and a coat. At that moment Hugh moved giving a snort but immediately went back to sleep. Holding her breath, she stood still hardly daring to breathe, her body was racked with pain, she just had to get out of here before he woke up. If only for the child she was carrying she could not put up with this treatment anymore, her baby would be better off without a father than one like him. She realised she not only didn't love him, but she had lost all respect for him as well and this was the end of the road for her and Hugh Grainger, she could not believe that he was capable of treating her in the way that he had. For the sake of the child she was carrying she had to put an end to this relationship. How she would go about it she wasn't sure but she needed to get out while he was asleep, somewhere that she would be safe.

Picking up a bag she quietly opened her vanity case and took out all her bankbooks plus her passport and placed them in her bag, along with some night clothes, only stopping in the kitchen for a few seconds longer to wipe the blood from her face. Dressing herself quietly, for each movement brought a fresh spasm of pain, and at the same time listening carefully for any movement in the bedroom. One thing she was almost certain of was that when he had been drinking, he slept quite heavily and most times would not wake until the morning. And then quietly going into the lounge holding her breath as she eased the draw that held their medical file easing it out and placing it in her bag, she took a moment to grip the sideboard top as once more a wave of pain engulfed her body. Once she had fought through the pain, she quietly made her way to the door picking up her small travelling bag as she was already clutching her hand bag, she could not afford to leave that behind.

Opening the door carefully she looked toward the small hall that led to the bedrooms leaving it open in case he heard the click as she shut it. Holding her breath as she slipped into the hallway looking behind her, she slipped the flat pumps she was carrying on to her feet. Maisie managed to get to the lift, she didn't know how, but fear must have given her strength and couple of times she had to stop, as a spasm of pain gripped her body. Reaching the lobby where the night porter was, trying to keep her face down as she asked the night porter to call her a taxi.

'Here are you alright love? he asked'.

Yes, just call me a taxi please,' she asked.

'Are you sure? You don't look to good to me missus'.

'Yes,' she replied, it took all her time to hold it together, she just didn't want to break down here, her instinct was to get to safety, she certainly didn't feel safe at all whilst she was still in this building, her legs were shaking like jelly, but she had to stay awake and not lose her sense's. The taxi soon came and she instructed the driver to take her to the nearest hospital. Leaning back against the seat she gritted her teeth as the waves of pain came and went, feeling sick and dizzy, the pain was getting unbearable and by the time the taxi arrived at the hospital she had lost consciousness. Turning to speak to her the taxi driver realised he had an emergency on his hands.

'Crikey love you just stay there I'll soon have someone to look after you'. Running into the hospital he shouted, 'Quick can someone help me I've a lady that's passed out in my cab, she looks in a right bad way. Quick you need to bring that trolley with you outside. This way,' he directed.

'Outside of the entrance,' the nurse shouted to a porter, 'depending on how poorly the girl is we will need to get her on to it, where's your cab?'

'Just by the door. Please hurry she looks all in.'

There was a flurry of activity as they transported her into the hospital, taking in that she was pregnant they took her straight to the maternity ward. Looking at another junior nurse, she said, 'quick page Dr Jones.'

The older nurse commented, 'it looks as if she's been hit by a brick wall, and by the look of it we need to deliver the baby as well as patch her up.'

From then on there was a flurry of activity. The hospital nurses and doctors worked tirelessly to deliver the baby and to clean the blood from her face, she also had internal bleeding, the doctor declared, 'it's a wonder either of them are alive, the baby is struggling. Still we'll find out what's happened to her when she comes too.

But at the moment it will be better to keep her sedated for a short while, because her body needs to heal and any more trauma won't help it'.

The nurse bustled after the porter who pushed Maisie to a side ward, quickly setting up a drip to keep her sedated, while her weakened body started to repair itself. Throughout the night there were nurses checking her condition, the doctor couldn't understand how she had taken such a beating and managed to get to the hospital, when asking the taxi driver where they had picked her up he had given the name of a well-known apartment block and said he had picked her up at the door. The doctor had also had photographs of her injuries taken for future reference for whoever had beat her needed to be taken off the streets and he also would have to report the incident, however he would wait to see if she made any progress first and could tell them what had transpired.

Maisie woke to find a pleasant faced nurse checking the machines and drip that was attached to her, 'so you're back in the land of the living, how are you feeling honey,' she asked.

'What about my baby?' she whispered, her throat was hoarse and sore. 'Please my baby, my little girl?'

All I can tell you is she is holding her own at the moment, a little poorly but holding her own'.

Maisie took her hand down to her stomach, 'you mean she has been delivered? When can I see her?'

'Concentrate on getting better, Maisie isn't it, we will look after your little girl, now have you a name for her? 'Yes Grace, My Little Gracie'.

'How did you know my name?'

'We found it in your handbag, don't worry its locked up in the hospital safe, along with your passport and the other valuables. Now you need to sleep, sleep is a good healer you are certainly looking a little better than when you arrived here, rest a little more, and when you feel you can eat a little, just ring this bell,' she said indicating the push button, 'and we'll come running, we need to see you on the mend. When you feel like talking about it, we'll sort it out'.

Maisie spent a month in hospital and Gracie was there just two months, throughout that month she was treated with nothing but kindness, and Gracie was quite poorly. They had already told Maisie it would be a miracle if she lived, this broke her heart, her first baby and it would be a matter of how long, the one thing that might have been good from her marriage and she would lose that too. Sitting there in the hospital she realised what she must do. Her marriage had been a sham she needed to end it, she realised that trying to make it work was a waste of time. Asking the nurse if there was some-one she could talk to as she needed help and advice, they arranged for her to see a hospital social worker.

With tears in her eyes she went over her eighteen months of marriage with a gentle older lady who, gave her time to talk when she began to be emotional. And telling her how Hugh had treated her was very difficult, would they think it was her fault? She still felt it was partly her fault. The social worker who was named Emma assured her that it was not at all her fault, some men were bullies and would never change, they should never get married. Telling Emma that she needed somewhere to stay, and asking if there was someone who could go back to the apartment with her to collect her clothes and any belongings that she wanted to keep.

'We can arrange that Mrs Grainger.'

'Please don't call me that, I'm Maisie I never want to be called that ever again, I'd also need a good solicitor, I would like a quick divorce and I know in America it's possible'.

'We can arrange all that for you Maisie, but the state you were in when you arrived at the hospital should be a matter for the police, we can't let him get away with this because he will only hurt someone else'.

'No, I can keep that as a lever, my trump card, my lever to extricate myself from this marriage'.

'How will it do that? 'asked' the social worker.

'It will, he won't want his employers to know how he has acted'.

'Are you sure'.

'Yes, very sure. I'm sure he won't still be at the apartment but I don't want to risk going there on my own'.

'Will you know where he would be for you to have the divorce paper's served to?'

'Yes, I think I do, but will you promise not to tell anyone until I have served the paper's to him?'

'Yes, I can do that, but only until the divorce is over, and then I can't let it lie'.

'I know, but I want to get this divorce over and then concentrate on Gracie until,' Maisie voice petered out at this point and there was a hint of a tear in her eyes.

'So where is he then, just in case you forget to tell me after the divorce?'

'St Augustine's hospital he works there.'

'He's a doctor then?'

'No, he works in the research department and I'm sure he won't want his company to find out. I'm sure working in the hospital requires him to have a good character and this coming out would ruin it for him. So please can you refrain from letting him know where I am until I have the divorce well under way, and have a new address that he won't be aware of, that way I'll at least have a chance of extricating myself from this sham of a marriage. Please,' she appealed.

Emma nodded her reply, 'well let's get a plan of action in place then.' Emma replied.

So, after spending around an hour with Emma she agreed for Emma to find a solicitor and guide her through the steps she must take, Emma also agreed to find her a safe address and it would be as near to the hospital as possible. Once this plan of action had been agreed on and Emma had told her she would, with other people guide her through each step of the way, Maisie felt quite calm and turned her attention back to her little girl. Now she had started the ball rolling it was just a matter of being patient and things would sort themselves out, Emma appeared to be trustworthy and helpful, she had plotted every step for Maisie to follow and she would walk every step with her. On her own she would have struggled to achieve what she had to do. She realised she would be forever grateful to this quietly spoken woman. With her help perhaps she would be able to forget this episode of her life.

When Hugh woke up, the next day he was still suffering a hangover, going into the lounge he saw the blood on the carpet. God, he thought, I hope I haven't killed her. He quickly went into the kitchen thinking he would find her there, then the spare room, there was no sign of her. The bloody bitch had sneaked out before he had time to stop her. Instinct made him go to the wardrobe and grab her vanity case where he knew she kept her bank books and a couple of pieces of expensive fripperies. The bloody cow had gone and taken anything of value with her. He could have pawned them for a bit of money, why he hadn't thought of that before he didn't know. He would have had a bit of ready cash then, now what am I going to do? He was already waiting for pay day Still Jodie would be glad he would think of something to tell her. And Maisie must be alright, she had walked out, hadn't she? He didn't think she would go to the police, she was frightened of her own shadow, her father always treated her like a baby, she'd had a taste of what a real man was like. Still picking up a case I might as well make myself scarce, get it over and done with and move in with Jodie. He was sure he would think of something to tell her to cover up the reason that he had no money until payday.

Quickly filling the remaining suitcases with his belongings and carefully checking Maisie's handbags she had left behind to see if she had left any money anywhere, to no avail. Maisie was quite a tidy person she would always empty her handbags after she had used them. Grabbing a case in each hand he quickly looked in all the drawers to see if there was anything left that she had forgotten. He left the apartment to join Jodie, who would be waiting in the usual place a couple of blocks away. As he walked the couple of blocks to Jodie's car a plan was forming in his mind. He was quite adept at being crafty and a plan had soon formulated in his head. By the time he reached her car he had his little speech firmly in his mind, all he had to do was sound convincing, he could get most women to believe him, why not Jodie? Once he was living with Jodie, he would have to keep his eye out for another distraction, heir and a spare so to speak. If he did, he would have to be more discreet, Jodie was a different kettle of fish to Maisie.

Chapter Ten
Returning to the Apartment

Just one month after Maisie had entered the hospital, she returned to the apartment with the social worker Emma and her husband Jed, he was off duty that day. He was a police officer and he also promised to hold back until Maisie had sorted her divorce, although after listening to his wife he would have liked to tear him apart, and then some more. As it was, he took Maisie's key and opened the door first, they had spoken to the janitor of the apartments who said he had not seen Mr Grainger since the day after he had rung for a taxi for Mrs Grainger. He had seen him leave with a couple of cases. He also hadn't paid the month's rent, and when Maisie said she would settle it he said, 'no you don't have to, the lease is in Mr Grainger's name and we have already contacted the hospital who have advised us that it will paid as soon as they have spoken to him'.

Maisie thanked him and made her way to the apartment. The carpet was still stained with blood he hadn't even cleaned it up. Masie went into the bedroom with Jed's wife Emma to pack her clothes whilst Jed took out his mobile phone and commenced taking photographs as evidence for a later date, he already had photographs that had been taken of Maisie when she was in hospital. He was certainly going to make sure that Hugh Grainger was not going to get away with this. Because if he did, he would only do it again to some other trusting woman and Jed was not going to let that happen if he had anything to do with it. Hugh Grainger was obviously a nasty piece of work, oblivious of other people's feelings and only bothered about himself. Jed vowed to make it his personal objective to take him off the streets or at least to stay away from Maisie whilst she was in America. He would make it his personal objective, people like Hugh Grainger were Jed's pet hate, if someone went to use their fists on Hugh's type they would run like a hare, Hugh was the sort who would only beat women, children, and the elderly, a coward.

Going into the bedroom Maisie stood and surveyed the room, she at once noticed the wardrobe doors open, there was no sign of Hugh's clothes, her wardrobe was open and her vanity case was on the floor along with the handbags she had left behind, they had all been opened. He obviously had been looking for her money and any odd pieces of valuable jewellery that she owned, she was glad that she had placed everything from it into her handbag. Her intuition had been right he had been livid when he found it empty, he thought perhaps she might have had some cash in it, Maisie thought I'm happy to disappoint him. There had been some expensive pieces of jewellery belonging to her grandmother and Maisie would never have forgiven herself if she had allowed Hugh to get his hands on them. She was relieved now that she had the forethought to completely empty her vanity case and take it with her. Everyone's first thought must be, to survive in the face of danger, her subconscious must have told her even though she needed to get out of the apartment she would need her savings and her valuables. If she was to get through this divorce, she also needed her savings to survive and of course her passport to go home.

At the moment she could not afford the luxury of thinking about the fact that she had so much to achieve. Then thinking about the day before Hugh hit her, she could not understand why he needed to ask her for money. Maisie herself had been paying all the bills and managing to put a little bit back into her account that she had spent from in the beginning, Hugh had not answered her when she had asked what he had done with his money and why he hadn't drawn some out of his own accounts. She racked her brain and still couldn't understand why! What had he done with all his wages; she had not seen a penny of it so where was it? She now realised he was utterly selfish and would never change.

Reaching for a case Emma said, 'it looks as if he has moved out already, was there someone else?'

'If there was Emma, I had no idea, it's not something you think about after only being married to him for such a short time. He did get annoyed with me when I said I couldn't believe that the hospital expected them to work so late, so I always backed off thinking I was being disloyal. And I'm glad I did now if I hadn't I suppose it would have been more beatings, I think that is why I must have had the instinct to back off so many times.'

Jed popped his head around the door to say he was nipping back downstairs he just needed to check something in his car, what he really wanted to do was to question the night Janitor, to make sure he was the one on duty the night that Maisie left the apartment. The Janitor quite willing gave a statement and signed it.

'It was such a shame for Mrs Grainger, he never seemed to be in, going out early morning not coming home until the early hours and mostly worse for drink'.

For Jed that was another little bit of the puzzle in place for when the NYPD prosecuted Hugh, and they would. Taking the stairs two at a time, he was back upstairs ready to carry the cases down.

'Are you two girls ready?' he asked.

'Yes.' they both answered. 'I think I never want to see this apartment ever again,' Maisie said, 'I have nothing but bad memories of this place it never felt that it was home, but I now understand it's not the place but the people that make it home'.

'I understand Maisie but you married him, when did he start getting aggressive with you?'

'I can't pin it down when, I noticed that there was something different straight after the wedding'.

'It was as if he needed to have his own way right from the beginning. And I know now that I was a little frightened of him, I would make excuses to myself for how he acted. I found it less intimidating not to voice my concerns, he seemed always to be manipulating me, I could see when not to ask him about anything, really it was easier not to rock the boat. I only knew how my mum and dad were together, there marriage was completely different they shared everything they had no secrets. I grew up in such a loving family I didn't think people could be like how Hugh was, I thought it was something lacking in me'.

'Most people blame themselves, I always think that if we could stand outside ourselves and watch we would realise it was not us Maisie, so don't blame yourself, you are worth more than that Maisie'.

'Thank you, Emma, you have really a good way of understanding people's problems. I don't think I would have got this far without you. Thank you for being there for me'.

'You are most welcome, but you would Maisie everyone has strength, it's just not being frightened of using it, and because you wanted to speak to someone showed that you weren't frightened, so it's not just me but your own strength'.

It only took a short time to finish packing and to check the apartment for any personal effects, this done she looked around for the last time, she could not help but grieve a little for what could have been. She had had such high hopes and had weaved romantic dreams about the marriage she had entered into, now it had all vanished into cold reality and she had to take the consequences. Who would have thought all this could happen to her in such a short time of being married?

'Right,' Emma said. 'Jed and I have found a small hotel near to the hospital this could do you for a while it's not as spacious as the apartment you have just left but it will suffice for a short while, it will also be safe the land-lady has housed many of my people I want to protect, so we are going to take you there before we have lunch and when we have had lunch we will take you back to the hospital. You can then spend some time with Gracie and tomorrow we have a solicitor who will come over and talk to you, he comes highly recommended and if you like him it's up to you if you engage him'.

'I don't know how to thank you enough Emma, you and Jed have given me strength to do this'.

'Maisie you already had the strength, you just had to use it, and I know this is hard but you will come out of this the stronger for it, knowing that we are here to give as much support as you need. Remember you have done nothing wrong Maisie. Everything that has happened is down to your husband, he obviously did not show his true colours until after you married him. But people like him have a way of hiding their true personality until they can't get their own way'.

The hotel Emma and Jed took her to was small, clean, and cosy, it held a bed covered in a pale blue spread, the carpet was gold, a small armchair, a side table, and a small television, the owner asked her no questions, but just welcomed her with open arms. Maisie knew she would be comfortable here and it was just around the corner from the hospital so she could be with Gracie in minutes, the rates for the room were very reasonable. The only thing that bothered her was how much the divorce would cost. Maisie voiced her fears to Emma and Jed.

'Don't worry,' Emma said, 'we will cross that bridge when we get to it' So after paying a month's rent for her room and leaving her case and a small amount of belongings Maisie went with Emma and Jed for lunch. It was a small restaurant on the sidewalk where they had a steak with salad, and apple pie and cream to follow, and the coffee kept on coming. Later they made their way back to the hospital Emma let Maisie go straight to the children's ward to Gracie. Emma had also persuaded Maisie to spend another week at the hospital before she went to live in the hotel. She wanted to make sure that Maisie had recovered enough strength to be on her own. Emma would still be there to support her, but she had many people on her casebook to work on as well as Maisie, but Jed would help to support her as well. Emma tried to see as much of Maisie as she could in her spare time, it was unusual do this however Emma was aware that Maisie now was on her own in a strange country, her other cases always had family around them so she did her best to keep her eye on her. And Maisie obviously appreciated it.

Chapter Eleven
Gracie

Maisie sat at the side of Gracie's incubator watching Gracie fight for her breath, she was small because she had been born early, her eyes were green, and her hair was a blond fluff, just like Maisie's whose heart was breaking as she watched her daughter struggling to hold onto the short thread of life that was to be her lot. The doctor had told her that it was just a matter of time before her little girl passed back into God's hands. Maisie wanted to hang on to every minute of Gracie's short life. If there was anything that she could not and would not ever forgive Hugh for, it was what he had done to their daughter, what should have been a wonderous time had only been turned into a nightmare, and why? Because of someone's selfish attitude of caring more about themselves than the commitment they had so loosely made. But why God, why did he marry me? Masie asked herself. True I would never have seen Gracie as she was, if I had never met Hugh, but in later years if I had married someone else who did know what commitment meant, Gracie might have still been her first child and lived, how wonderful would that have been.

Hugh must not have a heart at all, she in no way expected him to seek her out, but would you not think he would have known her due date was past and at least wanted to know his child was okay? A stray tear ran down her face, there was only her to grieve for the small child that lay struggling in the incubator fighting for each breath. Quite obviously Hugh had no feelings whatsoever for her or their little Gracie, what sort of monster was he, how could she have been so gullible to marry him? Thinking of how her mum and dad had nurtured her and her sister Gwen, how could people be so indifferent, she could not understand. Maisie thanked God that Gracie would never know that her father never loved her and would die ignorant of that shameless fact.

Sitting there watching Gracie, Maisie thought of how her father and mother would have loved Gracie and at the moment they didn't even know of her existence. Maisie had told them she was pregnant the last time they rang, they knew nothing of the nightmare she had been living. Her father would have been appalled at the way Hugh had treated his little kitten, because Gracie would have been loved by him and her mother, just the same as her and Gwen. She could not burden them with what she had to do, they wouldn't find out until she returned home and had secured her divorce. Maisie knew that it would just be her that would travel home and her heart felt as if it would burst with pain. But she made sure that Gracie's remains would go with her unless there was a miracle and Gracie had a turn for the better. How she prayed for that miracle, but inside she knew it wouldn't happen. Aware that she would leave America with Gracie in a small casket, how hard was that!

Every minute that Maisie had to spare she spent at the side of Gracie, willing her daughter to understand how much she loved her, blaming herself for what would be Gracie's short life. If she hadn't angered Hugh, he would not have hit her and perhaps Gracie would have had a chance of life. However, if she hadn't, both of them would still be in his hands and the sort of man he was he could have hurt not only her but Gracie as she was growing up, and would have understood and perhaps hurt more, when Hugh had beat her. Gracie was not aware and unable to think it was her fault, and that she was in the wrong. As she sat there, she could not stop the stray tears that ran down her cheeks to be wiped away, only to be replaced by another.

Maisie watched Gracie slowly fade away three weeks later, she took her last breath at just nine weeks old. Maisie shed tears until she had no more to flow, like any mother she would have swopped places in a heartbeat if she could. Hugh might have been her father but she Maisie had loved that child and would never forget her. Her little girl Gracie. The nurses wrapped her in a shawl and allowed her to sit and nurse her before they took her away, her small features were etched forever in Maisie's heart and she felt as if she didn't want to put her down, all too soon the nurse came back to take her away. There would be no next time to see because she would be encased in the small coffin that she still had to choose, Emma was there beside her when they took Gracie and she gently led Maisie away. One of the nurses had taken a photograph of Gracie wrapped in the shawl she looked as if she was just sleeping Maisie shed more tears for the kindness, they were all showing.

Emma and Jed also helped Maisie with the funeral, Maisie had already decided to have Gracie cremated, that way she could take Gracie back home with her in a casket. She could not bear to leave her in America with no one to love her or take care of her resting place. She only hoped that going back to God she would be loved. Right at the beginning Emma had also made a personal visit to the department store that Maisie worked at to explain what had happened to Mr Johnson, and what had transpired. It prompted Mr Johnson to visit her and bring some small items she had left at the office. He had also told her that if she stayed on in America that there would be a job found for her if she wanted one, Maisie told him her plans were to return home but thanked him for being so kind. All these were small things and also large things that Emma had done to make things less difficult for Maisie. This was because Emma and Jed thought she had enough to contend with. This had made Maisie feel that she would never forget the kindness she had been shown since she had left Hugh.

Gracie's funeral was quiet just ten mourners Maisie, Emma, Jed, four nurses and the doctor who had attended Maisie when she was taken into the hospital, and also Mr Johnson her boss from the department store along with another office worker. As she watched the curtains close, on the tiny coffin she gave a small wounded cry. At that moment she knew that nothing else in her life would ever hurt her as much, but she also had to be strong, she still had to attend the divorce court in two weeks. That would be the testing time, would he try to stop her? She didn't think so in two and half months she had not seen or heard from him, despite him being served with the divorce papers. As far as he was concerned, she did not seem to exist. An old saying ran through her head, marry in haste repent at leisure, that would seem to be true in her case she should have listened to her parents, they had been right all along.

She wondered if he even knew that Gracie had died. Even now she could not believe that he could have been so heartless not to find out what had happened to his child, and not even to attend the funeral of his own daughter! And then another thought popped up in her head (Never put off until tomorrow what you could do today), if she had made the decision to leave Hugh sooner Gracie might still be here. Yes, it was her fault as well she should have not let it get this far.

CHAPTER TWELVE
THE DIVORCE

For the next week Maisie spent her time going through the divorce plea, it would be on the grounds of cruelty and unreasonable behaviour. And her solicitor Andy seemed to think it would be a breeze, up until now Hugh had not put up any defence to stop the action, he seemed to think that it would be a matter of attending and the Judge signing it off. Maisie hoped so, she did not relish a long drawn out case. Just one more week and it could be over except for the decree. All she had to do was stick out the six weeks and she could go home. She had given her parents her new phone number, she had to have great restraint when she spoke to her sister and parents, no way could she let them know what had happened it would be easier to tell them when she was safely at home. So, it took a lot of skirting around the issues and because she had purchased a new mobile and she had given them that number, saying it would be easier for them to ring her on her mobile number, she would sometimes not answer her phone, worried that she would sound ill or upset and she was aware she needed for them not to worry about her.

Despite needing her family more than ever, she knew that if her parents were aware of what had happened to her they would be on the next plane over, and that was something she did not want. Maisie needed to stay strong, she was fully aware that if she had told them she would not have been able to cope as well as she had. And she needed to cope with this herself after all she was to blame for not listening to her parents who had up until then guided her along the right path. Once she travelled back home to her parents and family, she would, and only then would she be able to admit she had been wrong to marry in haste and repent at leisure. Maisie also knew it would break her mum and dad's heart once they knew the full story of her short marriage. She was dreading telling the whole story to her parent's and Gwen. However, she knew that they would not say I told you so, they would just welcome her back and do their best to help mend the loss of Gracie. And Maisie knew she that was one thing she would never get over, time healed she would in time get over her short marriage, but not her Gracie.

Later that week she stood looking out of her window as the snow began to fall, Large flakes beginning to settle and cover the pavements, every person below was laden with shopping to celebrate the festive period. And what have I got to show for my life, Maisie thought, nothing not even my baby, a stray tear made its way down her cheek. 'It's not fair,' she whispered, 'I should be buying presents if my baby was here, even though she wouldn't have understood now, Hugh had robbed her of everything. The fairy tale of a magical first night, the happiness of being a new bride. Having a husband to come home and want to be with her. The magic of watching their first child beginning to crawl and take its first steps. Please lord forgive me asking, but why was it in your great plan for me, why did you allow me to marry him. You gave me such wonderful parents and a great sister had you already given me too much? Walking over to the settee she sat down and began to cry huge sobs tumbling out one after another until she had no more tears left, exhausted she fell asleep and she dreamed of walking in a beautiful garden, standing there before her was her grandmother holding a child. Maisie my darling girl, don't worry I have Gracie with me, it wasn't her time to walk the earth, I will take care of her she will come to no harm with me. You need to look forward not backwards your happiness will come in many forms it may take time but you will live with the lord's servant on earth. 'Always remember there is a reason for everything in life, good or bad, your time will come and you will have great happiness you will love and be loved'.

Maisie woke up with a jolt feeling calm and at peace, she suddenly realised it was the knocking on the door that had woken her up. Getting up she went to answer the door, as she went stooping to pick a feather up of the floor not understanding where it had come from. Standing there was Emma and Jed. 'Come on Maisie you are not staying here and feeling sorry for yourself we are having a little get together at the hall down the road and I need you to help me,' she declared.'

I'd love to Maisie replied, suddenly she had come to her senses, she needed to look forward to the future and become useful again, Besides Emma and Jed had helped her so much without pushing her, now she could pay them back a little. I'll just swill my face and I'll be with you she gave a faint smile all of a sudden, she felt so much more positive than she had done since she met Hugh.

Following Emma and Jed through the door Maisie said, 'thank you Emma, I don't think I have thanked you properly for helping me so much'.

'Maisie seeing you fighting back and seeing yourself as a worthy person, someone to be treated well has been thanks enough'.

Maisie smiled her thanks. She would never forget the little girl that had briefly visited her life. However, she needed to live her life in a positive useful manner, she knew she would not be looking for love again, but if she could help people not to be used like she had been and find their way back if needed to, she would when she got home try to be useful and help people who needed help how, she needed to figure that out but one thing she was sure of she would never allow herself to be taken in again.

The rest of the night passed in a whirl of serving meals to the less fortunate of society and she thoroughly enjoyed the banter and chit chat with the needy and she realised everyone had problems just in different ways. Now the trick was to make sure you overcome them. She knew exactly what she would do when she went back to England, she would retrain as a social worker. She, Maisie needed to make her life mean something and have the satisfaction of helping people to overcome their problems. This way, if any of the blame for Gracie passing away was her fault, she would at least try to atone for it in a small way, or even a big way, but she would try. It would probably take some time to pass exams but after all anything was possible if you wanted it enough.

That night Masie fell into bed and slept better than she had since arriving in New York, again she dreamt of her Gracie and awoke with a feeling of peace and tranquillity. This time she couldn't understand how there was a small white feather at the side of the small pink casket that held Gracie's ashes, it puzzled her where it had come from. It didn't matter where it had come from, she hoped that she would have Gracie in her dreams forever that way she would always feel close to her.

One week later she sat in the divorce court on pins in case Hugh turned up at the hearing, if she had any thoughts of him caring enough to attend, she realised whatever had kept him out at night that once he had tired of the reason he would move on to next idiot. It was hard to relive the life she had been leading and to relate it to strangers, it made her feel a little unclean. Maisie listened, as the Judge dissolved her marriage, with the second party not attending or filing any objections against the facts stated. Hugh had not attended, so the divorce was granted. Six weeks to go and she would be on her way home. As the Justice had granted the divorce it was as if a huge weight had been lifted from her shoulders, it was just now a time of waiting for the decree, both Emma and Jed along with the solicitor hugged her and said, 'well done, now we will go and have a little celebration'.

Maisie gave a small smile and said, 'yes I feel a strong coffee is the order of the day, that will do me fine'.

'Whatever makes you happy Maisie, you have been so strong we are proud of you'.

'Thank you, all of you, I couldn't have done it without you'.

The day came to a close after the four of them left the coffee shop and escorted Maisie back to her hotel. Soon she could begin to reorganise her life, it now belonged to her again and not Hugh Grainger.

Sitting in her room she thanked god for bringing her back to her senses, and for bringing Emma and Jed into her life. Once she was back home, she could start to re-build her life again, the thought of seeing her parents and sister again made her feel so much better in herself.

The next six weeks were spent avoiding her parent's calls and Juggling her time between helping Emma and sitting in on some of her cases, she wanted to see how being on the front line with a social worker and her cases were conducted. Emma had asked permission from her peers, and sitting in with her had given her a great insight for when she went home. She would have to enrol on a course, but she knew inside this was what she wanted to do. Maisie would miss Emma and Jed however they had promised to keep in touch. Maisie learnt how to counsel the people with similar problems to hers, and getting them to realise themselves how they could have made problems better by looking at more than one solution to the problem and choosing the one that would have worked the best and at what point to leave before it got worse. The work that Emma did was interesting and most rewarding and it made Maisie more determined to make this her career when she went home. She realised that she would have to retrain but it would be worth it, and that you could not use the same solution to everyone each person reacted differently, so you had tailor the answer to each individual.

CHAPTER THIRTEEN
GOING HOME

Today was the day that Jed would pick her up and drive her to the airport, Maisie once again stood looking out of the window, she had not told her parents of the fact that she would be arriving back home soon. Looking inside her purse she still had the key to her parent's home so she knew that if they weren't in, she would have no problem gaining access.

Maisie had already said her goodbyes to Emma, because Emma had a busy week ahead of her and Maisie had promised her that she would ring her and confirm she had arrived back home safely. Gracie's ashes were already in a sealed box with a certificate from the American customs to transport them back to England. She had also given Emma her phone number and address back in England, she knew it was a friendship that would endure. Maisie would always be thankful for the way that Emma had let her get out her story without making a judgement on either side. She had encouraged her to use her own strength within to decide what to do. She had supported the way that Maisie wanted to approach her divorce as well as explaining that Hugh would have to be dealt with by the law, but only when Maisie had achieved her goals, then they would take Hugh on. Maisie realised that it would be a huge shock to him, he obviously thought he was above the law. Perhaps it would teach him a lesson although Maisie thought he might need medical help.

The knock on the door jolted her out of her thinking, she quickly went and opened the door, it was as she expected, Jed had arrived to see her safely to the airport.

'Are you ready Maisie,' he asked with a smile.

'Yes,' she replied hesitating before saying, 'I'll miss you and Emma, your help and friendship is what has kept me sane in the last few months'.

'Yes, but you have allowed us into your life and enriched it, by giving us satisfaction that one other person will be stopped from hurting any other people because you had the strength to stand up to them'.

'I can tell you that once I have seen you on the plane safely back on your way to England myself and another police officer will on our way to arrest Hugh Grainger, and then he will be charged for his previous bodily harm to you and in light of his offence in England, he won't be free for quite a while to hurt anyone else'.

'What do you mean Jed his offence in England?'

'The NYPD decided he had committed an offence in our country, that could not go unpunished and we always have to check if there is anything that he has been charged with before, obviously if he had no previous convictions it would have been a lighter punishment. So because he was from another country we had to check with your authorities and it seems that you have not been the only person he used his fists on, he got away with that with a slap on the wrist and a fine, but he was also warned that it would be a jail sentence if he came back to court for the same offence again'.

'You mean he will go to jail?'

'Yes, and then after he has served it, he will be deported back to England. He has only himself to blame, I don't feel sorry for him, it might make him think twice about hurting someone else again'.

'The company did not check for previous offences before he came to America, the company he had come to work for they would normally check before offering him the position at the medical centre, it appears they didn't on this occasion. So sadly, he slipped through the net'.

'Right Maisie shall we get your cases and get you to the airport and on that plane, you'll soon be safely home with your parents'.

Giving Jed a small smile she watched him pick up her suitcases she just held on to her hand luggage containing her precious cargo, her Gracie. Getting into Jed's awaiting car Maisie was quite sad that she wouldn't see Jed and Emma again, unless they travelled to England on holiday, they had been good friends to her, for she had vowed never to return to America again. the memories of her life there were not the ones she wished to remember. On arriving at the airport Jed saw her to the boarding point and it wasn't until she was safely through the passport control and boarding gate that he gave her a last wave and made his way back outside, secure in the fact that Maisie would be miles away as he and his colleague would be arresting Hugh Grainger. Going back to his car he was soon advising his colleague that he was on his way to join him, Jed had felt that he had waited a long time to right this wrong and he would enjoy doing it. Now the time had come he realised that Hugh Granger would be completely shocked, as quite some weeks had passed since he had beat Maisie so badly. he would think he was quite safe now.

CHAPTER FOURTEEN
THE ARREST

Arriving at the hospital with his colleague two hours later, they entered the building and made their way to the main office. Flashing their police badges, they said, 'we are here to speak to Hugh Grainger. We don't want him to be aware that we are here, could you please have someone to take us to him'.

Yes, of course,' the young women replied. Speaking to someone in the inner office a gentleman came out, extending his hand, 'Hello there I'm John Blooms, Hugh Grainger's manager how can I be of help'. Briefly Jed and Bud the other police officer advised him that they were there to arrest Hugh not completely disclosing the reasons why.

'My God, I knew he was trouble, we have had to warn him on several occasions about his behaviour, it looks as if it has caught up with him, that'll put it in perspective for him and his girlfriend, they are toxic together. Follow me'.

'So, he had a girlfriend as well as a wife?' He asked.

'Yes, they have been together almost since he first started to work here'.

'I pity his wife, although none of us ever met her, If we had a company get together, he never brought her with him, he was always with Jodie'.

Jed answered for him, 'She will be far better off without him'.

Hugh had stopped worrying, he had not contested the divorce, the first few weeks he had lived in fear that the police would call on him thinking that Maisie had reported him to the police. He smiled to himself what a stupid cow she must be, no one had come knocking on his door or at the hospital she was probably still blaming herself. She would not even known how to go about it, he wished he had made sure of some of her money before she went, if he had held his temper a little longer, he was sure he would have pushed her enough to have her money safely in his account. But never mind he had come up with a good story to tell Jodie and it appeared to have kept her sweet. Now he could get on with building a safe home with Jodie, at least for the time being. Silly as it seemed Jodie was very much like himself, the only difference was that she had daddy to produce the money as long as she was having a good time, and it appeared that she was behaving herself, she wouldn't nag him for her security, content that daddy would cough up what she needed it.

Hugh had moved in with Jodie the day after hitting Maisie, he had lied to Jodie telling her that Maisie had used what money he had in his current account and that it would take time to get money from his accounts in England, and that he would manage when his salary went into his account. Her reply had been, 'That's no problem. I don't care, I will have you here with me all the time now, just think of what we can be doing whatever, whenever we want and you won't have to leave to go back to her'.

'I won't, you are right and as soon as my marriage has been dissolved, then we can be married quietly and tell your parents after'.

'But of course, we will get married but not quietly, mummy and daddy will want us to have a big wedding',

'I'm sure if daddy likes you and of course he will. Daddy will insist on having a big wedding and he will want me to move to a bigger house, so don't worry about marriage yet we can have lots of fun in our little love nest here,' she said as she moved over to him pushing her body against his, leaving him knowing quite well what she wanted and at that very minute. Moving to her he began to kiss and at the same push her to the bedroom where they stayed for quite some time, only coming out to replenish their bottle of wine. By bedtime they were that drunk they were oblivious of anything and had not eaten that night both falling into a drunken sleep. Jodie's father believed in her having a job, he would have preferred her to work in his company but Jodie knew that wouldn't be such fun as living on her own, and working where she was, instead of being under her father's scrutiny. She could have whoever she wanted staying with her and her father wouldn't know, she was still his innocent little girl in his eyes. That was how she wanted it to stay as long as he didn't have any idea what she was like he would still continue to be the bank of mum and dad.

The fact that they had drank until the early hours of the morning, much later than normal and of course larger quantities than when he was with Maisie. When the morning came neither of them had completely sobered up, this made them later than usual getting to work. Hugh's manager sent for him, saying he needed to see him in his office. It was a much quieter Hugh that left his manager's office, it wasn't the first time he had been warned and this apparently was his last written warning. He couldn't screw up now, not until he had secured Jodie, she would be his meal ticket, so he needed to keep his nose clean or there would be no Jodie and no apartment to live in. He now had to watch his step and make sure he stayed on the right side of his manager and Jodie.

For next few weeks both him and Jodie slowed down a little on the drinking as Jodie had been warned as well, but they made up for that by making sure they did not go short of sex. It was around four months after moving in with Jodie that they were having their coffee break when Hugh's manager came in with two men, everyone in the group went quiet when they cautioned and arrested Hugh for assaulting his wife so badly that her baby came early, and consequently she had to spend a month at the hospital.

Jed told him, 'we are also aware that your wife divorced you, it was her wish that we did not charge you at the time. However due to your past record in England we have no alternative than to make a police prosecution'.

'But you can't do that,' Hugh blustered as he saw his security with Jodie fading before his very eye's.

'Oh! But we can,' Jed replied, 'and it will give me great pleasure, after seeing the state of your wife when she arrived at hospital'.

Jodie didn't look at him as they led him handcuffed from the hospital. Jodie knew her dad would give her anything that would make her happy, but not if she was misbehaving and had caused a scandal, to her father she was still his sweet little girl and she wanted it to stay that way. The fact that he lied to her about how he had told Maisie that he wanted a divorce, and she knew nothing at all about what he had done to Maisie, she realised that she had to keep her head down for a while because some of the hospital staff knew that Hugh and Jodie had become an item. Jodie was very shallow in her mind, she was thinking that if Hugh had tired of her she might have ended up being beaten by the same hands that had caressed her, no she decided she had a lucky escape and there was always more fish in the sea. After all she had never gone short of men or sex before, she would soon have another diversion. Which meant that she did not really love him and she could see that given time would have tired of him herself.

Hugh came up before the Justice's and was quaking in his shoes for he knew it would definitely be a stretch in prison, and he was aware that in jail it would be the survival of the fittest. His face was unsmiling as the Judge sentenced him to two years in prison. How at that point he wished he had kept his temper and ignored her when she started to complain about his coming home late, if he had he wouldn't be standing here, as it was he would be in a strange country without his freedom and no money when he got out, how he hated Maisie, he had been sure that she wouldn't have complained to the police. He would now have to be celibate for the next two years, he vowed if he ever came across her in the future, he would make her pay. As it was, he had to try and make it through next two years and he wasn't sure how he would manage that, even though he was hard he knew that in jail there was always someone harder. So, at once he knew he had to befriend someone who was tough or keep his head down.

That was the last time he saw or spoke to Jodie, she very quickly moved on to the next man, after all she was single and as far as she was concerned, she had not committed a crime; he was the married one. And in any case, he shouldn't have been so handy with his fists, and there was no way she would visit him in prison. If her father were to find out he would have had a fit, she had done well to keep her steamy life away from her father. He would pay her rent on her apartment and give her an allowance, but only if she lived a decent life herself, after all he was a hard worker himself and had made his own fortune by hard work and he expected input from his family into their own finances, so far Jodie had kept him thinking she took him seriously. So, he kept her allowance topped up and took care of her rent. And again, she would play the dutiful daughter until some other diversion took her fancy, when Hugh met Jodie, he was right, they were very alike only bothered about themselves. So, once more Jodie was on the prowl.

Hugh left prison after serving the full two years, there was no reduced sentence for good behaviour as he wasn't capable of good behaviour. And because he had not much money only the small amount that was paid into his account when the hospital terminated his employment, he had assisted passage back to England. Where he had no other alternative but to go back to his mum's, as he had no collateral. He was now worse off than when he went. He had been escorted onto the aeroplane by two plain clothes policeman who watched him onto the plane and also watched it take off. He probably would not be able to enter America again as now he had a criminal record there.

Sitting on the plane he knew there was nowhere else to go but his mother's and at the moment she was not aware of the fact that he and Maisie were no longer married. How was he going to explain that away, that bloody bitch had caused this he thought, no way in his mind did he think he had brought this down on his own head. If he ever set eyes on her again, she would find that it had been a mistake to cross him. Some day he thought I'll get my own back on that poor excuse or a woman, she was daddy's little girl, she didn't even know what to do for a man. Because of her he hadn't had a woman for two years, and if she had not had him arrested, he would still be having steamy sex with Jodie. He had to admit he did miss Jodie. What he would do to have been with her for just one day before they put him on the plane home. If he could think of a good sob story for his mother, she would perhaps let him have a bit of cash to tide him over, it had started to get harder to con any money out of her. She might have begun to understand what he was like, still he would think of something he was sure. As it was, he only had the clothes he stood up in, he had one or two things he left at his mother's but none the quality he had left at Jodie's. It was true that he would have to start from scratch, the bottom of the ladder. So it was a very apprehensive Hugh that got off the plane in London to make his way back to his mother's, he hoped she would be in for he hadn't even a key to let himself in, besides the fact that he had been in jail he hadn't spoke to her for over two years, he hoped she still lived in the same house or he would be in a mess.

Chapter Fifteen
Maisie's Return

Maisie waited for her cases to come around on the conveyor belt, reaching to lift her cases off she breathed a sigh of relief, that was one part of the journey over, all she had to do now was to get a taxi to the railway station. There was plenty lined up but quite a big que of people waiting, just as the last taxi moved forward the young man in front said, 'I'm going to the railway station, if that's where you are heading, we could share', he gave her a pleasant smile. But now Maisie did not trust men in general or trust herself she needed to concentrate on herself without getting involved. He probably didn't mean anything but she remembered how it had been just so easy for Hugh to pull the wool over her eyes, until she was looking through, rose tinted glasses, believing that life would all be a bed of roses.

'Thank you, but I'll wait for the next one,' she replied politely. The young man gave her a quizzical look and climbed into the waiting taxi.

The taxi arrived and Maisie was soon on her way to the railway station, when she walked on the platform, she saw the young man higher up on the platform. Once the train came in the porter helped her with her cases onto the train, 'there you are love, I'm sure someone will help you at the other end'.

'Yes, I'm certain they will,' so giving the porter a coin she sat down in the carriage, she had a magazine however she didn't open it. What Maisie didn't realise, even with the slight scar on her nose where Hugh had headbutted her face, she was still very attractive and smart. The pale blue blouse and the dark blue trouser suit she wore, fitted her slim figure well, the fact that over the last few months she had lost quite a lot of weight, her blond hair had been washed and brushed until it shone like gold. She wasn't quite the girl that had left for America, but she wasn't the girl that had suffered at Hugh Grainger's hands. She had grown up quite a lot since her short stay in America, she now did not trust people, she would have to get to know them first before she invited them into her life. And really, she probably wouldn't have any time for getting to know anyone as she intended to throw herself into a course to realise her dream of being able to help people as a social worker.

The journey on the train was soon over and after having her luggage put into another taxi it would be just a short journey to her parent's home and the people who would always love her, Gwen and her mum and dad. She had had a couple of hours on the train to reflect on her journey out of England, how different it had been, all her hopes and dreams had been trashed by Hugh Grainger. Pulling up outside her parent's home the taxi driver carried her cases up the drive to the door, taking out her purse she paid the taxi driver and thanked him, tears appeared in her, eyes home at last. Putting her key in the door she stepped into the familiar hallway nothing had changed the gold carpet stretching from the hall up the stairs. The antique coat stand, and the small marble table holding a fresh vase of flowers. She smiled when she saw her old slippers still on the shoe rack that was always under the stairs and the emotion was a little too much, Maisie struggled not to break down, she just stood drinking in the familiar smells and sounds. The cuckoo clock on the wall and she could hear the washer going in the kitchen, her mother was always washing.

Maisie's mind flitted to the fact that whatever God had lined up for her, he had delivered her safely back to England into the into the arms of her family. Giving a sigh of relief as she stood there in the hall. Too full of emotion to think straight, she just stood, with tears slowly starting to run gently down her cheeks.

Standing and looking around at everything that was familiar to her, the lounge door opened and her father came out to see who it was in the hallway.

He looked astounded, 'Maisie my little kitten what are you doing here, why didn't you tell us you were coming for a holiday? Where is Hugh sweetheart and why are you crying my little kitten?'

Those familiar words suddenly made Maisie fly into her father's arms unable to stop the tears of relief.

'Here give me that bag,' her Dad said.

Maisie just shook her head and clutched the bag tighter, tears chocking her making it impossible for her to speak, she was not ready to put Gracie down yet. Her father held her tightly and led her gently into the lounge, and pulling her down to sit on the huge cushioned settee that had seen them through the last 30 years. The gold colour was slightly faded but clean. Sitting within his arms as she gave way to her grief, he was unaware why she was crying so, whatever had upset her must have been huge for he had never seen his little girl so upset. Yes, in his eyes she was still a little girl, and it was breaking his heart to see her hurting so badly. All he wanted to do was to make it better, if she had fallen as a little girl and grazed her knee, he would have cleaned it put a plaster on and kissed her better telling her what a brave girl she was. He didn't know what plaster she needed or how to help her, until he knew what was wrong, he just couldn't help her until he did know, so all he could do was to just hold her tight in his arms until she calmed down. Then perhaps him and mum could coax it out of her.

Her mother was just as amazed to see her daughter home, as she took in the state of her daughter and sat opposite her husband, and watched him gently console her and rub his daughter's arm as he held her close, 'there, there, lass take your time, you're safe here with us, whatever it is you take your time nothing's spoiling. Then your mum can make a nice cup of tea and if you want you can tell us all about it. If not, it can wait until you do feel like telling us. Remember a problem shared is a problem in halved, it's easier to deal with then. Besides, think about you and Gwen you always fought to look the best, do you want her to see you with swollen eyes and patchy skin from crying? Nothing is that bad that you make yourself ill. And of course, Gwen will be in soon. You just get out whatever is bothering you and then you can tell your old mum and dad what it's all about. We are always here to help, we told you before you went away'.

Maisie's mind said yes, they had and she had chosen to ignore it, thinking that life would be wonderful, as it was,yes, she had left a life to go to America that had been wonderful.

Maisie sat with her head buried in her dad's chest for nearly an hour still clutching her travelling bag until at last she became quiet.

'Mum do you think that you can make that cup tea?' her father asked. 'I'm quite parched and I'm sure that my little kitten here is ready for a cup herself, am I right?' he gently asked his daughter.

Maisie whispered, 'yes,' after all she had suffered in the hands of, her husband, she should be able to find telling her mum and dad what had happened in her short life a breeze, after all she was safely away from Hugh and free. But would she ever feel free again. And no, she suddenly realised that it still would be difficult recounting the whole sad episode, up until now it had only been Emma, Jed and the court who had heard her sad tale. However hard it would be, she owed it to her parents to tell them exactly what had happened, and to say sorry for ignoring their advice. But it had to be done and she would pull herself together, it had been the relief of making the trip back on her own, but she had managed it.

Once Mum had made the tea and handed Maisie hers, they drank it in silence, she sipped it quietly until, her mum said, 'do you want to tell me what's bothering you. Because I don't think that the tears are just because you are happy to see us, you need to get it off your chest love'.

'Mum I think it would be better if I told you when Gwen is here because I don't think I could tell it twice'

'Okay love, would you like to go and freshen up in your room while mum start's the tea?' her dad asked, 'and you can give me that bag and I'll take that up with your cases'. Maisie looked at her bag realising that she had been clutching it tightly.

'No Dad you take my bags up, I'll keep this here until I go up, her heart was breaking for she would be taking the tiny casket out to tell them, it was going to be the hardest thing that she would ever have to do. To tell her darling mum and dad that it contained her daughter, who would have been there beloved grandchild. No if she took Gracie's ashes upstairs, she would be leaving her on her own, and she didn't want to do that yet, only when she felt inside that if Gracie was watching up above, she would realise this is where she would have been loved even if only in spirit.

So, placing it gently down at the side of the armchair' leaving it there happy in the knowledge that her parents would not look in the bag until she was ready to open it herself.

'I think if you don't mind, I will just go and wash before Gwen comes in and I can tell you what has happened after tea if you don't mind. You see I will have to be strong, and I can be, because I'm here with the people that love me, and where everything is familiar and comfortable'.

'That's okay, you take your time, freshen up and we'll listen to what you have to say afterwards' 'But we are so happy to see you, and just think how surprised and happy Gwen will be when she comes in'.

Maisie thought, yes Gwen would be happy to see her but they needed to have their tea first, for she knew that if she told her family of her heartache and life as Hugh Grainger's wife they would not feel like eating, they would be appalled at the way he had treated her. And when her dad knew she was aware of how upset and angry he would be, her mum and dad loved both Maisie and Gwen the same, but her mother's job had been to nurture them and dad's to protect and he would feel that he had failed, but that was not his fault but her own for not listening to their sound advice. One thing was certain, she wouldn't try running before she could walk again.

When Maisie came back into the living room, she had showered and changed from her travelling clothes into a fresh dress of dark blue, she wore no wedding ring on her finger, this had not gone unnoticed by her mum she had been aware of the fact when her daughter was sitting on the settee clutching the travelling bag. Just at that moment Gwen was heard calling from the hallway.

'I'm home Mum'.

Her father answered, 'were in here love'.

Gwen entered the room asking, 'whose bags are those,' and getting no further, she exclaimed in delight. 'Maisie what are you doing here. Why didn't you tell us that you were coming?' Then giving her sister a puzzled look, she took in her pale face and how she had lost weight, 'aren't you well?' She could not help asking as she moved forward to hug her sister, they both clung to each other tightly, and at the same time said, 'I've missed you so much'.

'Me too, me too, it's so good to see you'.

'I haven't been myself just lately, but I will be now I'm back here with you'.

'Now shall we have tea?' her mum asked, 'then we can all have a good chin wag about what we have all been doing since we last saw one another'.

'Yes.' after tea mum' Maisie answered quietly.

'I still can't believe you are here,' Gwen said again, giving her another quick hug. They went to the table, funny enough they seemed to sit in the same place as they had before she left for America just as if she had not been away. But Maisie certainly knew she had been away and hoped it would not happen to their Gwen, she hoped if ever Gwen met anyone that they would be honourable, gentle and loving, yes that is what she wished for her sister, not what she had recently endured.

She hoped with all her heart that there was someone out there for Gwen who would love and cherish her, someone that Gwen would love and respect for as long as her life.

Sitting at the table eating her mother's steak and kidney pie with fresh veg, followed by fresh fruit salad, they chatted and kept up small talk and Maisie was aware that they were all being diplomatic for they all must be wondering why she was no longer pregnant, none had asked about the baby or mentioned Hugh again.

'You haven't eaten much love, were you not hungry?

'It was lovely mum I haven't much of an appetite just lately, but I'm sure your cooking will help me get it back'.

'I'll help clear the table Mum,' Gwen said, 'and then we'll have coffee in the lounge.'

I'll help too Mum, Maisie said.

'No! you can sit down, you have had a long journey travelling back home, it won't take us a minute and I'll make the coffee, we can do the dishes later I've only to stack the dishwasher after, so that won't be hard'.

Maisie listened to the familiar sound of her mum bustling about in the kitchen, no one knew how safe and happy she was sitting here in her mum and dad's home.

It only took Gwen and her mum a few minutes to make the coffee.

'Here we are,' her mum said walking back into the room and placing the tray down on the coffee table, 'now we can have a quiet chat if you feel up to it'.

Maisie took a drink of her coffee. 'I don't really know where to start, except to say that you and dad were right I should have listened to you', I was thinking with my heart and not my head'. A stray tear ran down her face, 'and I paid the price, yes you were right. Hugh changed straight after the wedding, it was if I didn't exist, he left me night after night on my own for months and he would not talk housekeeping, we needed to budget for our accounts. I even had to pay the bills out of my own money. Every time I tried to talk to him, he became aggressive, so I would find it easier not to rock the boat. If it hadn't been for the fact that I got myself a job I think I would have died of loneliness. Even when I told him I was pregnant he shouted at me and asked me why I didn't make sure that I didn't get pregnant, asking me if I wanted it, and suggesting an abortion or that I got rid of my baby. How could he ask me that Mum, we were married can anyone tell me why? 'And when I did find the courage to ask him why he was never home at night, and came in so late he beat me, not on one occasion but more, the last time he beat me so bad I had to sneak out of the flat and get medical help'.

'And the baby?' her mother asked quietly.

'My Gracie,' she said and the tears began to fall again, as the words fought to come out, and she could not manage for a few minutes to speak, struggling not to get upset again, and her heart was still breaking if she allowed herself the luxury of thinking of her beautiful baby girl.

'Take your time my little kitten,' her dad said, he already had to control himself because he had tears in his eyes too. What had happened to the child to upset her so much? He felt her hurt and sadness in his own heart.

'My beautiful little girl; it was my fault for staying with him too long, my fault,' she said again, 'for staying too long, If I had not foolishly thought he would change she might still be here'.

'What happened,' her father quietly asked her.

'He beat me for asking for explanations as to where he had been and for refusing to hand my money over to him; something told me not to. When I got to the hospital I had passed out in the taxi, the taxi driver went in and got me help. When I eventually came to, they had delivered Gracie, and I must have been out for quite a few days. The doctor told me that she would probably slip back into the hands of god because she had been delivered so early and I had taken quite a beating, the stress and blows had not helped her, so you see it was my fault as well. I should have realised that he wouldn't change'.

'She struggled to hang on to her life but it was just too much for her and just nine weeks later she died. The nurses and doctors at the hospital were all so very kind to me, and they were stranger's and yet Hugh didn't even try to find where I was. I know you would have loved her, as you both loved Gwen and I, she slipped away and I had lost her. Why did God not make me listen to you and Dad?'

'Everything happens for a reason Maisie, don't cry again, the time for crying is over you must look forward now not back'. 'We'll see a solicitor tomorrow and file for a divorce'.

'No dad there's no need'.

'There's every need', he exploded.

'No Dad you see I'm already divorced, Emma my social worker helped me with her husband Jed, he was a police officer. By now I think Hugh will have been charged with assault, and apparently, he has done it before in England so he might not have got away with it this time. They held off until after the divorce, however once Jed had seen me safely on the plane, he and a colleague went to arrest him. I hope I never set eyes on him ever again'. Reaching down for her hand luggage she gently took out the little pink box. And the tears began to fall again and not just Maisie's.

'My darling girl her mum whispered'. And this time she was enfolded in her mother's arms and not her dads. 'You're safe with us my darling, he will soon be a bad memory, and time will heal. If we had known we would have been over and brought you back so he couldn't have hurt you anymore'. 'You should have rung us and confided in us sooner, always come to us, don't ever be frightened of asking for help, we will, always be here to help you'.

Maisie's dad was appalled at the treatment that Hugh had meted out to his daughter and wished that he and her mum could have made it better, but it would take a long time to heal the scars of what she had gone through she was home now and they would do every-thing possible to make it better. And they too hoped they never set eyes on him. For if her dad did, he knew he was older but he would have wanted to thrash him in the same way as he had hurt his daughter, but inside Maisie's dad knew that nothing could be settled with fists; it would only give a certain type of satisfaction.

CHAPTER SIXTEEN
RETURNING TO NORMAL LIFE

Maisie took time to settle down into family life, her mum and dad made sure they were there if she wanted them but also gave her space to grieve and forget her appalling treatment from Hugh. A month passed before she made her parents aware of what she was going to do, with some of her money that her grandfather had left her she was going back to college to be a social worker. Telling her mum and dad that Emma, who had kept her sane throughout her ordeal of Gracie's death and her divorce had been such a comfort and a tower of strength, that she wanted to retrain and help people, because without people like Emma there would be women that would not know where to turn, and would probably stay in abusive relationships because they didn't know any other way. Sometimes the lack of money kept them shackled to the life they were living. Yes, she vowed she would do everything in her power to help people that were enduring what she had. And for everyone she helped to become strong it would help herself to continue to be strong.

So true to her word Maisie looked through the local colleges and found a course that she could do by distance learning with two residential periods with tutors, the course would take her three years, two learning and one year as a trainee, working alongside a trained social work. This suited Maisie because she could go back to work and study at night time and she knew that Gwen would help to test her knowledge to make sure she had absorbed the course work. Gwen was staying close to Maisie, however when she suggested that they had a night out it was always no, she no longer trusted her judgement if she went out and met the opposite sex. But on the odd occasion she would be persuaded to go for lunch and to shop, but always would return for tea and then stay in with her mum and dad.

The thing that worried her mum and dad was that Maisie was no longer the bubbly confident girl from the past. She was quiet and didn't smile much. They knew she was still grieving, but so were they, not just for the granddaughter they had never known but for their not so little girl that they had watched and loved as she became the beautiful young woman that she had been. Someday she might be able to forget, but if they could have suffered the hurt for her, they would have. As it was, they could only stand by and endure the thought that Maisie had to grieve and get over it herself.

It was Just two months later that Maisie had the call from Emma and Jed telling her that Hugh had been charged and given a sentence of two years for assaulting her, taking into account the suspended sentence in England. Maisie's answer was he perhaps would learn that he can't have all his own way. And that he needs to change his ways. Throughout her short marriage she had only met Hugh's mother and father once, there had been no contact since, she wondered if they even knew that they were now divorced, he must have been very spoilt as a young man. The call then turned to how Maisie was now and if she had started her course, they chatted for around 30 minutes saying goodbye and promising to keep in contact and to keep her informed on her progress in studying. Emma promised to send her some more books explaining cases that she might come up against and help to point her into the right direction or give her some insight in how to deal with these problems.

Maisie found herself preparing herself for another interview, it was at the local solicitor's office she hoped that she would be successful because she could still be earning money and therefore pay her way at her mum's and save a little money. Again, she looked smart in her tan coloured suit and cream blouse. And she felt that after the interview she had done well. The solicitors rang her at the end of the next week offering her the position saying they would put her a contract in the post and would she sign it and return it as soon as possible. They also arranged for her to start work in two weeks, this suited Maisie because she was now ready to embark on her coursework as it had arrived. So, she was quite ready to balance the two, work and her qualifications.

Maisie balanced her days working at 'Johnston and Jones' solicitors and studying at night, she found that she really enjoyed the challenge of the work, it was interesting and enlightening the different aspects and situations again were challenging. However, when giving her answers to the projects she always managed to get it right, perhaps it was because she had gone through some of the situations herself and that she had a deeper understanding of the situations to help the person that needed help. Gwen would help her where possible and she was a great help when Maisie talked of ways to get the people to help themselves, Gwen would listen and come up with ideas herself and Maisie had to admit Gwen had a sharp mind and was interested in the type of cases that would crop up. She was a great help and Maisie loved having her around and listening to her banter, they were just as they used to be, only Maisie didn't realise how much quieter she herself was since her return to England. But Maisie was determined that she would do well and pass her course with flying colours, she couldn't wait to be helping people, so she was determined to complete the allotted time she had committed to, and so she stuck carefully to the three hours studying. Always saying no to a night out.

Before Maisie knew where she was, she had completed the first twelve months of her studying she had also completed her first residential and passed the first exams with credits. She was respected by the people she worked with at the solicitor's, however they could not understand why when a couple of young junior solicitors had asked her out, she always declined. Try as they might Maisie always said no. She spent her life now studying to help people to trust and respect themselves, and here she was, she still could not believe in her own judgement, and by now she should do. She realised that inside she must have been frightened of being hurt again, Maisie had her heart ringfenced no one else would ever get through. On talking to Gwen, she had made her promise that she would listen to her mum and dad and make sure she took it slowly, even if she thought that she was madly in love and couldn't live without him, make sure you are ruled by your head and not your heart. Try and find someone like dad, yes that's the answer she said almost to herself. If she chose someone like her dad then she would be sure to have a good husband, but how would you know they were like dad she wondered. Thinking how her dad was, it was not easy to work out, Hugh had always been charming, but yes there was a difference. Charming was not being caring or loving and her dad was respectful. Thinking back, she had overlooked all these qualities because he was one thing charming. And being charming was not enough.

Maisie continued to work hard and study at night time, and still her parents worried about the fact that she never went out to any social events. Gwen was forever asking her to go with her but Maisie's answer was always the same, 'I need to complete my studies, when I've done that, I will have more free time'. So, Gwen spent more time staying in and helping Maisie to complete her assignments on the pretext that Maisie would get through her exams that much quicker, and that Maisie would have to go out with her then. So, night after night on coming home after work they would both have their tea and then closet themselves in the dining room with Maisie's books and study. Gwen declared that she herself could be a qualified social worker at the end of the course, she had learnt so much.

Soon it was once again the residential course, this one was a breeze, most of the other people studying made sure they celebrated at night time and once again Maisie declined to join in, which made her more uncomfortable when the examiner once more gave her top marks with credits. At last she was waiting for the results of her last exams, which she passed with flying colours. Now she had to wait to see where she was to be sent for her last twelve months of training and eventually, she could give in her notice at the solicitors. She would be sorry to leave as they had all been very good to her even though she did not mix with them much. She had now reached her goal and because she had done distance learning and gone to work, her grandfather's money had not been spent. Which meant that if she had to train further afield, because you had to go where they sent you, she could buy a flat or a small house, for she would need somewhere to stay and she would prefer to buy than rent that way she would have some collateral.

'Now Maisie,' Gwen said, 'we will have to look at going out, you have done your studying now so no more excuses'.

'All right Gwen we will have a day out soon I promise,' Maisie said.

Maisie would never forget what Hugh had done to her and her little girl, however the last two years had helped her to come to terms with it. She still could not let go of Gracie's little casket of ashes, as she could not bear to part with them despite her parents gently telling her it was time to let go and put her little girl to rest.

'It will help to heal your heart Maisie my little kitten, you can still visit her at her resting place'. 'Trust me Maisie,' her mum said, 'it will get easier once you put her to rest'.

'Mum I understand what you are saying but I'm just not ready to let her go yet. I couldn't stand the thought of her in the ground, I know I'm being selfish, but

I would feel as if I don't care like her father didn't. At the moment I need to keep her a little longer, you do understand don't you Mum?

'Yes love, but promise me you will think about it'.

'I will Mum,' Maisie said, giving her mum a hug and kiss. She knew they meant well but for the life of her she needed Gracie with her at the moment and just couldn't let go.

CHAPTER SEVENTEEN
MAISIE'S SOCIAL PLACING

Maisie's placing came through two weeks after her exam results, she would start in two months and it was to be in Chester, which would be a little too far for travelling home at night to Southport. So, she decided to travel to Chester with Gwen, they could then look for a small semi or a flat. She preferred a semi because she would like a garden, she loved flowers and hoped that she could grow some, and possibly some vegetables. What she didn't realise was that being a social worker could take a lot of time up and gardens did too. But determined that a house could be made into a home better than a flat this is what she would look for a house.

So, on Saturday morning they decided to ring all the estate agents in Chester, and get them to forward her the details of houses they had in her price range. She had already booked a week off and Gwen had done the same. That should be enough time to choose one, the conveyancing could be done by the solicitors she would be leaving so she would be there until the week she took up her post with the social services. The house would have to be vacant possession so that she could move quickly. Once that was done Gwen said, 'come on let's drive down there today, we can start looking while we wait for specifications to come through. Then we can have lunch out and a walk around to spot any interesting places when I come down'.

'Okay bossy boots' replied Maisie with a slight smile, give me a little time to get changed. The day was cool, it was a November day and she wanted to dress in something smart but warm. So, she was soon ready in a black pair of slacks, black sweater and a red short mohair coat. With matching black slip on shoes, bag, and gloves.

When Gwen appeared, she said snap she was almost dressed the same with black sweater, slacks and red coat, it was a different style and her bag and gloves were red, but they were almost identical in their matching colours. Getting into Gwen's car, she had insisted on driving, her logic was that Maisie would not be able to come home until Gwen was willing to drive, she was intent on Maisie having a day out, and she meant a day out, not half a day. They engaged in small talk as they travelled and they were soon on the motorway. Gwen was a good driver and they arrived at their destination quickly. Gwen had kept up a running commentary as they drove, Maisie always answered but did not initiate any conversation herself. And Gwen thought if I came across Hugh, I could cheerfully rip his head off and use it for a football myself, what he had done to Maisie was awful, he had crippled her emotions. Very soon Gwen was pulling into a car park taking note of the street they had walked onto to ensure they would find their way back. Chester held many, many, estate agents and soon they had covered at least half a dozen, nothing jumped out at her so Maisie said, 'let's just stop for a cup of coffee and get a second wind, we can have a look through these again and see if we have missed anything'.

There were one or two that would have fitted the bill but for some reason Maisie hadn't been drawn to any of the pictures. 'Okay Gwen said let's try along the other end of Chester, we perhaps might have a little more luck there'.

So, strolling arm in arm up the street they stopped when they spotted another estate agent's shop on the other side of the road. Crossing over carefully they began to look inside the window. 'Look' Maisie said staring into the window 'there a two bedroomed cottage on the outskirts of Chester two bedrooms, lounge, small dining room, kitchen and bathroom with a separate toilet downstairs shower. It's in my price range Gwen. Let's see if we can look at it, it's in a row of five so it's not lonely and I can get my car on the front'.

'Of course, we can, come on' she said linking Maisie's arm once more, she said 'let's have a nosey'.

Walking into the estate agents they were soon arranging to view the cottage, the estate agent said, 'have you a satnav?'

'yes,' Gwen answered. 'Well I can't leave the shop until my colleague comes back from lunch can we say in around an hour'.

'That will be fine we can just have our lunch and make our way there'. So, agreeing to meet in one hour they could see a little tearoom across the road.

'That will do Gwen it looks quite clean, let's go back we can just about fit our lunch in'.

Crossing the road once more, they were escorted to a table, looking at the lunch menu they ordered an omelette with salad and a bowl of chips and coffee after. Both girls enjoyed their meal and made their way outside. Looking in a shop window they passed Maisie said, 'look there's a sale on we'll have a look in here when we come back.'

Gwen gently said, 'but you still have all your wedding presents from when you got married Mum put them in the loft. I know how you feel but the presents were mostly off our family not Hugh's, so he won't have tainted them, it makes sense to see what you have before you buy anything. Come on Maisie don't let that vile man spoil everything, we can get through this if we stay strong as a family'.

'You are right as usual Gwen, I need to forget and get on with my life, the wedding presents are just item's no different than I will have to buy.

'Come on let's go and have look at what might be your castle and my weekend holiday home"

Maisie managed a small smile at this, yes things were going to be different know she, felt more positive than, she had in a while. She intended to make this new career work it was a new start and she intended to make a success of it. Hugging Gwen's arm again in apprecia-tion she did not have to tell her how she was feeling, Gwen already knew, she vowed she would not let anyone spoil Maisie recovery she was still very fragile and Gwen could see this even though Maisie pretended to be strong.

Pulling up outside the small cottage, Maisie realised it needed some love, it had a small garden at the front, which was mainly lawn, she could make a small feature in the front perhaps a circle of flower's in the middle of the lawn. The cottage rendering itself was painted white and needed a fresh coat, the door needed repainting and it would lift the front so much. The man from the estate agents had already arrived.

'There you are,' he said. 'I know what you are going to say it needs a little TLC but that could soon be achieved, it's just decorating really'.

'Yes,' Maisie answered, 'decorating, some new carpet and kitchen cupboards. And possibly a new toilet and basin,' getting carried away with how she could improve it.

There was a small hallway with the stairs directly in front of the door they had come through, the paper was tired and outdated.

'I've just done a damp test as I've gone through,' said the estate agent, 'and you can see that there is no damp; that's a good sign. Now the lounge is a good size, it's not massive, but not too small and the bay window lets in plenty of light'.

The cottage was double fronted, and directly opposite the lounge door was another door this was the dining room, a little smaller than the lounge, but big enough for a dining table and a sideboard. Once again, the young man did a damp test to show that it was just cosmetic work that needed to be done. At the end of the dining room was a door that led into a medium sized kitchen, there was another door leading to a small passage where there was a loo and a downstairs shower. It all wanted painting and tiling but it was doable. Again, damp tests were done to show her she didn't need to worry over that. Now that just leaves the upstairs, at the top there was a sizable landing which would take a small sofa bed that was if her mum and dad stayed as well as Gwen there was also a medium sized bathroom, again it had a shower, sink and loo with it not having a bath it looked bigger. Maisie had thought new loo's, that would mean two, she expected in an older cottage that they would need renewing and she was right. And there were two bedrooms this would be enough. For her she looked through the back window it had a back garden, but it definitely was a mess very overgrown. Maisie felt that the cottage felt nice.

'Would you mind if I just have a word with my sister?'

'Gwen, I like this if I could make an offer what would you say?'

'Go for it, Maisie I like it, try knocking £10,000 of. If you look at the sign it's being sold because it has been a snatch back because of non-payment of mortgage. Go for it'.

Going back to the estate agent he said he would put it to the vendor, he wasn't sure whether or not they would get back today but he would ring them as soon as he could, so giving him a phone number they said their goodbye's.

'Right said Gwen I feel a shopping spree coming on, then another coffee'.

'Shopping,' Maisie said, 'I will have to leave that until I see if they accept my offer, I might need my money for that, I have a good feeling about that house. It feels a little like it will be a whole new start I hope, but I can stretch to another coffee'. Maisie and Gwen strolled around the shops linking each other's arms, Maisie thinking that this was the first day of her new life, looking around the big department stores she saw lots of things she might need, but she satisfied herself with picking up brochures on furniture. Gwen ended up with quite a few bags from the ladies department. As they were strolling around that department Maisie, spotted an amber coloured woollen dress. 'Oh, Gwen that's nice,' pointing at the dress.'

'Try it on Maisie, so I can see what it looks like on,' Maisie asked the shop assistant for the dress in her size, going into the cubicle she put the dress on and asking Gwen how she looked.

'Just like you did two years ago, my beautiful sister'.

Turning to the assistant Gwen said, 'we will take that please'.

'No Gwen, I need to keep my money for my house, I don't know yet what I'll need'.

'Well,' said Gwen, everyone has housewarming presents and I'm not giving you a boring kettle you are having this dress, no argument's'.

'You know you are the best sister ever Gwen'.

I know, you don't have to tell me,' she laughed. '

Right coffee's; my treat. I can just about afford that' Maisie smiled as she said it.

'You are getting to be quite a scrooge,' Gwen threw back.

'I know living with Hugh made me that way, but I'm sure eventually I will get over it. Now coffee,' she said pulling Gwen back into a tearoom they were passing. 'Could you eat a scone as well?' Maisie said.

'Please,' was Gwen's answer, 'we need to enjoy today, but I warn you, you will get sick of me taking over your spare room at weekends'.

Just as they decided to have a refill of coffee Maisie's phone rang, it was the estate agent to say her offer had been accepted.

'That's great', she said, giving them the solicitors number that she worked for, they may as well deal with it for her and she would not have to keep making appointments to sort her conveyancing and contracts out, she would be on hand, And she was a first time buyer and she didn't have to wait for the vendor to move out. She could possibly stay at a bed and breakfast for around a month while she had the main rooms decorated or updated, mainly a bedroom, the kitchen, and the bathroom. Everywhere else could wait and be done as she went along.

Come on we better get home and tell Mum and Dad, we can take them down to see it next week the estate agent will let her take them in, she felt more excited than she had for a good while. Please God make this period in my life be happier than the last two years. Going back home Gwen and Maisie were that excited about the house that their mum and dad were just relieved to see Maisie being positive over the future.

'It looks as if you might need your uncle Ted and your good old dad to help you kitten. Gwen, Mum and you can do the cleaning before we decorate for you.

'Now your mum and I have been talking and we want to treat both you and Gwen the same, we gave you £10,000 towards your house funds it's hard for me to ask have you still got it?'

'Yes Dad, that was something that I did not give to Hugh he tried to get some money off me but I couldn't understand what he was doing with his money as he never gave me any. And I paid all the bills out of my wages, he rarely came home for tea, only having breakfast in the morning. Wine was the only thing that I bought with what little food I got for myself'.

'Wine, who was that for? asked her dad.

'For Hugh, he would get really angry if I had none in'.

'Why, I wasn't aware he drank so much Dad, but I never let him have my savings. What I spent on rent in the beginning when I wasn't working, I tried to, put back and I managed to put some back Dad so most of it is intact'.

'Good Mum and I decided to give you another £10.000, so Gwen, we will give you your £20,000 to put in a bank in your name for when you decide you need to fly the nest, we won't spend it, and we have enough for now'.

'Dad you don't have to do that,' Maisie said with tears in her eyes.

'No, we don't have to my kittens, we want to its only standing in the bank and when we've gone you will have the house and what money is left'.

'Both your mum and I will feel more contented that you have that little bit of security'.

Both Maisie and Gwen said they couldn't thank them enough. Monday she would call into her bank and see what deposit she needed to put down, the smaller the mortgage the less years she would have to pay, it made sense. In her mind it was important to pay it off as soon as possible. She would have to keep a modest sum for furniture and any repairs and a little over for emergencies, but she knew she had been raised to value what she had and not to waste.

The following week her father and mother plus Gwen went with her to view the property again, she arranged a survey and there were no glaring problems, as the estate agent had said. She had paid the deposit to her solicitor and also knew what the, solicitors fees would be, they had given her a discount because she worked for them, even though she had given her notice in. Her signing of contracts would be in two weeks, exactly one month after she said yes to purchasing it, the day she would finish working for them. One of the older ladies she worked with was making her curtains, they had measured all the windows and chose the materials and she was already hard at work making them. Maisie had paid for a small suite in green and was having arm covers made to keep the arms clean. She had chosen a plain gold coloured carpet and her father was going to decorate the lounge, while her uncle Ted concentrated on the bedrooms.

Maisie had spent quite a bit of her money on the deposit, leaving her enough money to furnish the cottage and a modest sum left over for a rainy day. She would start her training next week, looking around the lounge her father had made a great job, the gold curtains were now hanging at the windows, and the room was carpeted in the same gold shade. The walls were a delicate shade of gold making the room look warm and inviting, and finished with a pale green settee. There was a gold and green hearth rug a corner cabinet with a full tea set that her aunt and uncle had given her, there was also a coffee table holding a vase of flowers. Maisie, her mother, and Gwen had given the kitchen cupboards a thorough cleaning. The paintwork on the units had come up like new so she did not have on spend money on new cupboards. She realised that the wedding presents had been mostly from her family and saved her quite an amount of money and it wasn't as if she had used them when she lived with Hugh. The bathroom and bedrooms had been painted and decorated a new toilet downstairs, upstairs it and a new shower had been a must downstairs, it all look really homely.

Now all she had to do was make a success of the vocation that she had chosen, now everything had been done in the house, her mum and dad needed a rest. She had urged them to leave the garden she could get to that later. They gratefully fell in with her suggestion and they said the front garden was okay for now, the back garden would be a project for later, after all they weren't getting any younger. Maisie had already someone engaged to paint the front of the house and she was quite pleased now that she had got this far.

CHAPTER EIGHTEEN
BLANCHE HUGHES

Maisie settled into her new job, the social worker, Blanche Hughes, she worked with was really nice, and she would always discuss and work through the case notes with her before seeing the client so that she was aware of the counselling in advance that they would use in particular cases. All though she was a little older than Maisie they soon became firm friends, very often Blanche would call on Maisie for a cup of tea, and spend a little time. They would talk about their lives, Maisie confided in Blanche about the life she had spent with Hugh and Blanche could totally understand why Maisie had decided to become a social worker. Sitting looking through the window Blanche said, 'your back garden looks as if it needs a little work before the winter sets in'.

'Yes, Dad and my uncle Ted really worked hard decorating and getting the inside done, but they need a little rest at the moment and said they would get to it in the spring'.

'Look Maisie you can tell me to butt out, but my brother Matt loves gardening and he always has a little time to spare in the week, he will come and tidy it up before the winter',

'I really don't know about that, I'm sure you'll understand Blanche I'm not sure I'm comfortable with someone I don't know around'.

'Don't be silly Maisie you will hardly see him he very often works at night, so he would be here a few hours when you are working, and when you do see him I'm quite certain you will like him, and a cup of tea if you're around, would be all he would charge. Try it and see, if he does get in your way and you find he does, I'll tell him to leave it, let's face it everyone likes to give a little help sometimes in their life, don't they?

'Yes of course they do, that's why I'm training to be a social worker,' said Maisie it was just as if a light bulb had gone on and she herself still needed to be helped, she had to trust people a little more. And her mum once said that you had to accept help gracefully as well as give it, so she would try it.

True to her word when Maisie came home, she could see that someone had been digging in the far end if the garden, and that someone must have been Matt, Blanches brother, there was no one there and it looked as if he had marked out a patch to grow veg, she noticed that the ground within this area had been cleared and dug over. This was a good start and Maisie decided to put some money each week into a tin to help pay for plants and some extra to pay Matt a little money, Maisie liked to pay her own way and wanted to make sure she gave him something for his trouble. After all gardening was hard work and she was glad that her dad would be spared doing it for her, as he wasn't getting any younger and that way the job would be getting done sooner rather than later.

When Maisie went to work Blanche gave Maisie a small bill for winter veg that matt had purchased the plants for. There was winter cabbages, sprouts, onions, and potatoes to start off with as the season's changed then they could plant the seasonal veg that came along and he also had purchased some kerb edging, this would then isolate the veg from the lawn. Because Matt was doing the work and hadn't asked for any payment, she was putting some money in the box for him, but it wasn't like paying a gardener the set amounts they charged, so it was doable, a real help and made it easier.

Each day over the next month there had been a little more done, the veg patch was clearly defined with the edging stones around the patch, the lawn had been neatly cut. The small patio had been cleaned and was free of weeds. Maisie marvelled at the fact this had all been done without her even seeing anyone. It was cold now, but in the summer, she could see herself out there filling the borders with flowers. And a small table and chairs to sit by and enjoy the late sunshine. In one way she was glad that the work was being done while she was out, but she felt that she needed to thank the kind man who had done the work in the garden. Confident that she would see him eventually so that she could thank him face to face she was more than happy with the work that had been done and wanted him to know. Blanche's brother must be very kind hearted.

Not meeting Matt was taken out of her hands, it was Saturday morning and her mum, dad and Gwen had arranged to visit, mum and the girls were going to have a day in Chester shopping while dad spent the day on some small jobs that he knew wanted completing. They all arrived at 10 o'clock this was the time they had arranged. Maisie was up and ready arranging a tray with teapot and cups ready to make them a cuppa as they arrived. This was the first time Maisie's mum had turned down a cup of tea she said, 'if we stay drinking tea now most of the morning will be gone and we have loads of Christmas shopping to do, what do you think Gwen? Well we can have a drink of tea or coffee while we are out and dad can have some sandwiches ready when we come in'.

'Oh! can I?' their dad said, 'putting on me again'.

'You know we all love you Dad and you enjoy looking after us both,' Gwen and Maisie chorused together.

Slowly they could see their beautiful daughter returning, she was still quieter than she was before she married Hugh however every now and then she gave a rare smile it was like a ray of sunshine and made her mum and dad aware that everything heals in time and they looked forward to the time when Maisie would smile from the inside as well as the outside..

Maisie's dad was working on the landing painting the stair rail, when he went into the bathroom to wash his hands, wandering into the spare bedroom he saw a man repairing the back fence, knowing that Maisie had someone to do the garden he thought the least he could do was to nip into the kitchen and make a cup of tea and offer him a biscuit with it, after all it was quite cold out today. Putting two mugs of hot tea on a tray and a plate of biscuits he went outside.

'Hello there you must be Matt. I thought you would like a cup of tea'.

The young man standing there had kind, pleasant face, what Maisie's dad would have described as honest and open. He had deep blue eyes and he was about six foot. His smile was kind, 'Yes, I'm Blanches brother

I love gardening in my spare time and Blanche asked me to help out. So,' he smiled, 'here I am, the fence needed repairing and next week I wanted to weather seal the fence. I had a little time over this morning so it would be just enough time to do the repair, I've nearly finished now, I have a little work on this afternoon and I need a little time to get changed'.

'Well here you are lad, a hot cup of tea, do you take sugar?'

'No just milk is fine, and I'll have one of those biscuits if you don't mind, they look freshly made'.

'They are, Mum made them and brought a tin for Maisie'.

'Does your wife do much baking?

'Yes, she does quite a bit, her apple pies are famous'.

'Next time I come I'll bring some apples, we picked and stored quite a few, I can leave some with Maisie to pass on, we always have too many to use'.

'My wife, will appreciate that and I'm sure she will send you a pie to try, thank you, I'll leave you to it now I'd better get on now or the three of them might accuse me of slacking,' Maisie's dad said with a smile. 'When you finish your tea just pop the cup on the side in the kitchen and I'll wash it with mine. I better get some work done myself, I hope I see you again.'

'Yes!' said Matt holding his hand out. Maisie's dad gripped it firmly, thinking this young man appeared to very pleasant and kind, and he was certainly doing a good job. Maisie's dad had the impression of great strength of character and gentleness around this young man, a quiet bearing. Yes, he liked this young man, to be fair he was worried that a stranger that Maisie had not seen or met was doing work at Maisie's house, but now he had met him he felt no qualms about him continuing to work at the cottage. Yes! he was pleased and could see himself enjoying a chat with him if he was here when he visited again.

When Maisie's dad had finished his job in the bathroom and he came down stairs the garden was empty and both cups had been washed, put on the tray and the biscuits recovered with cling film. Smiling he placed another two cups on the tray in readiness for his three girls to come home. Mum, Gwen and Maisie were soon back and enjoying the fish and chips they had brought back with them and chatting away about the Christmas bargains they had managed to pick up in the sales. Although there was laughter and fun around the table her father noticed that Maisie had withdrawn back into herself and he knew why, it was the day before her Gracie had died, he noticed the date on the small pink casket and his heart was hurting for his daughter. If he could he would have borne all the hurt for her, however, she needed to grieve for her baby however long it took, and it would probably be easier when she could part with Gracie's ashes, but he could see she wasn't ready yet. It would take a little more time, and a little more patience. He hoped it would not be too long, his girl deserved some happiness. He wanted nothing more than to hold her and take her hurt away and he couldn't, so it hurt him too.

Once they had finished tea Gwen said, 'what shall we do now, have you still got your monopoly game?'

Maisie shook her head gave a small smile. 'We'll just have to watch the television, 'I'll have the control,' their mother said, or it will be football or boxing'. After another hour Gwen said had we better get a move on it's getting late, and I'm sure Maisie needs her beauty sleep as much as I do. After more hugs and promising to come over for tea with the three of them they left, leaving Maisie to lock up and think about her child. She slowly made her way upstairs to sit on the bed and picking up the casket she let a tear slide down her face. 'Why lord, what did I do to deserve this, why did you take my baby?' she whispered, 'my Gracie'.

Wearily putting it back on the cabinet she went to take a shower, tomorrow was another day, it was Sunday and she would spend the time reading over her case notes and prioritising her work load in readiness for Monday, that little bit of preparation helped her so that she was ready and knew which scenario she would use with Blanche running over it with her before the appointment's.

Getting into bed Maisie was tired but couldn't go to sleep, she must have eventually fallen asleep as she awoke suddenly to the phone ringing. It was Emma in America saying she had rung to see how she was getting on. They spent around thirty minutes chatting and at the end of the call Maisie promised she would ring Emma over Christmas. Emma had rung her because she was aware that it was the anniversary of Gracie's death, if she had lived Gracie would have been just three years old, she wanted Maisie to know that someone, however, far away was still thinking about her and cared about how Maisie felt. Emma hoped that her call had in some way made Maisie feel less isolated and better in herself, she was aware that it would take a while for her to get over what had happened to her, it had been a real test in her life. Maisie had appeared to be genuinely pleased to hear from her. Sunday arrived and Maisie walked to the bottom of the garden her father had briefly told her that he had spoken to Matt and said he appeared to be a very nice chap, genuine and trustworthy, and kind.

Maisie couldn't help but say, 'to have all the things you have mentioned to his credit, he must be a saint Dad'.

'Maisie,' her dad said reproachfully, 'that's not worthy of you, stop and think, you have to understand that everyone is not like Hugh'.

'I know Dad but I thought Hugh wonderful, and I know I have to get over putting everyone in the same category, but it will be a long time before I trust anyone else. You see Dad you only see what you want to see, because I didn't listen to you, I didn't have time to look beyond the outside,' she said. 'And he was very charming Dad and I didn't look beyond that'.

'You will my little kitten, you will, it will just take time and a little healing. Not everyone is bad, do you think your old dad is?'

'No! never Dad, that's what I found so strange, I kept thinking how you and mum were with each other and comparing how Hugh was with me. He was unkind, and aggressive, and never there. I felt so alone, when I had been to work and came home either you or Mum or both of you were here waiting to take care of your family. You and Mum made our house a home, whereas the apartment in America was just a house, you were never interested in drinking every night, you were just our wonderful mum and dad. Perhaps I had been given too much already having such a wonderful family I will always appreciate what I have with you, Mum and Gwen'.

'Promise your mum and I that you will stop looking back at what has happened and that you will give people the benefit of the doubt. Yes, sometimes you will get hurt but you gain so much more by trusting people and seeing the good that's there'.

'I will dad, I will,' she said painting a smile on her face. She realised she would have to be more careful when with her mum and dad, they could read her moods and she did not want them to worry about her. That she could not live with, because she would be punishing them and that would be wrong of her, Maisie knew that they worried about her. So, she would do her best to ensure that she showed a different face to them despite how she felt.

It was Sunday and if Matt came and she saw him she had decided to try and be a little more grateful for what he was doing, he had so far not charged her any money for the work done and he had been kind and unassuming. So, looking out of the kitchen window she had decided to sit at the table and watch to see if he came. It was a cold day and she could at least make him a coffee or a cup of tea. After all his sister Blanche was a really nice person and whenever she could she would call around to see Maisie, in fact they were fast becoming good friends. Her father's words had begun to hit home, and once more they had talked of putting Gracie's ashes to rest, but Maisie would not budge on that particular memory, she was not willing to let go. If she did intern her beloved child's remains, she was frightened of forgetting and she did not want her memories to fade, despite the sadness of what had happened. Making herself a sandwich for lunch and a cup of tea she sat once again at the table, for some reason slightly disappointed that Matt had not appeared. When six o'clock arrived, she realised that the mysterious Matt was not going to appear, it was too dark to do gardening. So, drawing the blinds she turned the oven on to warm the casserole that mum had brought over yesterday for her Sunday lunch. The work she needed to go over on her cases for the week done, she was aware of all the problems that the clients in the cases had.

After she had watched the television for a couple of hours Maisie looked at her watch and decided to go to bed so that she would be fresh and alert for work the next day. That night she dreamed, but it was not about her Gracie or a nightmare about Hugh, she dreamt of a shadowy figure in her mind it was Matt and she wanted to see his face, to see what her dad had seen but he wouldn't turn so she just couldn't see him.

CHAPTER NINETEEN
MEETING MATT

Over the next week Maisie threw herself into her work, all the time she kept thinking of her father's words, he had made her more aware of other people's feelings. At last, she was trying to be as kind to the men as to the women and listening to both sides of the arguments. She also felt more at peace inside. Yes, it was as if part of the cloud of hurt that had surrounded her had lifted, she still hurt a little inside but not as much as before. Each time she went home she realised that it was too dark for Matt to be working in the garden, she suddenly thought did he not go to work or was he a gardener full time, if so he must be losing money doing her garden, she must at some point speak to him about it. When, she didn't know, or how, she couldn't work out, as up until now only her dad had seen him, and for some reason she was quite curious. He sounded a paragon of virtue if such a man existed. After sitting in with Blanche on some of the cases she had said, 'how can there be a God when he allows people to treat women in the way that they do, if there is a God why does he?'

'I know one or two people who would disagree with you Maisie. They would say everything happens for a reason and eventually they will find out sometime later in their life'.

What Maisie did not know or understand was that Blanche already knew what had happened to Maisie, and admired her for how she had taken her life back and turned to helping other people, also because she had chosen to confide in her, Blanche, and that Maisie had accepted her as a friend. She also knew that Maisie would at some time in her life understand and turn back to her faith. Her parents were good people, before you were passed as a social worker your background would have been checked.

The week passed quickly, Saturday came around in no time, she had promised her mum and dad she would go home for a meal, looking at the time she realised that she needed to get to her mum's early as her aunty Vera was visiting as well. Having a quick shower and dressing in her black slacks and jumper, she carried her blue coat and a blue scarf, the same shade as the coat with silver motifs on and placed it with her handbag. Going into the kitchen she put the kettle on and made herself a cup of coffee. Once she had done this, she sat at the table watching the birds in the garden. Suddenly the back gate opened and a man walked in, this must be Matt she thought, but instead of stopping down the bottom of the garden, he carried on up the pathway. He stood and gently knocked on the door. Maisie was very reluctant to open the door, when she did, she was lost for words she was looking into the pair of bluest eyes she had ever seen, they seemed to see into her very soul, he at the same time looked kind and gentle with a firm smiling voice.

'You must be Maisie,' he said. 'I'm so pleased to meet you Blanche has told me so much about you. I can't stay to do much this morning as I have a wedding on'.

'Oh, that's fine,' Maisie stuttered lost for word's, 'you've already done so much you will have to let me know how much I owe you'.

'Nothing I'll get my reward from another being, and besides I have it on good authority that one good deed deserves another, so here are the apples for your mum's pies and your dad told me she would send me a pie when she bakes again. I really am looking forward to that'. 'I will be around to do a little in the week and I might see you on Saturday, in which case I will hopefully cadge a cup of tea off you'.

'You will be welcome,' was all she could say.

'Would you put the basket by the car, I'm going to mum's in a few minutes,' she said.'

'Give me your keys and I'll put them in the boot for you. Your dad I'm sure will get them out for you,' he gave her that lovely smile again. Reaching for her car keys Maisie passed the keys to him. He was soon back with the keys saying, 'I'm sure to see you again soon take care'.

Maisie smiled back not answering, once again stuck for words. She knew she would not have come to this conclusion without her dad's help, but he did appear to be a really nice man, she could understand now what her dad had meant, there was no way she should be tarring everyone with the same brush.

Driving to her mum and dad's her mind kept wandering back to Matt, her dad was right he did seem quite nice but she had thought Hugh nice. How wrong can you be, no she would make sure she was polite and pleasant up to a point, but she would no longer take people on face value, because what you see is not always what you get.

Maisie was soon there giving her mum and dad a hug. Gwen had gone to work this morning but would be back at lunch so Maisie said she would prepare the salad for her mum while she baked. 'Oh, Dad Matt has sent some apples for mum and he said he was looking forward to testing your apple pie Mum'.

'Then he shall have one'.

'I'll just go and get the apples from the car then,' her dad replied whilst giving Maisie a keen look. If he was right Maisie seemed to be struggling in her mind with something, he hoped it was a glimmer of recovery he thought.

Maisie's mum baked steadily through the morning, the biscuit tins were soon filled and a couple of fruit cakes along with her famous apple pies, the rest of the apples she cooked and filled air tight jars to use another week. In a tin she put Matt an apple pie, half a fruit cake and some biscuits in a small tin, to ensure they stayed crisp. Her mum had also done a goody box of pie and biscuits for her along with some ham she had cooked for lunch and tea. This would do for her sandwich's for work through the week. Her mum was making sure she did not go short of home-cooked food through the week, forever looking after her girls. The fact that she did proved what a good mother she was.

Altogether she spent a pleasant day with her mum and dad and Gwen, all too soon the day was over and she needed to go back home, she would take the pie and cake to work and give them to Blanche to pass on. Once she was at home she wondered if she would see Matt on

Sunday. Once more watching the television for a couple of hours she decided to go to bed.

All too soon the morning was here, lying in bed she allowed her mind to wander back to the days in America reminding herself to never get into that position ever again and for the life of her she could not understand, She had not thought this way for a bit, she had pushed it into the back of her mind and didn't want it to creep out again but she was fighting to control her mind. Was she worried that she might forget her darling Gracie? She needed to hang on to her memories of Gracie, it was the memories of Hugh she never wanted to think of ever again. She thought she was incapable of hating anyone, she was ashamed to say she could hate, and it was Hugh she hated more than anything, a man who had turned what was good in her life and rendered her to being a commodity in her makeup, that she had never had before in her life, Hate; she Maisie, was now capable of hate and she couldn't say that she liked the idea as she had been brought up to love not hate.

Sunday was much the same as last week, Matt never appeared, he must treat Sunday as his day of rest, for some reason she felt disappointed that he had not appeared, she knew she hadn't missed him as she had sat in the kitchen with her folders going over the work she had to complete this week. She had been in the kitchen at breakfast, dinner and when it had started to become dark. Maisie had made her mind up to offer him a drink and one of her mum's biscuits. Oh well, she thought that had taken a lot of courage on her behalf to think about it, but perhaps it was just as well because had he been nice to her she probably would have rebuffed him, now why did this seem to bother her. Perhaps if she could come to some agreement on paying him for his work, she wouldn't feel so guilty. Yes, that must be it she needed to pay and it would not bother her so much. Throughout the week Maisie's mind kept wandering to Matt and she could not shake off the feeling that she was disappointed because she had not seen him, he had said I might see you Saturday, it was now Tuesday and Saturday seemed a long time away.

Whatever's got into you Maisie it obviously means a lot to you to pay this man and then you can stop worrying about treating him right. Try as she might as the week by, he kept invading her thoughts. Maisie had passed the pie, cake and biscuits on to Blanche for Matt, 'saying my mum sent these and she said she has made good use of the apples'.

'Matt will really appreciate this home baking it's not one of his best skills, cooking is not quite him. Thank your mum for him and I'm sure he will thank you when he sees you'.

'Yes,' Maisie replied, feeling that she was letting this young man invade her life, and she was not quite sure how she felt about that. Trying quite hard to quell the feeling that she was looking forward to Saturday Maisie set to and tackled her work, it was important and she wanted to pass her training.

Saturday arrived and Maisie had a feeling of anticipation turning down her mum's invitation to go over it was decided she would get cracking on her housework, washing and ironing, however Gwen would come over for tea and spend the night with her, they needed to get their heads together on choosing a present for their mum and dad. She had set to on Friday night doing her hoovering and dusting so all she was left with was her Ironing, it was a bright day but cold, Maisie had set the fire in the lounge but stayed in the kitchen, it was by far the warmest room. After washing her dishes, she stood by the ironing board ironing. Every now and again her eyes would go to the window until she saw him arrive. Having just finished the ironing she put the board away and put the kettle on, he again did not stay at the far end of the garden but came right up to the back door.

Maisie had already noticed signs of the work he had done through the week. He had on a thick dark overcoat and a maroon scarf, he looked quite smart, he didn't look as if he was dressed for gardening and Maisie at once felt a pang of disappointment. Once again, she was amazed at the fleeting thought that passed through her mind. It must be because I was going to try and bring up the conversation of paying him and I can tell he won't be here long enough for me to bring it up, once again I will have to wait for a better opportunity. This must be the story of her life, pinning a small smile on her face she opened the door to his light knock.

'Hello Matt,' she said still smiling.

'Good morning Maisie, I've picked a few potatoes and veg until yours are ready and dad keeps a few hens so he's sent you a few eggs'

And I'd like you to thank your mum for the cake and pie that she sent your dad was certainly right her baking is incredible'.

'Thank you I'm glad you enjoyed it, would you like a cup of tea, I'm just making one'.

'That's a lovely idea its quite parky out here. I won't be staying to do any gardening today but I'll be back in the week, I've a feeling that it won't be long before we have snow and then we won't be able to do much until February'.

Once again Maisie was amazed at the thought that went through her mind that would be almost three months and she liked the feeling that he was there through the week, even though she had only seen him a couple of times.

'Come in out of the cold I've only to pour a cup'.

Pulling out a chair he sat at the table, his blue eyes following her as she got out the cups, putting them on the table she said, 'we'll stay in here if you don't mind, I haven't lit the fire in the lounge yet, my sister Gwen is coming for tea and staying over for the night'.

'It's very comfortable in the kitchen I always like sitting in mum's kitchen,' he said.

'Yes, I'm afraid when mum is baking Gwen and I are always in there with her'.

'I like the thought of that,' he said. 'It means that you and your sister must be good cooks as well and I'm sure I will be sometime in the future sampling your cooking,' he said, but this time holding her eye's with his, and giving her a deep look as if he could see what she was thinking. Lifting his cup and finishing the last dregs he said, 'well time waits for no one especially me'. I would prefer to be staying a little longer but I have work to do, no doubt I will see you next Saturday, or if you have a day off in the week I could catch you then, now I'll see you soon Maisie,' and with another smile that made her heart flip he opened the door and with a wave he walked smartly down the garden path, waving once more as he shut the gate behind him.

Maisie stood for quite a while looking outside, she had been sorry to see him leave and much to her surprise she had felt comfortable in his company, yes she knew and liked Blanche his sister but for some reason she felt drawn to him and she could not analyse why, she really didn't know him well. But again, the thought appeared in her mind that she had not been drawn to Hugh, he had flattered and charmed her almost at once, she had been thrown off her guard and mistaken it for love. She felt as if she could trust and make a friend of Matt without any strings being attached, yes she tried to convince herself that was it, he was like Blanche she could make a friend of him, and her dad was a good judge of character he liked and appeared to trust Matt after just having met once. The rest of the day went well Maisie made a chicken casserole, new potatoes and some of the sprouts that Matt had carried around for her were added to the meal, Followed by some of her Mum's apple pie and fresh cream.

They sat down and ate when Gwen arrived, Maisie had put a light to the fire in the lounge so that it was warm in the room after they had done the dishes, taking their coffee in with them they chatted the night away and stayed up quite late reminiscing over old times as children, some happy memories and some sad, particularly the one's when they had lost their grandparent's. The next day as Gwen made ready to leave Maisie promised to have lunch at her mum's on Sunday the following week, for in her mind she knew Matt would perhaps call on the Saturday and she felt that for some strange reason she had to be in, in any case that was the day she needed to do some of her chores. Straight away she thought that was not altogether the truth as she did some of her chores after work. Sunday passed with no sign of Matt so after having her evening meal of leftover casserole from the day before and a couple of hours of television she decided to take a book upstairs and read in bed. After making sure everywhere was secure she took a shower and retired, it was in bed that she thought of a way to repay Matt without offering him money, she would buy him a gardening book and some sort of garden pack with him liking gardening so much he perhaps would like that. Maisie relaxed in bed feeling much happier because she had decided how to thank him, she fell asleep more contented and happier than she had in a while.

CHAPTER TWENTY
CHRISTMAS

Shopping once again; the week passed with Maisie in her mind counting the days until Saturday, the week to her seemed to drag when she went home at night, throughout the day it seemed she didn't have enough time to give to her cases, and could have done with more to give to them, but Blanche had warned her about trying to give more than she could.

She had said, 'we all want to help everyone and be there for them, but we must have their input on how they could make things better for themselves, they had to be able to learn to be independent', that was why Emma had said Maisie had been strong, it was not just her help that had got her through a very upsetting period of her life, but Maisie herself coming to grips with the situation she was in. If she hadn't Emma would not have been able to give all of her time to her as there were new cases arriving all the time as a social worker she needed to help until they could help themselves. So, knowing this she decided to allot just so much time instead of most of her spare time when she was on her own this would achieve a little time for herself.

Maisie and Gwen had come up with a Christmas present for her mum and dad they had put halves each to a new three-piece suite. Maisie had booked a meal for her dad and mum and herself for Christmas Eve, saying that Gwen was to be there as well, Gwen would cry off at the last minute saying she had to work and she would nip back home and let the delivery men in and at the same time arranging for them to take away the old suite. Maisie had already got Gwen a small present as they had decided to cut back on what they got each other to make sure they got the suite their mum wanted. They had gone shopping with her and on a pretext had wandered into the furniture store and began to look at suites her mum looked at a cream suite that had taken her eye, 'now that one is nice' she said' dad and I have had ours since we got married, still knowing your dad he will say there's a good many years left in it yet, and I suppose he's right, but it's nice now and then to have something new'.

'He has agreed to have a new carpet I've got to pick some samples up and see if we can have it fitted before Christmas as our present to each other'.

'OK mum let's have a look, you choose what you like and ask them if they can get it in say the week before Christmas. Take a sample home for dad to look at, you know he will leave the choosing to you, and if he likes it, it will be looking very nice for Christmas'.

'Yes, I think I will girls, let's go and look in the carpet department. Maisie's mum was torn between two carpet samples so she decided to take the two and get dad to help her choose, the sales man had given her a card with their phone number on she could ring for them to come and measure up for them assuring them that they could have it fitted for Christmas.

Every Saturday morning it became a ritual for Matt to call and have a coffee or tea with Maisie even though he did no gardening that day, they would have around 45 minutes to an hour, but he did plan with her what she would like planting in the summer, he said if her funds would run to a small greenhouse she could grow tomatoes and lettuce and the flower's that it had become obvious she would like to grow. And I grow cucumbers at home they grow quite easily in a greenhouse, Maisie soon got caught up in his plans for her garden. Very often she would look up and he would be watching her and he looked as if he was comfortable, you could say he made himself at home. When their eyes did meet Maisie had a hard time in dragging hers away. She was trying hard not to get involved and she had told herself Matt was just a good friend; however, she had never felt this way before he was kind and she knew she could trust him, in her mind this was enough, yes, friendship was enough. She was still none the wiser why he was always busy on a Sunday and on most Saturday's, she did wonder what he did for a living, she did not like asking Blanche in case she thought that Maisie was being nosy, so Maisie satisfied herself with the fact that he was a good friend and she wanted to keep it that way. He was the first man other than her dad that she had trusted since Hugh. And Hugh was fast becoming a faint memory. Maisie had managed to push him out of her mind and was realising that all men were not like Hugh. She was regaining her faith in human nature.

The only present Maisie had to get now was the present for Matt, she had purchased a new Filofax for Blanche with a pen in it, and the same for Emma and a tie for Jed, she had already posted there's to America, now time was running short so she took a rest day in the week to finish off, having her father to go with her, she had told him that Matt would take no money for his work and she would like to get him something useful and that she had thought of a gardening book and some sort of garden tool.

'I'm sure we can find something suitable at the garden centre'. First of all, they made their way to the book stand and there they purchased a good gardening book with a description of all areas of gardening. From there they went to look at some stainless steel, garden implements, they purchased a spade, a gardening fork and her dad threw in a new rake from him, he had seen Matt a few times now and he really liked him. Her dad even helped to wrap them up in the card board box that they came in, and even helped to cover it in Christmas paper, adding a huge bow that had her mum and her dad in stitches. That looks amazing I'm not sure the bow will fool him he will know by the size of the box what they are.

'Look I've been thinking Matt has been really good to you perhaps he would like to have a meal with us over Christmas or even the new year. Ask him and ask his sister, she might like to come too if she's not busy'.

'I will Dad but I think they live with their mum and dad and would probably like to be with them, but I will ask just in case'.

'You do that lass, now how are you going to get this to him?'.

'If you put it into the boot of my car for me, I will take it to work and ask Blanche to put it in her boot then she can pass it on with strict instructions to give it to him on Christmas Eve'.

'That way he won't feel inclined to get me something and I can pass Blanche hers before we go home for Christmas'.

'That should sort it out'.

When Maisie went home that night it was early and still daylight and Matt was just finishing his last check on the garden it was only two weeks to Christmas, 'would you like a cup of tea Matt?'

'I'd love one Maisie I'll just put these in the shed and lock it and I'll be in'. Taking his shoes off at the door he sat in his usual place, his eyes watching her as she made his tea, I've been shopping with my dad but I wanted to get back before it got dark, oh and my dad wondered if you and Blanche would like to join us for a meal over Christmas or New Year'.

'That is really nice of him to ask Maisie, but Christmas is my busy time of the year. I will at some point need to have a word with your dad so I will keep it in mind, and I most certainly will be dining with them at some time in the future. Now I must go, but if you will be in Saturday morning I will be calling in for my customary cup of tea, that's if you don't mind?'

No, of course, I don't. I'll look forward to seeing you,' she replied, unable to drag her eyes from him.

He was giving her a strange look.

'Now I must be going,' he stood up and hesitated gently holding her shoulder's he looked once more in her eyes and gently kissed her on the cheek.

'Goodnight,' he said gruffly.

Maisie stood and watched him and whispered, 'goodnight'.

He smiled back at her as he put his shoes back on, 'lock the door up Maisie' and he gave another smile and closed the door. Maisie locked the door and could not understand why he kissed her on the cheek, her insides was fluttering like a trapped bird, something was trying to enter her mind and she was pushing it back out, no please don't spoil my friendship with him, I really value having him around, however her brain was saying you are close enough. Standing with her back to the door a stray tear ran down her cheek. Why am I so upset, lots of friends kiss you on the cheek when they leave each other or even meet on the street, it was just a friendly kiss. Don't spoil what you have got, Matt only meant it in a friendly way, don't mention it, just act natural when you see him again remember you are a grownup. And most people these days would give you a friendly peck on the cheek, they do don't they she thought.

When Maisie went to work the next day, Blanche was happy to take the present for Matt and had promised not to give it him until Christmas eve. 'Now Maisie, she said, there is a charity occasion on at the local hospital and we are expected to go, Mathew will be there'.

'Who?' said Maisie.

Blanche gave a little giggle, 'I mean Matt, I've not called him Mathew, for years? It's a nice name but Matt suits him too, you will come, won't you?'

'Yes, of course I will, how dressy will it be?' asked Maisie, 'smart but casual, now I will be going with Matt but he has somewhere to go after so will you be okay meeting us there?'

'Of course, I will that way if one or the other of us has to shoot off we can without upsetting anyone else's plans'.

'That's great. but I promise you we will at some point have a night out with Matt or even you and him if all three of us can't make it, I happen to know he would love that Maisie'.

'Oh, me too,' Maisie said, not really taking in what Blanche was saying.

'So! remember Tuesday next week, pop it in your diary now,' Blanche said repeating the hospital and the time.

Maisie dutifully wrote it down she had not been out for a while and suddenly she looked forward to it and Matt would be there to look after herself and Blanche. Maisie threw herself into the week and Saturday was soon upon her, as usual she looked forward to Matt calling for his cup of tea. When at last he arrived, he said at once that he could only stay for a short while as he once more had a wedding.

'That's a shame I was looking forward to a chat,' and he could tell by her face that she was genuinely disappointed. 'Don't be disappointed Maisie I'm sure we can make up for it in the near future,' he said as he gulped is tea down. 'I just couldn't let Saturday go by without seeing you, now if I don't see you before I'll see you Tuesday at the charity night'.

Turning her to him he looked deep into her eyes, then pulling her to him he hugged her and kissed her on the temple. Holding her tight he whispered, 'Tuesday my love'.

It was said so low Maisie thought she was hearing things and just smiled her goodbye to him. What had he meant? She found herself over analysing what he had said and came to the conclusion that she had not heard what he had whispered to her correctly? Maisie decided to ring Gwen to see if she had time to come over and they could have lunch out and do a little shopping, and of course they could make sure they had everything in place for Christmas Eve and her mum and dad's present being delivered. Gwen answered the phone and declared that she was just going to ring Maisie to see if she could come over and spend the night as she realised that there would not be a great deal of opportunity to plan how Christmas and their plans would pan out.

'That would be great, what shall we have for tea? I don't know about you but thinking of all the goodies we will be eating over Christmas we need to be a little careful until Christmas Eve. Okay salad and an omelette that won't take us long to do',

That night Maisie and Gwen spent a pleasant evening reminiscing back to their childhood and they talked about when their father first called them his little kittens, it was because they had tried to curl up in the dog basket together and he had called them that ever since. She also told Gwen about the charity night that she was going to, and said, 'you know Gwen I have not been out for so long and suddenly I am quite looking forward to it. I think I've put the whole sorry episode of my marriage behind me'.

'I know I'll never forget my Gracie, and it will always hurt that I didn't get to know her, but the hurt gets less'.

'You know Maisie that's the one thing that worries mum and dad, they think she should be put to rest; they love you and even though they did not know Gracie they love her too'.

'Think about it Maisie, their belief in God makes them think she needs to be put to rest. Promise me you will think about it'.

'I will it's just that it will be so final, I don't want to just forget that she existed, that would be awful'.

'I know but you have to start living again, and at the moment I know you want to help people and I applaud you for that, but you must also live your life again and more importantly help yourself. Gracie will always be in our thoughts but all we want for you is a normal life again and a little happiness, Now tell me to mind my own business, but this Matt; you like him, don't you?'

'Yes, he really nice but we are just friends Gwen'.

'Are you sure you sound different when you talk about him?'

'It's just that I feel comfortable with him, that's all nosey'.

'Well remember we had this conversation then,' Gwen laughed. 'I think the lady protest's to much'.

Maisie immediately threw a cushion at Gwen and it found its goal, they both ended up doubled up with laughter. And it had been a long time since she had laughed this way.

CHAPTER TWENTY-ONE
HUGH'S SHOCK RETURN

The day of the charity night arrived. Maisie dressed in a sea green fitted dress, it had three quarter sleeves, a straight skirt and the bodice hugged and flattered her figure. She had taken the trouble to use some green eye-shadow and was wearing the antique emerald bracelet, ring, and matching earrings belonging to her late grand-mother, on her feet she had black patent heeled shoes and carried a black patent clutch bag. For some reason she felt a small shiver of anticipation. Tonight, was the first night in more three years that she would be going out to a social event. All she needed now were her black gloves and winter cream coat. Looking at her watch it was time to go. Checking around the house to ensure everything was neat and tidy, she set the alarm and went to her car. Maisie had a feeling of anticipation she thought she was really going to enjoy tonight, yes, she was certain she was.

Arriving at the hospital Maisie locked the car and went to the entrance, where she found Matt and Blanche waiting for her, Blanche hugged her straight away, and Matt leant forward and kissed her on the cheek, taking her arm he gave her a quick look and Maisie found her heart skip a beat. All of a sudden she felt as if she was someone who had been reborn, Matt was so nice and kind and he appeared to like her, she felt worthy and wanted, she had not felt that for a long time .He was a really good friend and she wanted him to be around forever.

'Let's find a table, shall we?' Matt asked.

'Yes. But I want a drink, what about you Maisie?' asked Blanche.

'Just an orange juice will do me thanks,' Maisie answered.

'You look really nice Maisie I am quite proud to be out with two lovely women,' he said giving Blanche a quick look making sure he included his sister.

'Well Maisie might only want an orange juice, but I want wine'.

'Alright stay here and I'll get the drinks,' said Matt, 'that small table there will be big enough for the three of us'. Striding away he made his way to the bar. Around ten minutes later Matt returned with a tray of drinks an orange juice, glass of wine and a coffee.

'Don't you drink Matt?' Maisie inquired.

'Not a lot. I need a clear head most of the time'.

His answer puzzled Maisie, how did gardening need a clear head?

Maisie had seen her uncle many a time working in the garden after having a night out on Saturday. At that moment a couple walked past, 'we'll see you Sunday Matt,' they said with a smile.

Maisie was just about to ask him what he did on a Sunday when a familiar voice said, 'Why! Maisie darling what, a coincidence meeting you here sweetheart how wonderful, I was just thinking about you'.

Maisie, was horrified and shocked to the to the core, unable to speak as she stared into the glittering eyes of Hugh. Suddenly Matt said in a tight voice, 'shall we go and refresh the drinks Blanche?'

Blanche silently nodded her head at Matt, the way that Hugh had approached puzzled both her and Matt.

'We will be about 15 minutes Maisie,' Matt said looking at her, giving her an inquiring look. When Maisie didn't answer he turned and walked away with Blanche.

'Who's that?' he asked Blanche.

'I haven't a clue, but he seemed to know Maisie well. We'll perhaps find out when we have the drink's'.

'I can't wait he,' said in a thoughtful voice, Maisie looked a little startled'.

'Yes, she did go quiet,' Blanche agreed.

'Well you look well Maisie, despite the fact that you saw fit to walk out on me taking my child with you,' he said. 'Did you not realise that as a father, I have right a to see my child and have access to see her, it was a little girl on the scan was it not?'

This shocked Maisie to life, 'you dare speak of our child, you who beat me so badly that she had to be delivered before her time'.

'Now come on Maisie you are exaggerating'.

'You may think you can get away with telling people that Hugh, but I know what happened to you when I left, I have press cuttings of your case'.

'I will still insist on having access to my child, you can't stop that my dear wife,' he answered.

'I don't think that any court in the land can give you access to our child's ashes that rest in a small pink casket, where you put her'.

For one minute Hugh's eyes showed a glimmer of shock then he hissed in a low voice, 'you owe me, two years of my life you bitch, I know it was you that put the police onto me, I intend to get my own back, you see if I don't'.

'Will you go away or I'll get security to make sure you leave me alone?' Maisie answered quietly. 'Now go and crawl back under whatever stone you crawled out from'.

'You may think you have seen the last of me, but you better make sure you are looking over your shoulder in future, for I will be there when you least expect it,' he said. 'Making that last comment he smiled and strolled away.

Seeing Blanche and Matt paying for their drinks at the bar, he walked slowly towards them, this is a good place to start he thought, it was obvious that the man had the hots for Maisie he would just introduce himself and see what happened from here. Turning on his most charming voice he said, 'I'm so sorry to have interrupted your night, Maisie asked me to pop over and ask you if you could give us a little space, you see I'm Maisie's husband, Hugh Grainger and we have decided to give it another try would you mind"

'No not at all,' Matt said in a gentle voice, 'it was nice meeting you,' he said without a smile. 'Nodding his head, he said 'come along Blanche Joe and Eva are over there It would be a good time to say hello to them'.

'Matt should we leave him with Maisie on her own I don't like the look of him'.

'Neither do I, however I won't and can't come between husband and wife whatever it does to me'.

'But Matt you and Maisie had something special'.

'I know you see I like her, really like her and I thought she was beginning to like me, but if she still loves him, I can't get involved and neither must you. So, I suggest we call it a night, Maisie will be okay she has her husband'.

Blanche looked at her brother and her heart went out to him she had realised a few weeks ago that he was falling for Maisie, but as he said he needed to be open and above scandal in his job. Marriage was sacred to him and if they were going to try again, he should not interfere, it wasn't as if he had spoken to her about how he felt, so he must step aside. He had gone this long and not fallen for any woman, but now he had fallen hard he realised he had to walk away, he couldn't say it didn't hurt because it did but obviously, she was not for him. At no time had she given either himself or Blanche the impression that there was any chance of trying again with her husband, certainly Maisie had played it close to her chest. He had been quite busy for the last week and the one thing that he had looked forward to was tonight because he was to spend it in the company of Maisie, he had been trying to make sure he took it slowly so that Maisie would start to trust him and as usual he had taken it to slowly. He had been aware of the circumstances that turned Maisie into a social worker and inside he couldn't for the life of him, under- stand why she would give her marriage another chance what he had heard about Hugh did him no favours. But there again love could conquer anything. How lucky Hugh was, because he, Matt would have done anything to make sure she was happy, he had even stepped back at once to make sure she was happy. Now he must come to terms with how he felt and he knew it would be quite difficult for him to do. But come to terms he must.

Blanche left with Matt, he dropped her off at home. 'I'd better go and work on Christmas Eve's programme, goodnight Blanche,' he said and made his way back to his car, giving a last wave as she entered the house. Sitting in the car Matt wondered if he would be destined to be on his own, for at that moment he knew he would not love anyone else, when Blanche had asked him to lend a hand in Maisie's garden he had not realised that he would meet the woman of his dreams, only for them dreams to be dashed beyond redemption.

Blanche herself did a lot of thinking that night, she knew it would be impossible not to tell Maisie how Matt felt, after all she would be seeing her on a daily basis and with the friendship that she and Maisie had, Matt's name would be sure to crop up in conversation. Maisie did not realise that everything that had happened to her in America, Blanche knew about and when faced with the trainee social workers folder she had been interested in having Maisie train with her, she had asked for her to be placed with her. She now knew that she must ask to swop her trainee. Looking at the clock to ensure It wasn't too late to ring her superior and ask if she could swop. Once she had spoken to the head of her department and it was decided that she swopped trainees with another department and it would commence directly after the Christmas holidays, that way there would be no awkward moments to get over with Maisie and herself, and she would not breach Matts confidence and hopefully he would get over this period in his life. Blanche would miss working with Maisie as they had become such good friends and she would miss their friendship, just as much as Maisie would but she had to do it for Matt, she was appalled that Maisie had decided to give it another go, Maisie had told her a little about it, however Blanche had looked the case up and had seen that he had treated Maisie even worse than she had told her, this is what puzzled her about giving him another chance.

Maisie was patiently waiting for Matt and Blanche to return after standing for almost an hour as Maisie couldn't see them anywhere, she was quite worried, spotting a colleague she walked over and asked casually if they had seen Blanche. 'Yes, her and Matt were just leaving when I came in, after all its his busy time of the year'.

'Oh! I didn't realise they had planned to go early I was just about to leave myself, Goodnight Mary and have a lovely Christmas,' she said trying to hide the hurt she was feeling. Blanche and Matt were important to her if they had said they wouldn't be staying she perhaps wouldn't have attended, and might not have had to come in contact with Hugh. Leaving the hospital and climbing into her car she was soon driving out of the hospital grounds. Maisie was understandably upset that they hadn't told her they were leaving; it was a very disappointed Maisie that left the charity evening.

Arriving back home and letting herself back into the house, she went into the kitchen to make herself a cup of tea. Taking it into the lounge she tried to analyse what had happened tonight. She was strong enough now to cope with the fact that Hugh had turned up, she was not fazed by that, but it had hurt her deeply that Matt and Blanche hadn't just come over and said we are leaving now we have another engagement elsewhere. Maisie would have understood and would have left the same time as them, she was not up to going for nights out yet on her own. The night had hardly begun, surely it would have been better for them not to attend if they had no time at all because they had left almost as soon as they got there, thinking about its puzzled Maisie why.

After taking a shower Maisie went to bed, picking up her book she decided to read for a while her eyes began to droop so she put the book down and decided it was time to sleep, being tired she fell asleep quite quickly. Maisie was soon pulled from her sleep by the phone ringing. Who on earth could that be she muttered to herself, reaching for the phone at the side of the bed, she said 'Hello'?

When there was no answer she again said 'Hello,' for which she was rewarded with a snigger. Putting the phone down she was now quite unnerved whoever it was had the desired effect. Maisie sat shivering on the side of the bed, after 30 minutes she thought it must be teenagers having some fun. Climbing back into bed she turned the lamp off and snuggled down just as she began to drop off the phone began to ring again, once more turning the light on she answered it again, this time the caller just said, 'Tick, Tick, Tick,' and in a muffled voice said, 'time is ticking away for you'; and gave a strange snigger. By this time Maisie was getting quite upset, 'you're a coward whoever you are. Why don't you try someone who is bothered, cowards don't frighten me whoever you are! You are wasting your time. I will inform the police if you don't stop this silly behaviour,' and she quietly placed the receiver down, but inside she was shaking.

The rest of the night Maisie never closed her eyes, she made up her mind that if the same happened the following night she would unplug the phone and set the burglar alarm before she went to bed, she also found the pepper spray she kept in the drawer and put it under her pillow so that she was ready for any eventuality that was thrown at her. Someone was playing tricks on her and she was not going to allow them to frighten her. And she was going to her mum and dads for Christmas, but she wanted to be here if Matt called on Saturday. That day Maisie forced herself to go to the shops and get any of the last bits of shopping, she needed. Making her way back to the car she was sure she saw Hugh walking on the opposite side of the road, taking another look he was nowhere in sight she must have been imagining it, last night must have made her jumpy. Taking her time going back so the day would not drag, she got back about six o'clock and it had already gone dark. Making sure she locked the door behind her she carried her shopping into the kitchen a began to put it away, turning around she saw a figure walk across the window. Walking across to the kitchen window, she turned the outside lights on there was no one outside at all, the gate at the end of the garden was shut. Whoever was on the phone last night had really made her jumpy, so drawing the curtains to, she put the wireless on and made herself some soup and salad to follow. Once she had eaten her meal, she made a cup of tea and went into the lounge to watch the television for a while. Because she had slept so badly the night before she decided to have an early night. Checking the doors and unplugging the phone she went upstairs and placed her mobile on the side cabinet so she had a phone by her, she also put an old hockey stick just under the edge of the bed. She was determined that whoever it was she would not let them frighten her, she had been frightened of her own shadow in America and she would not let it happen again.

Suddenly she thought Hugh! He had just turned up could it have anything to do with him, it couldn't, could it?' she asked herself. Well if it had been, he would soon find out she was not a push over. She would come out fighting and if it was him, he wouldn't win. Climbing into bed she felt under the pillow to make sure the spray was still where she had put it. But as it happened no calls disturbed her that night, she slept well. She had decided to take no chances she would in future set the alarm every night. Saturday came and things had settled down and she told herself that, she would still be careful and on her guard, she wouldn't leave it up to chance. Once completing her chores, she set a tray ready for Matt's visit. When he didn't arrive for eleven o'clock Maisie felt really disappointed, when there was no sign of Matt, two hours later or Blanche. And it was usual for Blanche to phone her and she hadn't, she sat pondering on what she could have done to upset her. They both were perfectly ok until they went to the bar.

Gwen Rang her on her mobile as she sat thinking, 'Maisie I've been trying to ring you and your phone is just not ringing out'.

'I'm sorry Gwen I must have knocked the plug out when I was cleaning the lounge. I'll have to watch what I'm doing.

'I was just checking that we are still on track for tomorrow, you are taking mum and dad out while I take delivery of mums new suite and you are staying over for Christmas'.

'Of cause I've not forgotten I will be there first thing in the morning, I'm looking forward to staying at home for the week and being with my family'.

'Great I'll see you tomorrow then bye'.

'Bye Gwen'. Maisie had been quite truthful she was looking forward to staying at home for the week, she would have a little peace of mind and whoever had rung her in the middle of the night would cease to when they realised, they would not be getting an answer.

That night Maisie woke up thinking she could hear someone knocking, but as she looked through the window the next door lights came on and their dog began to bark, Maisie opened the window as she saw Joan's husband and son from next door come out into the garden, when she called down he said he had been woken by a knocking and it sounded as if someone was knocking on the outside wall but he couldn't see anyone in the garden, but their Billy heard it as well.

'Don't you worry Maisie we will have a good look around and if there is anyone messing around out here, we can always set the dog on them'.

'You get back off to sleep, we'll keep our ears open don't you fret lass goodnight then'.

'Goodnight,' Maisie answered. Maisie was not disturbed again that night, whatever it was that had woken them up there was no sign of anything in the morning they thought it must have been someone going home. The next day Maisie awoke tired and out of sorts, the disturbed night had upset her nerves and, she needed to pack a case to go to her mum and dads.

Once she arrived there Maisie had a full day ahead of her, she would be taking her parents out and then the rest of Christmas Eve would be spent preparing for the next day. Looking through the window she noticed it had been snowing, walking over to the window she could see footprints in the snow. So, there had been someone outside last night, she needed to make next door aware. Whoever it was she would be away for almost a week and they would keep a check on her house over the next week. Quickly she went and took a shower, once dressed and ready she had a bowl of corn-flakes and a strong coffee. When she had washed her cup and bowl, she nipped upstairs packed her case and put on her outdoor clothes. Popping around next she asked to speak to Harry and at the same time telling Joan that last night someone had been in her garden and they must have come back after everyone had gone back to bed.'

'Harry,' Joan shouted, 'can you go next door and check the garden with Maisie?'

'Why what's happened? he asked.

'I really don't know Harry just that there must have been someone making the knocking last night and they went when you came out, up to then it hadn't snowed so they must have come back when you went back to bed there are foot marks all across the lawn, come and have a look'.

'Now you lead the way Maisie let's have a look'.

'Your right Maisie we are going to have to keep watch over our house and yours'.

'It looks as if someone is up to no good, don't you worry, me and our Billy have a security camera we will get it set up so that we can see the perimeter of your property as well as ours, we'll set two screens up so we can watch whenever we want'.

'Do you need to get anything else Harry, I'll leave you some money if you do?'

'No, we have more than enough cameras and screens so we don't need anything'.

'Have you secured everywhere and set the burglar alarm?'

'I have,'

'Then you go and enjoy your week at your parents, have a lovely time'.

'I will and all of you enjoy Christmas as well, you do have a key, don't you?'

'Yes' we have'.

'Well here's a small present for you, Joan and the boys, and I'll see you when I get back'.

Waving to them as she got into the car she pulled out on to the road and made her way to her parents. As planned Gwen cried off giving the excuse that something had come up at work so she couldn't have lunch out with them, but would get back in the afternoon. Maisie pretended she was upset she hoped she had given a good performance and her mother and father believed her.

Maisie's mum grumbled about Gwen having to work whilst they went out, 'she should be with us it's really too bad,' she said.

'Now mum don't worry, if something comes up you have to deal with for lots of things can happen when we least expect it, you wait and see, anyway I'm here I'm sure you will enjoy your day with me'.

They made their way to the restaurant that Maisie and Gwen had booked, the restaurant was full of people, some having their company lunch out. Standing and waiting to be shown to their table, the waitress came and escorted them to where they were to sit, it was near to the window, just as they, sat down she was not imagining it now, Hugh walked past the window and looked directly at her giving her a big smile and nodding his head. The look on Maisie's face prompted her father to say, 'are you okay Maisie you've gone white?

'I'm fine dad I didn't sleep very well last night, but I'm sure I will tonight,' trying to put on a convincing smile whilst inside her heart was pounding, it was just as if he knew her every move. Picking up the menu she started to ask her parents what they were going to have.

'Well her mum said they do a lovely lamb tagine here and if we have something hot now, we can have a little buffet tonight and can help ourselves as we watch the celebrations or a good film on television'.

'If Gwen hadn't gone to work,' her mum commented, 'she would have had the lovely hot meal that we all have just enjoyed, as it is, she will have to have finger food the same as us. Maisie kept her parents out as long as she could after having a walk around the shops and getting some bits and pieces that she'd forgotten. Taking them later for a coffee, she also took her time making sure that the shop had had plenty of time to deliver mum and dads suite, that they didn't know about. Maisie could not stop thinking who it had been in her garden.

'Is something wrong Maisie? her mum asked.

'No Mum I'm fine just running through a case that I have on at work'.

'Well don't love, put your work away until after Christmas, you can't carry everyone's problems'.

'No Mum your right, let's just enjoy our Christmas together'.

Giving her mum a big smile that she hoped it would mask how she really felt. Maisie tried hard to lighten the mood so that her mum and dad would enjoy their day out, aware that her mother's face told her she didn't quite believe her. The last thing that Maisie wanted was to worry her parents. Looking at her watch she said, 'shall we make our way back home, we do have things to do, you especially mum?'

'Ok let's go and see what has to be done, the sooner we do it the sooner we can relax and enjoy sitting and watching television'.

Maisie and her parents made their way back home, dad opened the door and ushered her mum in Maisie held back as they went into the lounge the gasp of astonishment from their mum and dad was well worth all the walking around the shops, Maisie would have wanted to be in the house relaxing without a worry. Worrying about her mum was ok, but she needed to find out who it was that was playing tricks on her, it was an added worry that she could do without.'

'Merry Christmas Mum from me and our Maisie.' she heard Gwen say.

'It's lovely and it matches the carpet, how did you know I really wanted to have a suite?

'Doesn't matter mum we just did'.

'Now I'm going to get fish and chips for my tea, I know you won't want anything hot as you have had a hot lunch'.

'See you in minute, our Maisie be a darling put me a plate to warm'.

Throughout the rest of the day their mum kept going into the lounge to look at her suite, it really had made her Christmas.

'It's just what I wanted,' she was heard saying.

The rest of Christmas went well but Maisie's mum and dad sensed that Maisie was holding something back. She decided to speak to her again over putting Gracie's ashes to rest, if Maisie did this, she would perhaps find peace of mind. All too soon Christmas was over, and tomorrow Maisie would be going home. The thought of going back was hard she knew that she had to or lose that strength she had gained in leaving Hugh and come what may she did not intend for that to happen. Besides if she couldn't help herself, how could she help anyone else. Determined that she would not let anyone bully her again, she pinned a smile back on her face when she hugged her mum, dad and Gwen and said that once she went home, she would see them the following week and a week soon goes. They in turn promised to see her in a week. Feeling a lot less brave than she sounded she said let's make sure we enjoy our last day together, we have to go back to work in a couple of days.

Chapter Twenty-Two
Returning to Work

The next day Maisie made her journey back home to her cottage, everything looked the same, putting her case down she went into the kitchen to make a cup of tea. Later sitting by the fire and watching the television she decided to turn in, after all she needed to be up bright and early, she had to go to work tomorrow. Going upstairs and putting her case down she quickly unpacked and began to put clothes back into the drawer. As she closed the drawer her eyes alighted on the top and then she let out a gasp, Gracie's casket was always on the small side table at the side of her bed it was now on the large chest of drawers that she kept her clothes in. Holding her breath, she was aware of her heartbeat thumping away in her chest. There was no way that she had moved it, only Joan next door had a key, someone had been into her house, how she asked herself. Racking her brains how could anyone get in, she trusted Joan they had kept a spare key for her since she had been here, and in her heart, she believed it would not be her. Her mind went back to the night she saw Hugh at the charity night, but how could he get in? Giving herself a mental shake, she told herself not to be silly had she not dusted in her bedroom before she went her mum's? But to be on the safe side she would have another word with Joan and Harry She would make sure that Harry and Billy had set up the camera's that he had mentioned before she went her mums. Moving Gracie's casket back to where it belonged, she checked that she had the pepper spray under her pillow and the old hockey stick under the bed. Climbing into bed she turned the light off but did not shut her eyes to go to sleep, her mind was far too active.

It was a tired Masie that dragged herself out of bed the next day to go to work, she took a shower hoping that it would wake her up by having it cold, and in this weather, she struggled to do it. Rubbing herself dry and dressing in a dark navy trouser suit and brushing her hair, Maisie felt more presentable to face work. Thinking that she could perhaps talk it through with Blanche when she got in work. Making her way to next door she knew they would be up, she knocked on their door. When Joan opened it, Maisie asked Joan if she could speak to her husband for her and ask him if he would keep the security camera's on now, she was home and that she would feel more comfortable knowing that they had it trained on her back and front doors. Joan was really helpful she said that they would make sure it was on all the time in fact, Harry had put up a couple of extra cameras' outside, they were small, but they would now give a wide view of the outside. Maisie thanked them and said I will see you later tonight. Giving her a wave as she climbed into her car.

On arriving at work Maisie made her way to the office she shared with Blanche to find a much older lady sitting at her desk, 'Hello Maisie,' said with a smile.

'Where's Blanche?'

'Hello, you must be Maisie,' said the woman. 'My name is Edith I'm afraid that Blanche has had to transfer to another trainee so you will be training with me for the rest of your placement, I'm sure we will get on well'.

'Oh, why did Blanche have to transfer,' Maisie asked. 'I believe it was personal, so I couldn't really say, so would you like to walk me through the case notes you are working on then we can compare how we could deal with the scenario's'.

'Yes, of course,' Maisie replied a little confused as well as hurt, why had Blanche not told her that she would no longer be working with her. It wouldn't have hurt her to mention the fact before their Christmas holidays that way she would have been kept in the loop and have expected the change and been prepared for it, this way she was unprepared and had to talk to a stranger if Blanche had told her she could have run her theories through to ensure she was on the right track. Puzzled and upset inside she collected the files and went through them individually and very carefully gave her opinion of how they should proceed. Edith was very thorough, asking questions to ensure that Maisie was following the rules correctly. To be honest she could see that Maisie would make a good social worker at the end of her training and that she didn't judge people, she listened, and would help them to make the right decisions for themselves whilst ensuring they were not in danger and understood the plan's that they put together with the people involved.

That night Maisie went home still puzzled at why Matt had not visited her on Saturday and why they had left the charity night and most of all why, Blanche had swopped trainees. That night she went to bed and set the burglar alarm to ensure if any one tried to enter her home she would be aware of any trespasser's; she was a little apprehensive, however she slept throughout the night with no disturbances. The next day when she got up the garden gate was open and it hadn't been the night before. Maisie went down and the bolt was hanging off, now she realised she could ask her dad to come and fix it but she wasn't ready to involve them in her speculations, she had a feeling that Hugh was responsible but she had no evidence. And when Harry looked at the gate, and said the wind could have broken it if it had not been bolted properly. Of course, that must be the answer, it wasn't shut right.

'Don't worry Maisie I'll go down and purchase another stronger one and fix it today for you'.

'Well make sure you give me the bill for the bolt and the fixing. I can't keep on putting on you'.

'I will save the bill, and you aren't putting on me, it's a pleasure and we love having you next door to us, you are a good neighbour'.

'Thank you Harry I don't think I would know what to do without yours and Joan's help'.'

'Yes, but you have been a good friend to Joan too, so accept our help gracefully, we might need your help ourselves one day, now go to work it will be sorted when you get home, have a good day'.

'You too Harry and thanks again,' giving a wave she got into the car and drove away.

That night when Maisie came home Harry had been true to his word the gate had been repaired and he had put the receipt through the door, this again made Maisie feel more secure. The night was cold and they had more snow, so Maisie had her tea when she came in and settled down to her case notes. After a couple of hours studying her notes, she felt as if there was nothing more, she could do on them. So, taking a shower and putting on her nightdress and dressing gown Maisie settled down to a couple of hours television. At last she felt tired enough to go to bed and get some sleep, so setting the alarm she had no trouble tonight in going to sleep. That night she dreamt of Matt, he was standing a little distance away and didn't answer her when she called, he made no effort to speak but just watched; he looked sad. Throughout the day Matt kept popping into Maisie's mind, she had to admit she missed him even if it was only a couple of weeks since she had seen him. Still it would be Saturday in a couple of days perhaps he would find the time to pop around, it wasn't as if they were in love, he was a good friend and she would like to hear from Blanche as well.

Maisie had tried a couple of times to ring Blanche's mobile but she didn't answer, still perhaps she was driving. Maisie as always was making excuses for people, what she really needed to do was to get Blanche's phone number at work and her extension number, yes that's what she would do. Feeling a lot better when she went to work the next day, she managed to look up Blanche's works number in the internal phone book of email addresses and phone numbers. Maisie did try to ring her only to be told that Blanche was on holiday so she asked when she would be back and the young woman that answered said she was not sure. Maisie then decided to leave it a couple of weeks and then try again, there was obviously something wrong and she wanted to get to the bottom of it, she had counted

Blanche as a good friend and she wanted to know what had happened to change that. The next week passed without any more incident's, the garden gate stayed locked and there were no more footsteps in the snow and no more midnight phone calls. If fact three weeks passed without any more problems, however Matt did not call again to have his cup of coffee on the Saturday mornings. She felt as if she had lost something really important to her. It suddenly hit her that it had been almost as bad as losing Gracie, for every time she thought about him, she had this screwed up longing inside her stomach and she asked herself why. And then she would close her eyes and ask God why do I need to be punished again, am I destined to lose everyone who brings something good into my life? I thought I had made lifelong friends, what have I done to deserve this punishment. Please God tell me and I will try to make it right. Maybe she had done something wrong in another life and she had to atone for it.

It was almost a week later she had tried to ring Blanche again only to be told that she was in a meeting by another young lady who said she would pass Maisie message on to her. Maisie also had a heavy work load that day so she was exhausted when she arrived home, so she didn't try to contact Blanche that night. She just warmed up some left-over casserole from the night before and after washing up she decided to go up and have a shower, Maisie had already checked that she had locked her doors. Once she had done this she sat and dried her hair and when she had finished, had every intention of going back downstairs to make a milky drink and read once more the work she needed to complete. But instead she sat down on the bed and put her feet up just for five minutes she thought, she lay there turning over why it was that she needed Matt in her life.

Her mind went back to the last Saturday when although he had called, he said he couldn't stay as he was very busy. He had gently held her and kissed her brow and she thought he had called her his love. It hit home then that she was falling in love with him and she had vowed never again to be that vulnerable. The past few weeks since Christmas had been so stressful she allowed herself to give into her feelings why did she have to fall in love again and complicate things up to now she had been steadfast in her determination to make her career enough for her now once again there was something that she wanted badly and she made up her mind she couldn't have it. Eventually she cried herself to sleep, she had not bothered to go back downstairs to turn the lamp off in the lounge, but when she went into the bedroom, she had put the lamp on, and she had every intention of going back downstairs. So, she lay there in the gentle glow of the lamp. Maisie must have been asleep for around three hours when she woke up to not knowing what had woken her. Then she felt his breath on her face.

'How! did you get in here, get out!'

He hissed, 'No you bitch, you owe me and you'll pay one way or another you bloody bitch, two years of my life I lost because of you and my job and girlfriend',

'So, all the time I spent on my own in the apartment you were with another women. I knew there was something you were spending your money on. I saw precious little of your wages, so I don't owe you anything, now get out before I fetch Harry'.

Suddenly! Maisie galvanised into action she grabbed her pepper spray from under her pillow. To late Hugh grabbed her arm and held her down by the throat, throwing the spray over the other side of the room he kneeled on her stomach and punched her around the head until she was half unconscious.

'Now! You useless cow, have you been missing a man? You won't when I've finished with you, you'll perhaps be better at it, bloody stuck up bitch, so I'll just give you a little of what you've been missing'.

He began to undo his trousers he had released his hand from Maisie throat to undo them'. Maisie at last began to get some air in her lungs and the red mist began to clear. She was certain that Hugh was going to rape her. Filling her lungs as full of air as she could, she suddenly screamed at the top of her voice. Hugh brought his fist down as hard as he could into her face, Maisie went out like a light. He reached down and ripped her nightwear from top to bottom revealing her smooth creamy body. In his mind he said, she will thank me for tonight when I get going, I can go some. He hadn't really been close to a woman since he left America and he blamed Maisie for that. Still there was no one to stop him tonight. He could take his time and he would make sure she knew he could do what he wanted. Besides, that quiet little runt she had been with was soon sent off with his tail between his legs, he didn't expect any trouble from him.

'You wouldn't give me any money, so you may as well be of use in a different way. Payment in kind Maisie I hope you have upped your game in the last two and a half years, don't disappoint me tonight or else I'll get my thrills in a different way, besides there is no one to help you tonight'. 'You'll be sorry you ever crossed me Maisie, by hell you will'.

Next door young Billy had still been downstairs in the small dining room studying, he was seventeen and still went to the local college, he heard their dog give a low guttural growl, so getting up he went to, see what was wrong, the dog hadn't barked he was just growling. On the way he had to pass the screen of the home security and he could see plainly that Maisie's outside light was on over the window showing that the back door was wide open and the garden gate was also open.

'Be quiet boy,' he said before quickly taking the stairs two at a time and rushing into his mum and dad's room, quickly shaking his dad until he was awake, he said, 'quick Dad it looks as if someone has broken into next door. The garden gate and the back door are wide open'.

Jumping out of bed he had woke Joan up, 'what's the matter' she asked.

'Somethings amiss next door. Quick Billy get Peter up. The more of us the better, Joan grabbed her dressing gown, pulling it on quickly they all met on the small landing. Grabbing whatever they could as weapons to protect themselves with, Harry told Billy and Peter to go to the front door handing him Maisie's key off the hook in the hall where they kept it. Harry and Joan went around the back.

Maisie was moaning, opening her eyes she found her voice once more, 'no Hugh you will end up in prison again don't touch me'.

'Shut up you bitch'.

Maisie screamed once more and Hugh's fist came down on her again. All at once all hell broke loose as three bodies hurled themselves through space, taking Hugh by surprise, and as he tried to fight them off, he was outnumbered, he had to let go off his trousers and they fell around his ankles tripping him as they went. Joan was quickly on the bed cradling Maisie head on her chest and at the same time pulling a cover over her to shield her nakedness.

'My poor, poor girl,' she whispered. 'how could he?'

Peter and Billy were sitting on Hugh and pinning him to the floor, their dog was slowly growling at the side, and Harry stood over them with a cricket bat. Harry also had a mobile phone in his hand calling the police. Soon the police car sirens were heard as they pulled into the lane and stopped outside the cottage, they were soon inside and putting handcuffs on Hugh Grainger, he started to bluster that he was Maisie's ex-husband and he had been invited; he was a coward to the end.

Well we'll find you a room for the night to cool down in and until the young lady is able to corroborate your story, that's where you will stay a guest of Her Majesty. The next minute the ambulance sirens could be heard, one of the officers went out of the room to guide them up to the bedroom the paramedics were soon with Maisie and confirmed that Maisie had sustained quite a beating. They gave her an injection for the pain, and gently got her on to the stretcher, examining her injuries they carefully tried to stem the blood from her mouth where her teeth had punctured her lips as he had hit her. Hugh could be heard saying he was sorry he hadn't meant to hurt her, inside he knew it wouldn't be a short stretch this time, because they would see his other two offences and he had been caught in the act this time. Why did he not think before he did thing's?

Harry gave a statement to the fact that he knew that Maisie had been having prowlers around so they had been watching the house, also that she was divorced and worked as a social worker in Chester, one of the police officers went through her address book and found her mother and fathers address and they said they would send two officers to speak to Maisie's parents, as she would need someone with her. Joan said she would quickly go with her in the ambulance, it wouldn't take her long to put on a track suit and she would be back around. Harry and Peter would secure the house, then they found the lock on the back door had been forced, that's how he had got in. So, it was obvious to the police that Hugh Grainger was not there by invitation. He was obviously a bully and he needed to be locked up for a long time and if they could throw the key away it would be all the better.

Once Harry and Peter had repaired the lock on Maisie's back door, Peter fetched a small bolt from their shed, which he put onto the back door to make it even more secure. Harry took the bloodstained bedding he had stripped from her bed and they carried it back to their house and put it straight into the washer, when Maisie came back to her home, he didn't want anything left to remind her of what had happened. They turned off the lights and set the alarm. How anyone could treat someone like that he didn't now, once he had put the washer on he told the boys to turn in as he was going to drive to the hospital to be with his wife, he was sure they would stay there until Maisie's parents arrived, she needed familiar faces when she came to.

So, getting dressed and putting on a thick coat he put a fluffy car rug in the car that Joan would be warm when they came home, it could be a long night. He also made a thermos of coffee. Just in case she needed a drink, getting into the car he made the short drive to the hospital where he found Joan in the corridor outside the side ward. He had carried the thermos in with him and Joan gratefully accepted a drink of the strong coffee. The doctors were still cleaning the wounds on her face, one doctor had assured them that the injuries would not leave any scars. The doctors that came out of the side ward said that Maisie was still under sedation and that they would keep her that way for a couple of days. They had set up drips to ensure that she was kept comfortable and they could sit in with her if they wanted.

'Yes, we will until her mum and dad arrive thank you'.

'Well we will get someone to bring you a cup of tea later then'.

Someone will be around to check on her through the night. Joan and Harry settled down to watch over Maisie, drawing two chairs up close.

Joan whispered, 'that's right love you sleep, we'll keep you safe and your mum won't be long now'.

'How could he Harry, she wouldn't do any harm to anyone'.

'It was a good thing that Billy looked at the security camera, and we were just in the nick of time, goodness knows what he was about to do'.

'The poor girl. Locking up is too good for him he needs stringing up'.

'I know lass he is obviously sick in the head'.

CHAPTER TWENTY-THREE
A POLICE VISIT

Maisie's mum and dad's house at that moment lay in darkness as everyone had retired to bed, the Police car came to a halt outside, a young women police officer and a man in plain clothes got out. Ringing the doorbell, they waited for an answer. Maisie's father opened the upstairs window peering down into the darkness he demanded 'who's there'.

'I'm sorry sir it's the police we need to talk to you please'.

'The police'.

'Who is it dear?'

They say the police'.

Getting out of bed Maisie's mum reached for her dressing gown, 'I'm coming down with you'.

'All right, it's probably nothing,' he said.

'It must be something or else they would not be ringing our bell,' she grumbled as she followed him. The next minute Gwen's bedroom door opened. 'What's going on'.

'It's the police they say they have to talk to your dad'.

'Couldn't they wait until morning,' Gwen said giving a yawn, 'some people have to go to work tomorrow'.

'No obviously not love it must be important it's the middle of the night'.

'Well let's hope they won't be long then'.

Opening the door, the plain clothes police officer said. 'my name is Detective inspector Johnson and this is WPC Harrington'.

'Would you like to sit down Mrs. Redman, and could you sir'.

'Spit it out man, and stop pussyfooting around what's the matter?'

'Well sir there is no easy way to say this, but there has been an incident at your daughter's house'.

'My Maisie's!' he asked in amazement.

'Can you tell me Maisie has been in touch with her ex-husband Hugh Grainger, recently?'

'In touch with him never! she never will again after how he abused her in America, she would never let him near to her again. Maisie lost our grandchild because of the beating that he gave her, she still hasn't got over that why do you ask?'

'So, he has abused and beat her before?'

'Yes, But!' Maisie's dad did not get any further.

'Now what are you saying is Maisie all right? He hasn't hurt her, again has he?' Gwen asked butting in before her dad could answer'

'I'm afraid he has gained entry into her property while she was sleeping and beat her badly and if it hadn't been for the quick intervention of her neighbours, God knows what else he would have done'. 'They have taken her to the local hospital in Chester, so if you would like to get yourself changed, we'll take you to the hospital'.

'Is she going to be all right her dad asked'.

'Yes, I'm sure she will,' the young detective said. 'The hospital told us that they didn't think that she will have any scars and that's good, I would think she is quite pretty like you. Are you her sister?' he asked Gwen, giving her an admiring look.

'Yes,' answered Gwen struggling to answer. 'Can I come too?'

'Of course, I'm sure she would be pleased to know you are there. Maisie probably will be under sedation but it will be nice for her to have someone there when she wakes up'

'Make yourself a cup of tea if you want, it won't take us long to get ready,' Maisie's mum said.

Gwen gave him a smile through her tears. The WPC said, 'I'll go and make that tea, which way is the kitchen'.

Gwen showed her the way and left the young detective to wait in the lounge. When they all came back down the police officers were just finishing their tea, and the WPC carried the cups back into the kitchen, washed and stacked them on the drainer. Waiting for the three to put on their coats and lock up they helped them into the car.

It wasn't long before they arrived at the hospital, 'I'm just going to have a word with the doctor and then I'm sure he will come and have a word with you'.

While the detective was with the doctor Harry and Joan came out and explained what had happened. 'If our Billy hadn't needed to finish some course work to take to college the next day we would have missed it, Mum, Peter and myself had gone to bed and Billy heard Jasper growling, so he went to see what was the matter with him when he spotted Maisie's garden gate was open and the back door was wide open'.

'How did he see that?'

'On the home security screen, we set it up as Maisie had been having phone calls in the middle of the night and she thought there was a prowler about'.

'And she never told us, why?'

'It was probably because she didn't want to worry you, you know she loves you and her mum. After all everyone wants to protect their parents from worry'.

'But if she had told us she could have been spared the hurt, she could have come back home and stayed, with us, her family'.

'I don't think she was aware of who it was or else she might have done. Well now you are here I'll take Joan home, but if you need anything let us know, we will come back tomorrow night to check that's she's Ok, my Joan has become very fond of your Maisie, she's a really good neighbour, good night then,' Harry said extending his hand to Maisie's father.

'Goodnight and thank you both so much, I know we will never be able to thank you enough'.

'Come on lass,' he said to Joan, 'let's get you home'.

Tears rolled down her father's, mum's and Gwen's cheeks as they sat at the bedside of their lovely daughter, her face was bruised, swollen, and stitched, it was her mum's turn to say, 'why has he, up there, let this happen to Maisie? We know she wouldn't hurt a fly, so why had she to suffer a bully like that. I hope everything that is bad will happen to him he deserves nothing less'.

The young detective appeared again with the doctor and Maisie's mum and dad were listening to what the doctor was telling them about Maisie's injury's and how long she would be kept sedated. Leaving the young detective to speak to Gwen.

'I'll have to go back now but here's my phone number, when you, your dad and mum are ready to go give me a ring then I'll come back and give you a lift home'.

'That would be great,' answered Gwen, 'wouldn't you have thought he would have learnt his lesson after going to jail last time? And in America at that'.

'So, he's done this before'.

'Yes, twice he beat Maisie when she was married to him, and another woman at home before they got married'. I hasten to say Maisie didn't know about it.

'Look I know I shouldn't ask but after this is all over and he's safely locked back up, would you mind me taking you out for a drink?'

Gwen looked up at him and said, 'Yes I would like that'.

Gwen, her mum and dad stayed there until the doctor said, 'we are going to keep her sedated for another day, so if I were you, I would go back home and get a little bit of rest and a shower. Have something to eat and then come back. If anything happens, if she comes around and we think it is safe to leave her awake we will, and of course send for you immediately. Now go and make sure you three are okay, she will need your support after this'. '

Come on Dad, it is sensible, we need our strength to support her'.

So, thanking the doctor and getting him to promise to contact them if anything changed in her condition, they made their way home. After a shower and a drink, they tumbled into bed. For all of them sleep didn't come easy, they all were worried about Maisie and just couldn't switch off.

'Why didn't she tell us love?' he asked his wife.

'Because she loves us and didn't want us to worry, besides she probably didn't know he was back. And who would have thought that he would have dared to touch her again after doing a stretch in America. The problem is some people never learn and believe that everything that they do is right'.

When Gwen woke up, she rang her works and asked for two weeks holiday, she was certain that Maisie would be on the mend after that, she just needed to be there too if Maisie needed her and there was her mum and dad to think of as well. Looking into her diary she found the number of Maisie's work and rang them to say she would be off sick and when Gwen could get in with a sick note she would. She didn't tell them what had happened they would cross that bridge when they had to. At the moment, she felt it more prudent to wait until Maisie came to and they knew the full facts. What Gwen did not realise that incidents like this are always reported by the police and the hospital to the authorities and would at some time would make it to her place of work and of course because she was a social worker it definitely would get there.

Over the next two days Maisie's mum, dad, and Gwen took turns to sit with her, and Harry and Joan came and did a turn as well. They couldn't settle until Maisie was awake again, it was towards nine o'clock on the second night that Maisie opened her eyes, it was her dad that was sitting at her bedside.

'Dad she croaked,' her throat was still very sore where Hugh had nearly choked her.

'Don't try to speak my little kitten just rest, we can talk about it when you are feeling better'.

The WPC that had been waiting outside popped her head in and asked if she was okay and Maisie nodded her head.

'I won't be long sweetheart,' her dad said and went outside to see the police women.

'Look you can tell your superior that Maisie has come to, but could they leave questioning her until tomorrow she can hardly speak? Her throat is black where he must have almost killed her, make sure they don't let him out'.

'They won't sir not with his track record'.

'Good, he needs locking up for good, the world would be a better place if he was not on the loose'.

Going back into the private room that Maisie was in he said, 'Don't try to talk yet love, you can tell us all about it when you are feeling a little better. You know you should have told us, but we can go into that when you have your voice back properly. Whether you love us or not, it is our role in life to worry about you'. Maisie nodded her head next time she would.

The next day Maisie found herself giving a statement once again to the police this time she left nothing out and she certainly was not going to blame herself for anything, she was once more determined that he would not get away with what he had done. The young detective that had driven her family down to the hospital popped his head around the door and said, 'can you give your sister a message for me?'

Maisie nodded her head in answer, 'tell her not to forget her promise to go for a drink with me, and for what it's worth, when you have got rid of them bruises and stitches, I bet you are just as pretty as your sister. I do hope that Gwen remembers my invitation I will get to know you and your family too then'.

He seemed a nice young man, but she hoped if Gwen did go out with him, she would take it slowly and make sure whatever she did that she was careful. If Maisie thought that she underestimated her sister, who had already made her mind up that anyone she got involved with would definitely wait for her scrutiny and approval and she would take her time in getting tied up, they would have to work hard for her favours. She felt for her sister and was appalled that he had managed to find her.

Maisie was soon on the mend, the doctors had been right, she still had the small scar across her nose but the other blows had hit the side of her face and he had bruised her stomach where he had kneeled on her stomach. Also, where her teeth had gone through her lip, she had been assured you wouldn't see it especially if she wore lipstick. She herself sent in a hospital sick note and they had put on the note personal stress through accident, they had put that in conjunction with making sure nothing would get into the press until Hugh Grainger was charged with actual bodily harm, aggravated assault, and also breaking and entering. This was to make sure any of the jury were not swayed in their judgement before the trial, but again the police thought the case would be cut and dried and that he would be put away for a long time. When Maisie came out of hospital, she went back to stay at her mum's, she no longer wanted to be on her own at the moment. At her mum's she would be loved and cosseted by both her mum, Gwen and of course her dad when he came home from work. He told her in uncertain terms that he was disappointed that she had not kept him in the loop. In future she needed to tell them her worries, however small or large they were there to help and protect both her and Gwen.

Maisie was soon back up and working, no one mentioned why she had been sick, she still had bad dreams about that night and she could still see Hugh undoing his trousers to rape her, the thought that someone could watch you and get you on their own to do that made her feel sick. No way could she have stood for that man to touch her she would have preferred to be dead. Trying not to think about it Maisie had not gone back to the cottage, she had just gone with Gwen to pick some clothes up and to see Harry and Joan and of course to bring Gracie back with her. But her mum had spoken to her saying, 'promise me that when everything has been settled and Hugh is back behind bars could she please put Gracie to rest'.

'You will never forget, but you need to stop grieving and give her back to God, when you fret about leaving her on her own in your room'.

'If you interred her ashes, you are placing her back with other children in heaven. Think about it, would me or your father advise you to do something wrong? It's the right thing Maisie whichever way you think about it, arrange to put her back to rest we will help you to arrange it love'.

'I will mum but after we have settled this business with Hugh, I need to be sure that he won't hurt me again'.

When Maisie was at work sitting in the office she looked up to see Blanche go in to their superior, Maisie tried to watch for her to come out for this was something else she needed to sort out, it would be another thing that she needed to clear up so that she would not be worrying about it, if she could speak to her she could perhaps clear it up. Maisie still thought of Matt and she could still conjure up his face when she was thinking. The phone rang and she had to turn around to answer it. Once she finished her conversation, she turned to see Blanche look back at her office and she thought Blanche had seen her, but she turned quickly and went back out of the building, Maisie felt more hurt than ever for she could not think what she had done to upset her. She now realised that whatever it was Blanche did not want anything more to do with her, so it was another phase of her life she needed to put behind her. It wouldn't be long before she would hopefully pass her training and perhaps, they would find her a placement, at the moment she was travelling backwards and forwards to her mum and dads to get to work she preferred to do this than go back to the cottage.

She had thought long and hard that she could no longer live in her cottage she would put it up for sale. Hugh had sullied her home and left her with bad memories, so she had decided she would put it up for sale and start afresh again. And yes, after the court case Maisie had made up her mind to put Gracie to rest. She would use the small church she had seen on the edge of Chester something told her that Gracie would be happy there, yes she felt better now she had made up her mind and she had hoped to still be somewhere placed in Chester or in one of the departments on the outskirts and perhaps at some point she would see Matt again, even if only from a distance. He seemed to be more on her mind just lately than ever, she wanted to know what he had meant when he kissed her, was it a promise, if only. Maisie now knew her mind was changing, she knew everyone was not like Hugh, he was sick and needed help and to be put away for as long as it took, he should not be let out to hurt anyone else. Maisie thought it would be foolish to ever think that he would change, he would always be a threat to women she hoped when his case came to court the judge would take this into account when sentencing him.

The weeks passed and suddenly it was the beginning of April and Hugh's case was to be heard At the crown court it was quite lengthy and she had to recount everything that had happened since arriving back from America, statements had been sent to say that after only working at the hospital for one month and when he had only been married for six months, he had been having an affair with a women called Jodie Farrell that had continued throughout his marriage Maisie had the courage to leave him after divorcing him in America. There was also photographs of her injury's inflicted on her in the recent assault in England, these were passed over to the jury to examine. All the time in court flanked by her family Maisie did not turn her eyes away from him, she kept her steely glance trained on him and she did not flinch, she intended to show him how strong she was now and that he could never hurt her again. Whilst inside she was quaking, no way would she allow her mask to fall, he might have been abusive to her and battered her, but she was beginning to believe again. He needed to know she would never back off and that she was capable of standing up to him. Because she was so strong and did not avert gaze, Hugh himself looked down and couldn't face her.

The Jury then retired after the closing speeches of the prosecutor and the defence; Maisie had to wait until the next day to hear the results of the case. The jury were all in agreement and he was found guilty of all charges and sentenced to eight years in prison for actual bodily harm, assault, attempted rape and an extra two years for stalking and breaking and entering premises unlawfully. The judge told Hugh, 'and that is a lenient sentence for such an horrific crime and the fact you took a young girl as your wife and treated her in such away, I won't be as kind to you if you ever come before me again.'

'Take him down,' the judge ordered.

On leaving the court Maisie her mum, dad and Gwen went for lunch at a nearby hotel, they were not actually celebrating, but hadn't eaten much that day. So, Maisie's father said, 'we'll have a good cooked lunch'. I will pay and then mum and you two can have a rest tonight and we can have sandwiches later for our tea, I will get them ready, and I think that there is some of mums homemade fruit cake left. You three have been so strong today you deserve that rest'.

'Yes, because I have a date tomorrow night,' Gwen said.

'You have?' they all said together'.

'Yes, with that nice young detective that gave evidence for the police, he asked me out months ago but we had to wait for Maisie's case to come to court so that he did not compromise himself as he was on the case'.

'But he has rung me most days to remind me, he's been very patient so I thought I'd give him a go'.

Maisie said, 'good for you our Gwen. you were right to wait, if he's been that patient, he's a keeper'.

Their meal came and they all had a roast lamb dinner with all the trimmings and finished with lemon cheese cake and cream followed by coffee.

Over the next few weeks Maisie went to see Joan and put her house up for sale, she told her she would keep in touch because she had been informed that she would be staying in the Chester area. She had completed her training for the beginning of June, herself and Gwen had decided on having a holiday at the end of June that would take her into the middle of July. So, she was going to see the local vicar to arrange the internment of Gracie's ashes now she had found the strength to at long last part with her little pink casket. Maisie intended to find herself a house nearby the church so she would be able to visit her Gracie's resting place, yes she would never forget her little girl, but now that period surrounding Hugh Grainger was over she could start to heal inside and forget what had happened and start to love herself again and hopefully begin to trust people they were definitely were not all like Hugh.

Gwen and Maisie's holiday arrived but by this time Gwen and Grant, her young detective, had definitely become an item and had decided to get engaged at Christmas, Maisie was so pleased that Gwen had not been like herself but had listened to her mum and dad's advice, once again she asked herself why she didn't and why things had to be different for her, but as her mum had said everything happens for a reason, her grandmother had once said whatever doesn't kill you makes you stronger. She smiled to herself for the first time, it had certainly made her stronger and it would continue to do so. She wouldn't ever let herself be dominated by another person marriage and life should be give and take, not one person should dominate another.

Grant had told Gwen to go and enjoy herself he would be waiting here until she came back, 'I love you,' he told her, It was obvious that Gwen and Grant were very much in love and had taken the time to plan their life and not just jump in with both feet. Packing their cases, they were soon on their way to Majorca, it was the first time that her or Gwen had left England since Maisie had come back from America. Maisie thought that probably it would be the last for her and Gwen together, because if she married Grant next year she would be going away with Grant. She hoped from the bottom of her heart that Gwen would be happy and funnily enough Maisie knew inside that she had come across and had captured a good man. She knew her sister would be happy he appeared to be like her dad in many ways and fitted in with the family well.

Maisie was more than pleased with Gwen's choice. Her only regret had been that she hadn't been as fortunate, and wondered if ever she would have someone to care for her in the same way. Hugh's mother put pen to paper and took it upon herself to say how sorry she was that Hugh had treated her so badly and had said that he was having a bad time in jail as the other prisoners had attacked him and he was at the moment in solitary confinement. She also said that she was glad that his father had passed away last year and would not see how their son had turned out. Maisie thought that Hugh had deserved everything he got and then chided herself that two wrongs don't make a right. it was Hugh's mother that Maisie felt sorry for he was still her son.

Maisie at last knew that if his mum could write to her in this way, she hadn't done anything to blame herself for what had happened within her marriage. Maisie was slowly regaining herself esteem she would never wonder again if it was something that she had done.

The holiday was great, Maisie for some reason appeared to have turned full circle she was happy to go out with Gwen at night for a drink in the bars and in the daytime sunbathe on the beach. They had plenty of comments and admiring glances, but Gwen had only eyes for one person, her young detective, and although Maisie had come a long way in the last few months, she hadn't come that far for her mind was on her lost friend Matt. As she lay there in the sunshine her mind kept thinking of his eyes as he gently held her arms before that strange kiss it was like being touched by a butterfly then before she knew it had quickly flown away. She now wondered if she had dreamt it, as it was so long since she had seen him.

That longing was suddenly back in her stomach, that feeling that she had lost something precious it must be because she had valued his company, but how she missed him. Would he ever reappear. No because if he did, he would find her house was up for sale now. So, he wouldn't do any gardening at her house, if he found that she was not living there.

The rest of the holiday went to quickly, however Maisie was glad she was going back because Matt would not know where she was if she was not back in Chester. But she knew he would not seek her out, it must be that for some reason, Blanche thought she Maisie had done something to upset her. And Matt had thought she had too, she could think of no other reason for him staying away. Maisie thought I wish whatever it was that they thought I had done they would tell me. I would never have done it. I miss both of them so much. Suddenly Maisie realised that she was feeling sorry for herself again once more and she mustn't fall into that habit or else she would go backwords and that would not do her any good. So, she tried hard to draw on that strength that she had found during Hugh's trial. Why did she always see the good in everyone, and no seemed to care for her.

Two nights later Maisie found herself packing her case and trying to push more in than she had brought with her, they had both bought presents for their mum, dad, uncle and Grant they just couldn't go home without taking them a gift, Maisie had enjoyed her holiday, but was looking forward to seeing her mum and dad, All though Gwen had missed her mum and dad she was ashamed to say she had missed Grant more and couldn't wait for him to hold her in his arms. She hoped he had the day off when she arrived back, the thought of being with him made her want him and so far, they had controlled themselves really well. Both girls had a healthy tan that made them all the more attractive.

The next day they were up bright and early for breakfast because they had an early flight back, after breakfast they were sitting waiting for the coach to arrive to take them to the airport. They were still quite relaxed when the coach arrived and they found where they were sitting. Watching the scorched land through the window she marvelled at how green and pleasant England was, Maisie had enjoyed her holiday with Gwen, but she would be glad when she was back home in Chester and her life had slipped back into that, well-ordered and organized work and home. She would be staying at her mum and dads of cause until she sold her house and found a new home. Once back and if she had achieved her goal of a new home, she would make an appointment with the vicar at the church to have Gracie's ashes interned. Then and only then could she look forward to a different life she would do her best to put that period of life with Hugh behind her and look forward.

The next few weeks Maisie spent her weekends looking at houses accompanied by Gwen and sometimes Grant, he was always popping in to take Gwen out and he would say I'm on a weekend off this week so the three of us can have lunch out, and one or two times it had been the five of us and he included mum and dad. He was a really nice young man who understood what Maisie had been through and had no intention of leaving either her or her mum and dad to fend for themselves. Besides he said he did work shifts and Gwen and Maisie could keep each other company.

Maisie looked at lots of houses but there was always something wrong with them they were either too large or to small, so she looked at a rented flat. It was a really nice flat but it was rented and she couldn't make up her mind, after all if she purchased another house she would have collateral, renting would leave her with none and she needed to protect the money her mum and dad had given her, buying a house was an investment.

She already knew that the cottage she bought and was now selling would bring her an extra £15,000 in on top of the price she had paid allowing for a slight reduction, so it would be more if they paid the asking price. Maisie had updated it and the work her dad had done had made it quite appealing inside. But it was early days yet. Maisie rang the church and spoke to a young lady who said the reverend Mathew was away and would not be back until the end of September but she could pencil her in for the first week in October to arrange for the ashes to be buried, at least she could tell her mother that she had made some arrangement, but not finalised them quite yet. The young lady told her that the reverend had taken a six months sabbatical, something had been a problem for him so he had felt the need to take a break and reconnect to his faith.

Happy that she had done what her mum had asked her and that she would keep Gracie with her a little longer, it was like having a slight reprieve she knew it was for the best but wasn't sure that she felt ready, but she knew when it was done she would have the strength to carry on.

Maisie had moved to her new office and it was slightly nearer to her mums a little less driving for her, so she was still commuting the short distance from her mum and dad's, it didn't take long it was around an hour's drive, and mum would always have her tea ready when she got in. She toyed with the idea of staying there but had gotten used to her own space and she wasn't as outgoing as she had been, she liked a little solitude now and then.

So, she would continue to look for another house to do up, and it would be her little bolthole, her furniture was in her mum and dad's garage and in their spare room until she found somewhere, at least she would have furniture for the next house And would only have to do any jobs that needed doing, she hoped that when she did find one she wouldn't have a lot to do. At the moment she was having a rest from looking she had decided to deal with Gracie's ashes first. Going into her wallet she looked at the small photo that had been taken for her, Gracie looked as if she was just sleeping, she had shown no one of her family the snap, she had been too busy grieving. So, she decided that she would have a larger one for her mum and put it in a silver frame and one for herself as she would no longer have her little pink casket. Continuing to look at the small photograph of Grace Maisie tried to imagine what her daughter would look like now, she was aware that she would have had blonde hair and green eyes, she and her family had missed so much. Thinking about how babies cut their first teeth and take their first steps her first words. With a huge sigh she put her treasured photo away.

Chapter Twenty-Four
Hugh in Prison

Hugh Grainger was in prison and the word had got around that he was a wife beater and a rapist, a lot of the inmates were in prison because of theft, burglary, robbery, money laundering and fraud. All of these crimes are serious in themselves but lot of the men frowned on beating women and rape. So, a lot of the prisoner's held themselves above Hugh, to them their crimes were not as bad, so the tough ones spent their time giving him a hard time. Hugh had to be in solitary confinement quite a few times for his own safety. He vowed if and when he got out, he would make sure he never hit another woman again, by now he had been at the end of quite a few fists. And he would physically squirm when he knew he had to go back to his own cell. A couple of weeks ago three prisoners had him in the toilets, two put his head down the toilet until he thought he would drown while one kept watch he was so relieved when a prison warder came, but the one on watch kept him talking while the other two walked away. Hugh told the warder he did not know who had done it, knowing that if he had told him who it was he would have come off worse further down the line. He was a coward as well as a bully and at the moment he swore he would never use violence on anyone again. He hated how the other prisoners would lay in wait until the warders were not around. On one particular day four prisoners cornered him in his cell, he was only saved by another prisoner quickly telling a warder who came running and the prisoner's said they were only having a friendly chat.

The days and weeks dragged and he lived in fear of some of the other prisoners, when he was in any room he always tried to stay where the prison warders were. His mother was at her wit's end she no longer liked to visit him, but she did. She had always been aware that her son was a little wild, but she had not been aware to what extent. She would have liked to have gone and apologised to Maisie but she was too ashamed. However, he was still her son and as such a mother's love could not be turned off like a tap, it would always be there. However, the hard core of prisoners did not give up, he was found in his cell with stab wounds, it was touch and go if he would live, he was taken to hospital with an armed guard and there he would have, for the time being, around the clock surveillance. Hugh had been in hospital for three weeks but his wounds were too serious and eventually he passed away. When Grant told Maisie, she could feel no pity for him it was his mother she pitied, she herself had lost her child so she knew how she felt, and perhaps like his mother she would have no more children and suddenly she thought of Matt, a friend would have been better than nothing. She was destined to grow old on her own no children or partner.

Over the next few weeks Maisie, Gwen, and Grant had been to look at another five houses, Maisie did not see anything that grabbed her however Grant and Gwen saw one and decided to buy it and start to update it ready for when they got married next summer they had decided 17th June would be the date and Gwen could not wait until Christmas for her engagement ring, Maisie was really happy for her because Grant was a really genuine man. She wondered if she herself would ever be happy again and suddenly she wondered where that thought had come from, she then dismissed it immediately, she would never get married again and once more her mind wandered to Matt. If only she knew what she had done to offend him she would correct it straight away. She really still missed their quiet talks but had always been too quiet to question him on his life. So, all they talked about was the climate, her garden and general knowledge, Maisie always thought he had kind eyes that wrinkled when he smiled. His smile was what she had liked the most, he had a way of slowly smiling at her as if it was just for her. Maisie gave herself a mental shake, it was nine months since she had spoken to Matt or Blanche, that seemed like a lifetime and she could still feel the hurt.

The weeks passed and she was always busy trying to help someone or another of her case victims she knew her job and did it well. The social department were pleased with the work she did and she had to admit it. Every time she found a safe house for a battered wife and their children, she felt elated and that she had made a new life for women and sometimes men. Because out there, were men too that had an abusive wife. Maisie had never heard of this before she took up social work. but as it happened it was quite a regular occurrence, because she had been so looked after and loved by her parents it had come as quite a shock that people were so complex, she had led a sheltered life which had been fortunate for her in one way, but unfortunate in another as originally she had been ignorant to the distress that other people had been subjected to, so when it happened to her she was unprepared for it and blamed herself as many other abused people did.

It was only her natural instinct to survive that had got her out of her problems, but some other wives or husbands thought they were worthless and stayed to be battered and sometimes they had one too many beatings that resulted in their death. How lucky had she been, her instinct to survive had been strong and thinking back to when she had been brave enough and the sheer strength she had needed to enter the bedroom where he slept, he could have quite easily woke up and caught her, every time she thought of it she shuddered. Because the thought of what he might have done had he awoken and caught her. But now it was definitely all over, Hugh had now been lain to rest and could no longer hurt her, so she knew when she did find a new home, she would be happy and safe within, it was the memories of what had happened in her cottage that had forced her to sell. No way could she have seen herself sleep in that bedroom again, not after seeing the evil in Hugh's face.

Soon the first week in October arrived, in three days she had her appointment with the vicar to put Gracie to rest, her mother sat and talked to Maisie about what they must do. They needed to order a small plaque that could be placed on her resting place, also they would have a small reception of finger food for her family at home because her uncle's, aunt's, Gwen and Grant and obviously Mum, Dad, herself needed to celebrate Gracie's life; even a life so short. Maisie felt better when her mum had explained why yes, she needed to celebrate Gracie's life, she was right she should have put her to rest sooner. She would save the silver picture of her daughter and give it to her mum afterwards, she knew her mum would be pleased with it. Standing holding the little pink casket in her hands, she whispered, 'I'll always love you Gracie, but now is the time for you to be at peace within God's garden; one of his treasured blooms'.

This was the worst thing that Hugh had been guilty of, not even bothering that his child had died what sort of monster had she married? She was really glad that she was no longer connected to him, she pitied any women that had become involved with him before he went back to prison. She thought back to his mother as she had been in court when he had been sentenced. She appeared to be a broken woman, but she was a mother and she would still love him, but it didn't stop her hurting. Now he was dead and his mother would be suffering even more. Maisie once more turned her mind to her work files in a couple of days she would have everything sorted. Switching her attention to preparing her work for tomorrow she had a couple of home visits to make, and a couple of appointments with two women and a final meeting with the senior social worker. The next day everything went well all her cases for that day were on the right track, Maisie went home feeling at peace with herself, she was helping people to be strong and to speak out about abuse.

Tomorrow was Saturday she had her appointment with the vicar and she would feel better when it was over and she would know that the burial of Gracie's ashes would be final and her little girl would be in the hands of Jesus, she probably was with him already, but she had with the help of her parents to made sure. Hugh would be somewhere but she was unsure that he would be in heaven, unless God was really forgiving. If Gracie met her father in the hereafter would she forgive? Maisie knew she was being uncharitable but she hoped with all her heart that her little girl would not.

The next day Maisie declined her mother's offer to drive to Chester with her,' I'm sorry mum but I'd like to make the arrangements myself, I promise you when I have a date for having the ashes interred, we will do it together.

'You know it's for the best Maisie love, once we bury her ashes she will be at rest'.

'As long as you have the ashes with you, none of us will stop hurting, not only for Gracie but for you love, you need to start living again'.

'I know mum and once I have sold my house and purchased another then I will do my best to forget what happened and I will. You'll see Mum, but until then I'll be living with you and Dad and you'll probably get fed up of me'.

'Don't be silly Maisie when you and Gwen are living under our roof we know where you are it will be strange, and Gwen 's wedding will soon be here and then our little nest will be empty, we will want to come and stay with you'.

'Well if you do you will always be welcome at my home, I can't imagine my life without you and Dad in it, so stop fussing, both Gwen and I will always be flitting back home on different occasions. Besides Mum, both you and I know that Hugh can no longer hurt me again and it's sad that he had to lose his life for that to happen.

I might still have to look over my shoulder if he hadn't. I'll always be thankful for Harry's, Joan's and their boys help, without them she had no idea if she herself would still be alive.

Maisie had dressed carefully in her black slacks and sweater topped with her cherry red jacket, climbing into her car and driving carefully to Chester she pulled up in a side street by the church, getting out of the car and standing looking up at façade of the church Maisie felt a feeling of peace and tranquillity come to her. Looking at her watch she saw that she was early for her meeting so she wandered into the grounds to look around. Here Maisie found a whole section dedicated to children and the thought passed through her mind that Gracie would be with other children, like herself, that thought was comforting, so going into the church she sat in a pew, head bent and prayed that Gracie would be watched over by Jesus.

There had been a section that appeared to not have a plaque so she would ask the vicar if that plot was vacant. That way she would rest under the rose bushes. It would be a space filled with sweet smelling blooms in the summer that sometimes bloomed until quite late in the year, and perhaps the vicar would allow her to plant a special rose, there was one named Grace she had spotted when reading a gardening book, that would be the one she would plant. Maisie did not lift up her head as she heard footsteps walk down the middle of the pew's she had sat at the far side mostly out of view. She heard a door open and shut, looking at her watch she realised that it was still thirty minutes from her appointment. So, she sat where she was in the pew until the thirty minutes had passed, she had been told to come to the church and someone would be there to escort her to the vicarage that was in the grounds of the church. Maisie had spotted a building amongst the trees, but was unsure if this was the vicarage. Suddenly the door opened and an elderly gentleman came in.

Maisie moved from her place that she was sitting at, as soon as he saw Maisie, he asked, 'are you Mrs Redman?'

'Yes. I have reverted back to that name.'

'Oh, I see,' when the man smiled at her he reminded her of someone. 'If you come with me, I'll take you to my son. I used to be the vicar here, but when I retired my son took over and he is just sorting a few things out and he will have them done when we get over there. This way', and he stood back so that Maisie could go in front. As Maisie walked before him, she couldn't understand why she felt she drawn to him, he was tall with a thick head of grey hair and smiling blue eyes that seemed so familiar.

He opened the door and Maisie let out a gasp for standing there complete with his dog collar was Matt. She thought had he stopped doing her gardening because Blanche had mentioned what she herself had told her about her marriage, because if he had judged her, surely as a vicar he should keep an open mind. Holding his hands out he gripped hers and asked, 'are you well Maisie?'

'Yes, thanks Matt and you?' she answered in a stilted fashion, he appeared to look deep into her eyes, 'I'm so sorry Maisie, I didn't know you were pregnant'.

Maisie looked at him and said, 'I wasn't, Gracie died over three years ago, I just couldn't bury her ashes in America for I would have been leaving her on her own as I intended to return to England'.

'I see, is your husband not with you?'

She looked at him and said, 'Husband? He and I parted company over three years ago just before Gracie was born so why do you ask Blanche knew that so why ask?'

'I'm sorry Maisie. I didn't mean to pry'.

Maisie repeated again, 'but why do you ask?'

'Well the gentleman at the charity night introduced himself as Hugh Grainger your husband.'

'She replied, 'my ex-husband'.

'I must have got it wrong then, I thought he asked Blanche and I to give you some space as you were going to give it another try'.

'So, yourself and Blanche judged me and didn't clarify the comment, you both just left me standing on my own and when Blanche asked me to go, I was only going as she would be with me'

'Both of you really hurt me, leaving me thinking that I had done something to offend the both of you, now I know it wasn't me at all, but the both of you'.

At this point Matt's father who had just been standing and listening intervened, 'Look Matt you and Mrs Redman have a few things to discuss, I'll just go and arrange for a cup of tea to be brought in'.

'Mrs Redman,' Matt repeated, looking at her with a puzzled expression. 'No Miss Redman I have reverted back to my single name miss'.

Once started Maisie could not stop, 'it didn't matter that both you and Blanche really hurt me I couldn't help missing you, do you believe all strangers are as easily forgotten or was I just a stranger that passed in the night?'

'Please Maisie I wouldn't do anything to hurt you, please believe me'.

'Look this is getting us nowhere let's just do the job I came to do, arrange to bury my little girl's ashes, after that I can get on with my life and you and Blanche yours'.

'Okay we need to do that, but we must talk afterwards. For there is a lot more about my life and yours that needs to be clarified, I'll pop around the first Saturday after we have put her to rest'.

'No that won't be possible, you see my cottage is up for sale and at the moment I am living with my parents and it's not yours or Blanche's fault, so don't feel guilty about that. So, I won't be around to talk, be like me I just believe the friendship we had just wasn't strong enough, so let's just forget it shall we. I need to put Gracie to rest and unfortunately I chose this church, if you had you taken the time to tell me you were a vicar, I would have chosen a church further away'.

'As it is, I promised my mother that I would deal with her grandchild's resting place so I must go ahead with what I have arranged, the sooner I go over the details with you the sooner you will not have to see me again other than the day we put her to rest'.

'Please don't be so bitter Maisie, please believe me when I say it wasn't because I didn't want to see you again; quite the opposite. I can honestly say you have never been out of my mind over the last months, you are the reason that I went on my sabbatical, for no other reason. You must believe me and I will explain'.

'You don't need to Matt. I got the message loud and clear, both yours and Blanche's, so please let's put our personal feelings to one side and concentrate on the job in hand. Gracie's resting place. I thought I saw a small plot underneath the rose bushes, is that plot vacant?'

Matt did not answer straight away but looked at her with troubled eyes, 'Okay Maisie we will leave it for the time being, but whether you like it or not we will talk, and I think you will find you have misjudged me',

'Will I? I suppose you feel that I misjudged Blanche as well, will she speak for herself then or will she continue to look the other way when she sees me?'

'Yes, Maisie she will speak for herself, I promise you she will'.

Maisie and Matt spent another hour going over the details of Gracie's interment, they pushed the problem of not understanding to one side. When his father knocked on the door. 'I'm sorry son. your next appointment has arrived'.

'That's fine Dad', he gave his father one of those smiles that Maisie had missed so much. 'I won't be long now Dad, but what happened to our cup of tea?'

'Thought you might have preferred your extra time together, so to speak'.

'We needed a lot longer Dad, it's a pity I had booked another appointment, however I hadn't recognised the name. Whatever Maisie thinks, come what may Maisie and I will talk again whether she likes it or not'.

Matts dad said, 'I'm glad lad we have noticed, sorry I have to speak my mind'.

'Okay dad two more minutes please and I'll be out'.

Maisie just stood looking at them in amazement, did they not realise that she was still here. She was just going to voice her thoughts but too late.

Matts father nodded his head in answer and left. Turning to Maisie, Matt slowly moved to her, 'I'm sorry Maisie but if you insist on saying no to listening to me, I have to have something more to remember you by,' slowly he cupped her face in his hands bending his head and claiming her lips. Then stood back just looking in her eyes. All Maisie could do was stare at him this was why she couldn't get him out of her mind. With tears in her eyes she turned and went through the door, she was totally confused. Hurrying to her car and climbing in, it was a while before she could start the car up and move away. Half of her wanted to run back to Matt the other half denied what she was feeling, why her again. Why! What have I done for me to be punished so very much?

Why had this happened to her she had only just come to terms with one thing when another happens, when would she feel whole again? Driving around Maisie did not know where she was going only that she needed to be alone, her mind was in a whirl. She thought she would never bother about another man, but her heart was telling her different. She was aware that she had to get through the next month then she could perhaps forget and put behind her this whole sorry mess. Inside she knew she would never forget Matt and was ashamed of how candidly rude she had been to him. In that short time that she had known him he had become so important to her and because of Hugh, Matt was someone else he had robbed her of, if she had met Matt before Hugh how different her life might have been.

It was as if the whole universe was testing her strength and she wasn't sure that she had any left. Pulling into a layby she sat for quite a while and shed yet more tears. And she did pray to god to forgive her and asked once more why, why me lord? And the answer popped in to her head, yes! Why not you, why do you think you are any different than the next person. Drying her eyes, she tried to pull herself together, thinking yes that's the answer, why someone else. Perhaps for her to tread the path she had chosen she had needed to suffer as some of the people in her case notes had, or she would never have chosen this job. She would have continued to do her cosy secretary's job and never known that people in the world did suffer incredible hurt and hardship. Maisie's mum had said everything happens for a reason and perhaps this was the reason, she needed to feel to be able help. Drying her eyes and finding a moisture wipe out of her glove compartment she put on a little more makeup, realising the she must not look too upset when arriving home. If she was to get back before dark she needed to go now, because she realised once more her mother and father would be waiting for her to get back and wondering why it had taken so long. Starting the car engine she put the car in gear and pulled out as soon as it was safe to do so.

Letting herself into her parent's home she pinned a smile on her face to ensure that her parents did not know that she had been upset, if it looked as if she had been crying she hoped they would think that it was because she was going to part with her darling baby girl's remains. Whatever she thought of Matt she was glad that it would be him that would conduct the service, yes despite how she acted she had always known that he was a good man. And yes in her heart, where no one else could hear she admitted that she loved Matt Hughes and she loved him when she thought he was a gardener, and she still loved him now she knew he was a vicar, but it was a love she could not let anyone be aware of, least of all her family or Matt, it had to lie quietly in her heart.

But Matt had kissed her, what was he trying to tell her, she was so confused all she wanted to do was go back to him and ask his forgiveness. To sit quietly with him would have been enough. The lounge door opened and her mother was there, 'we were beginning to worry where you were Maisie, tea is almost ready and Gwen is due in'.

'I'm sorry mum I had a walk around the shops and I forgot the time'.

'I have arranged everything and chosen a plot for Gracie. 'I know she will be happy there in the children's garden there was a plot with rose trees. They will smell lovely most of the year, yes she will be happy Mum, you were right once more'.

Maisie's mother held her arms open and held her daughter in her arms, patting her back, 'you will see love everything will be okay, now come get your coat off and have a wash, tea's almost ready'.

Maisie smiled brightly and turned to go upstairs; she felt the need to say, 'I love you all so much Mum'. She also needed to make her mum think everything was okay and that she wasn't suffering, giving her once more a bright smile even though her heart was breaking. Because once more she knew she would never forget him, she was still amazed that she felt this way, and that he had kissed her, why! Nothing else of any importance would happen over the rest of the weekend and it would soon be work on Monday. She could throw herself into work and try to draw strength from it to see her through the ordeal of Gracie's interment.

Chapter Twenty-Five
Love Conquers All

Monday arrived and her new manager called her into her office, and introduced herself and asked her if she could tomorrow cover a case at her old office because until they replaced her there, they would be short of staff.

'Off course I don't mind, it will be good to see everyone there,' Maisie replied'. Not feeling the love inside she hoped no one had been aware of what had happened to her, still if they did, they probably would not mention it, and after all one day would soon go.

The next day Maisie went to her old office and in the middle of her meeting she saw Blanche go into their superior's office, when she looked up Blanche smiled at her, but at that moment Maisie in no way felt like smiling back and looked back down at her notes in front of her. The meeting was almost over so she decided to do one of the house visits that she had to do. Anything, was better than thinking Blanche might come into her office after her meeting. Quickly putting on her coat, gathering her briefcase and file she made her way to her car. No way did she want to have another argument with Blanche however large or small, Maisie felt as if she could not stand anymore. She was not in the mood for arguments or finger pointing, and Maisie knew that it would be herself finger pointing and not Blanche.

Blanche sat in front of her superior and listened to what she had to say, 'You are a good friend of Maisie, aren't you Blanche?' Her superior asked.

Yes, I am.' Blanche answered, 'although I haven't seen her in a while, but I was going to pop in before I go'.

'That's a shame because she has just left, what I wanted to show you is a report of a court case that we have just received, where the ex-wife was beaten quite badly after he broke into her home, if it hadn't been for the timely intervention of neighbours God only knows what would have happened'.

She then passed the file over, 'perhaps you would like to read it?' She said passing the file to Blanche. 'This must remain private, but as you are her friend would you perhaps keep your eye on her and make sure that she is okay in herself. Up until now she has not confided in any one. Maisie is a good worker however we can't have her overlooking her own health, so I will ask you if you could make sure she is okay in herself, and I'll keep my eye on her in the office she appears to be a very strong person, but even the strong can buckle under the strain. So, read it and tell me if we need to do anything else. Blanche looked up with a suspicion of tears in her eyes, 'no we don't need to do anything she is a very private person, but she will confide in me when she is ready'.

Blanche had sat and read the file and could not believe that Hugh Grainger had put Maisie through such abuse and she remembered how she had walked away from Maisie as a friend and as it appeared in her hour of need, her brother Matt had spoken to her since, but had not mentioned this particular incident to her, she could only think that Maisie had not mentioned it. Now Blanche really did feel guilty that she had walked away from her friend without a valid reason. Would Maisie ever forgive her? Matt had gone away to rid himself of his particular demons, however it had not changed how he felt, he loved Maisie even though neither of them had declared it to each other in words. Blanche hoped with all her heart that Maisie would forgive her and that she loved Matt, she would have to speak to Maisie to explain and ask her forgiveness. But how and when she would have a chance to do so she had no Idea.

Maisie kept thinking about how Blanche had smiled at her when she had been working at her previous office, she was now taking a week's holiday and it was Tuesday, on Saturday they would be putting Gracie to rest in the children's garden. Soon her little girl would surely be with God. Maisie would not forget but would tuck away her daughter in the corner of her heart. And at the service it would be the last time she would see Matt. It would be perhaps easier to forget this whole episode of her life. Surely God couldn't have any other trials for her to overcome she thought. Love was not for her she would have to resign herself to that. Although she couldn't stop thinking about him ever, like she thought she knew his dad when she met him in church.

In the meantime Blanche spoke to her brother in confidence, he too had not realised what Maisie had suffered once again at the hands of Hugh Grainger, his heart was breaking, he knew that he would not divulge to anyone else that he knew, even Maisie, but he knew he had to protect her and love her for the rest of his life. He would make sure, that he would insist on talking through why he had stepped away from her. He needed her with him for the rest of his life he would ask God for guidance. He was not used to asking God for anything for himself, but tonight would be the first time and if he granted him this one thing he would be satisfied and wouldn't ask for nothing else for the rest of his life.

Saturday arrived, it was bright and dry but cool, Maisie, her mum, dad and Gwen and Grant, her aunts and uncles all congregated at Maisie's mum and dad's house ready to take Gracie to the church. Waiting for them at the church door was a church warden to hand the order of service to her. As they walked to the front pew Maisie saw several people that she recognised from work, as well as her superior and Blanche. Harry, Joan, and the boys, and to her surprise Matt's father and it appeared to be his mother who smiled in her direction. Once they had taken their places in the pew she was gazing into those familiar eyes and Matt appeared to give her a flash of that special smile. 'Maisie,' her dad whispered, 'it's Matt why didn't you tell us'.

'Yes, I know!' Maisie replied sharply having to keep herself in check, she once more had to call on that newfound strength before her dad started to worry.

The service began with Matt warmly welcoming the family into St Michael of All Angel's Church, on the internment of Gracie Grainger; Maisie could not be cruel and take away her father's name. She listened to his words trying hard to push Hugh out of her mind, and Looking around she was astonished and amazed to see Hugh's mother sitting in the opposite pew on her own, how on earth did she know? Who had told her? Looking up at her dad she knew it had been, her dad and mum? And in her mind, she realised that it had been the right thing to do, yes, they had been right, it was her grandchild as well. Soon the service was all over and Matt was leading them outside to the grounds he waited at the end of the pew for her to join him, Maisie did not know which way to look, she felt as if everyone could read her mind. And she so wanted to keep her secret a secret.

Standing by the little plot of ground Maisie could not help but shed a tear, 'goodbye sweet little Gracie', she whispered, 'sleep tight'.

She suddenly felt elated, her little girl was at rest at last. Looking up once more she found Matt's eyes on her, she blushed and turned away. With Grant on one side and Gwen on the other she thanked Matt for the service and quietly said goodbye.

Matt looked into her eyes and said, 'no I'm joining you at your home for a cup of tea, both myself and Blanche'.

Gwen answered for her. 'You are most welcome, where is your wife? Gwen asked, 'not my wife I'm not married yet, my sister', he said smiling at Gwen.

She smiled back and said, 'I told her'. This caused Maisie to poke her in the side and say, 'shush be quiet'.

Maisie's heart was hammering against her chest, why had he to come to her home, she had suffered enough stress she just wanted a quiet cup of tea with her family. Why should she have to face another trial, it was time she had no more problems, Still with her family there perhaps Matt and Blanche would not broach the subject of their friendship, Maisie was at breaking point if she could just get through today and get back to work perhaps she could slot her life back into an orderly balance.

Maisie went into her parents' home and made straight for the kitchen to make tea, her mum had borrowed a large stainless steel teapot that would make larger quantities of tea than the normal pot would, Gwen joined her and put her arms around her sister, giving her hug she said, 'give him a chance he looks really nice'.

'So did Hugh and look where that got me'.

'Please Maisie, don't be so cynical. That period is over, don't make everyone suffer as well as yourself and if you don't care anything about him just tell him, but I know just looking at you two, there is something there and you are fighting it'.

Maisie just looked at Gwen and tears began to flow. 'Please don't cry Maisie I know today is difficult for you, but it could also become the first day of the rest of your life'.

At that moment the kitchen door opened and Matt walked in and he said, 'I thought this might be where you two were, is that the way out to the garden?' he asked.

'Yes,' Gwen said, 'could you get me Maisie's coat Gwen'.

She nodded her answer.

'Maisie was still crying in Gwen's arms. Walking over he said, 'I'll take over here and once we have Maisie's coat, we can finish this outside'. Matt walked over to Maisie and took her into his arm's, kissing her gently on the brow he held her close to him, 'shish don't cry my love, we can overcome this you'll see,' he whispered.

Gwen was soon back with a coat and Matts overcoat as well, Matt smiled and said, 'I can see that I am going to like being in this family,' at that point Grant put his head around the door, 'Gwen tea, people are spitting feather's in here'.

'Okay just tell them it will only be a moment,' going to the drawer she took a key out and handed it to Matt, who led Maisie to the door, opened it and they went outside. Maisie didn't protest but allowed Matt to lead her to the bottom of the garden where there was a garden bench, so sitting down and pulling Maisie down beside him he allowed her just to cry, he was aware this was what she needed to do to release the grief and emotions she had been so carefully controlling.

Matt must have been holding Maisie close for at least half an hour, before she became quiet in his arms. Once she had gone quiet, he asked, 'are you feeling a little better now?'

Maisie did not look up but whispered, 'yes'.

'Then perhaps we can talk'.

Shall I go first'.

'Yes,' was her quiet answer.

'Well where do I start, the day I came to bring the apples for your mum'. 'Up until then I had not even glimpsed you, I knew a little of what had happened to you and I was just intent on helping you, as my sister was very fond of you'. 'Believe it or not she sung your praises on how you wanted to help everyone not thinking of the strain on yourself'. 'She told me she had found a friend for life'. 'The day I knocked on your door with the apples for your mum I was smitten, but I knew I had to win your trust, and I thought I had'. 'So, the night we went to the charity occasion I was looking forward to your company'. 'Then Hugh Grainger turned up, because of how intimately he spoke to you, I decided to refresh our drinks, I did say we would be around fifteen minutes but you never answered'. 'So, when Hugh came over and said you had asked him to tell us to give you and him a little space', I was devastated'. 'As a man of the cloth I could not become involved in breaking up someone's marriage. So, I walked away',' Blanche knew that she would have to tell you how I felt if she continued to work with you and I had asked her not to tell you'. 'That way you would not be torn to know more'. 'So rightly or wrongly she asked to be transferred, that is the only crime she committed and she regrets it, she will always care about you'.

'Myself, it made me question my faith. for you are the only women that I have ever loved or will ever love'.' So, I took a sabbatical to try and strengthen my faith'. 'And yes, I did once again commit to my faith but I could not stop loving you, it took a lot of strength not to come and beg for your love'. 'Now that's just what I am doing now, please think about its Maisie'. Lifting her chin up with his hand he looked at her with such love. And the tears began to fall again as she stretched up to kiss him on the lips. Matt then pulled her close, his kisses were both gentle and filled with longing and passion. The fact Maisie stayed locked in his arms gave him the answer he craved. When he did speak again it was to ask, 'am I forgiven'

'Yes,' Maisie whispered shyly.

'And what about Blanche,' again nodding her answer she was content to sit and be held tightly in his arms. 'Would it be too soon for me to ask if you could put me out of my misery and tell me you love me?' asked Matt.

'No, I love you Matt, I think I have since I first met you, but I told myself not to love again, I love you Matt,' Maisie said, her head still buried in his coat, lifting her chin with his finger he looked deeply into her eyes and gave her his special smile as he bent his head to claim her lips once again.

Sometime later Gwen opened the back door and walked out calling, 'are you two going to come in before you freeze to death? I've just made a fresh pot of tea. In fact, dad's asking when his little kitten was going to join us again, do come in you two, there's lots of nights to come'.

Matt stood up and pulled Maisie up, keeping his arm around her they followed Gwen into the house where their mum was pouring more tea, 'go into the other room, and take your coats off. I'm sure you will find a chair to share between you,' she said giving them a brilliant smile. For no reason at all Maisie leant over and hugged her mum and her mum turned and hugged both of them. 'Go and get warm you both feel frozen. I will be in with the tea for you soon'.

Going into the lounge Grant walked over and took their coats and said the armchair near the fire is vacant, I'm sure you both will fit on there to get yourselves warm.'

'Thank you,' Matt said, 'I'm sure we'll both fit on there as well,' pulling Maisie by the hand he sat her on the chair and settled himself on the arm besides her. And soon they were enjoying a hot cup of tea, no one seemed to think it strange that Matt and Maisie looked as if they were an item, they just took it for granted that they were.

When it was time for everyone to go Matt and Blanche stayed and it was just as if he had slotted in to the family without even trying. Blanche had hugged Maisie and asked, 'can you ever forgive me?' and Maisie replied, 'there is nothing to forgive it's just another little hiccup in life, no doubt we will have many more through the years but I'm sure we will and can overcome anything now'.

When it was time to go Matt and Blanche said their goodbyes in the lounge and Maisie's dad said, 'you go to the door with Matt and Blanche Maisie,' at which Matt gave them that lovely smile. On reaching the door Blanche said, 'goodnight' to Maisie and said, 'I'll just go and wait in the car Matt'.

'Thank you, Blanche,' Matt replied, and he stood holding both of Maisie hands.

'I love you so much Maisie,' he said, watching her face. He knew now that she loved him, they both moved together and she whispered, 'I don't know how it's happened, but I love you too and I thank God you have come into my life'.

'It's restored my faith in him, because he had got something good lined up for me'. Kissing her once again he whispered, 'I'll be around sometime tomorrow or perhaps you would like to come down to our service. 'Yes,' Maisie replied, 'I believe I will'. Quickly kissing her again he joined Blanche in the car. Maisie stood and waved until they were out of sight.

Maisie joined her family in the lounge and Gwen said with a cheeky grin on her face, 'I told you I would remind you later and I feel I have to now'.

'Well I'll remind you Gwen,' said Maisie you need a little more practice with the washing up so come on, you and I will get most of it sorted out, mum has already done more than her share'.

Laughing the two girls went into the kitchen and cleared up the mess to give their mum a rest.

The next day after church Matt asked Maisie to marry him, Maisie's answer was 'yes please,' as she gazed into his eyes. Inside her heart she knew that Matt would never be like Hugh and that like Gwen had stumbled into someone who would love and cherish her just like their dad. They would grow old and grey together and build lots of happy memories. Maisie also knew that cruelty and abuse would not exist within her marriage, only in her working life, and that she would fight along with her clients to make their life better.

Matt said, 'find out when we could speak to Grant and Gwen, did you say they were to be married on July 17?'

'Yes,' replied Maisie. 'Well how would you feel about a double wedding, would that give you time to get everything we need, after all we have got a home, the rectory and you and Gwen do seem quite close and Grant seems a really nice man, so'.

'I can't think of anything nicer,' Maisie whispered as Matt pulled her into his arms.

Gwen was over the moon that Matt had suggested a double wedding, that meant they would celebrate their wedding anniversaries together and Grant and their parents were happy about it to, it meant only one reception for the two. Matt and Maisie had decided that they would also get engaged at Christmas so they both had a ring. Then their mum, Grant's mum and Matts mum would set out to choose wedding dresses, bride's maids, and the mother's outfits together. The grooms, dads and best men would shop for their own.

July the 17th was soon upon them, both Maisie and Gwen looked beautiful in matching cream dresses, the bride's maids were dressed in pale blue with darker blue sashes, with bouquets of blue and white roses, the headdresses were tiaras. It was obvious to Maisie's mum and dad that Maisie and Gwen would now be well looked after, there was no misgivings or worry as there had been at Maisie's first wedding. They were content with both of their little kitten's choice.

Three years later Gwen and Maisie were sitting in the garden at the rectory watching their children. Both Maisie and Gwen had two children each, Maisie had a little boy, Mark and a little girl, Yvonne, they both had dark hair and blue eyes. Gwen had two boys, Ian and Peter; she was pregnant again she wanted a little girl. Maisie suddenly held her fingers to her lips as she remembered her dream and her grandmothers words,' you will live with gods servant on earth' and here she was, she hugged herself with happiness as they watched the other two boys in their life try to play cricket with tiny bats, big kids themselves.

'Thank you, God,' whispered Maisie, 'you have provided me with a rich tapestry of life, some good scenes, some bad, but always for a reason.

THE UNINVITED GUEST

Olivia was shocked into awareness by something furry rubbing against her leg, quickly turning the light on she found herself staring into the green eyes of a Siamese cat!

'Where did you come from?'

The next day she took the cat with her to her shop, placing a notice in the window; found one cat contact giving her phone number. A good looking, man came into the shop whose presence disturbed her, introducing the cat to him he named it cream puff. Becoming involved with him Olivia soon became upset by his duplicity.

The Uninvited Guest
By Barbara Anne Machin

CHAPTER ONE

Olivia Bancroft stood at the lift reading the notice, *Out of Order*. This was the third time this month, so walking over to the stairs she looked up, her flat was on the fourth floor and her feet were killing her for she was wearing three-inch heels. She was of average height, five foot six, slim, with titian coloured hair that fell to her shoulders. Her skin was like a peach, flawless and with her almond shaped green eyes it gave her quite an intriguing look; she had been shopping on the way home. Right now, she just didn't feel like climbing those stairs, looking down at her feet she removed her shoes resigning herself to climbing the stairs. It seemed to take her forever to get to the top. Standing at the door she stopped to get her breath, putting down the bags she found her key and opened the door, picking up the bags she walked in and placed them inside the kitchen on the work surface. She then returned to close the flat entrance door. Slipping her coat off she turned and hung it on the hall stand, making her way into the kitchen she put the kettle on to make a much-needed cup of tea.

Carrying it into the lounge she flopped down on the settee at the same time as putting her cup of tea on the coffee table, she leant back and closed her eyes to relax. Olivia was very house proud, at twenty-seven she had lived on her own since finishing university, she now ran a small florist in the High Street and it was doing very well. The flat had belonged to her mum and dad, they had an arrangement that she repaid them back as an interest free loan, her grandad had also left her a little money which she had ploughed into her florist shop, working for herself was rewarding but also hard work

She had furnished her flat with care, choosing a plain gold carpet with an antique red leather suite with gold and red cushions and at the windows gold curtains. Her small coffee tables and display cabinet were in yew wood, the room was finished with a gold and red Chinese washed hearth rug. Everywhere was neat and tidy. However tonight she was too tired to appreciate it as putting her head back to rest she had fallen asleep it had been a busy day. Olivia jumped unawareness of how long she had been asleep, she didn't know it had become dark outside. She was certain something had touched her on the leg, there it was again, something furry. Jumping up she quickly turned the lamp on.

Looking into a pair of green eyes that were staring at her Olivia gasped in amazement, 'where on earth did you come from?'. The cream Siamese cat once more rubbed against her legs, purring.

'Well we will just have to find out who you belong to. You must have come through the front door because I'm too high up for you to get in any other way. Well I haven't had my meal yet so I'll let you out on the balcony for tonight and then you can share my evening meal, but don't leave me any presents in my flat, or whoever you belong to will get the bill'.

Going to her French windows that led onto a small garden balcony where she grew a small selection of plants Olivia waited patiently for the cat to relieve itself.

Letting the cat back in she went into the kitchen and found two old bowls filling one with milk and the other with some chopped chicken she placed them on the floor. The cat at once ate the chicken and drank some milk. Preparing herself a chicken salad she sat and watched the cat wash his whiskers.

'Now I wonder what your name is, someone will be missing you; I can't call you my uninvited guest can I and if I put you out you might not know where to go back to. You can stay tonight but tomorrow you need to go home. Have you got that?' she said.

The cat just stared up into her green eyes.

'Right I'll find a box and put a towel in it, that's the best I can do for you to sleep in okay?' Placing the box in the corner of the bathroom, 'you will be better in here, it's got a tiled floor'. Picking the cat up she stroked his soft silky fur.

'So, I think I'll turn in now, so you will have to as well. Your domain for the night has to be the bathroom, so I'll just have a shower and then it's all yours'.

Slipping into the bathroom Olivia quickly had a shower before returning to the lounge.

'Come on sunshine,' she said. 'In, you go'.

However, the cat had other ideas. As Olivia tried to pick it up and put it into the bathroom it kept walking away. In desperation she sat on the settee and encouraged the cat to come to her half an hour later the cat was sitting on her lap. Holding it in her arms she got up and took it to the bathroom. Placing it in the box in the bathroom she quickly shut the door, hoping that it would settle down. Clicking the lights out she made her way to the bedroom and taking off her dressing gown she flopped down on the bed, she felt quite tired.

Once in bed Olivia was treated to the most peculiar sound of her uninvited visitor wanting to leave the bathroom, the sound of the cat meowing was just like a baby crying, she knew she could not stand that. She would get no sleep and tomorrow would be a busy day, flowers for two weddings to be done and deliveries made.

Getting up once more she said, 'you've won,' picking the box up, she said, 'come on'.

The cat followed her into the bedroom without a problem, she could see that whoever owned her allowed it to sleep in the bedroom. Placing the box on the floor she went to pick it up and put it into the box, she was saying it in her mind as she did not know if it was a boy or girl. As soon as she turned the light out, plonk! It jumped on the bed.

'Do you know what cat? I'm too tired to argue with you anymore but you are definitely going tomorrow'.

CHAPTER TWO

Waking around six o'clock the cat was purring in her ear as soon as she opened her eyes, it started to run to the bottom of the bed with its tail held high.

'I suppose you want to go out do you?' Olivia said, 'don't mind me will you', getting out of bed she walked to her small roof garden and let the cat out. 'When you've left and someone has claimed you, I will have to spray some disinfectant out here, you nuisance,' she said.

Coming back in she looked in her fridge to see what she could give it to eat, there was still a little chicken left so she chopped it small and placed it in the old bowl she had washed from last night before filling the other bowl with milk. Putting the coffee pot on she went to the bathroom to wash and get dressed. When she returned, she felt more awake and alive, she had dressed in her usual black jeans and T-shirt with her shop logo on, going into the kitchen she made herself some scrambled eggs and a small slice of toast, once more sitting at her table and watching the cat wash its whiskers.

'Now I can't leave you here today, you will have to come to work with me and you will have to stay put. Do you get it cat, no roaming off? Whatever is the matter with me talking to a cat, I will end up being known as the cat women if I'm not careful'.

Standing there with her hands on her hips, yes it could work quite well as the door to the back room was a stable door and as long as she made her shop assistant understand to keep the cat the other side of the door it should work. Taking her phone out she took a picture of the cat and then taking a small memory stick she copied it off, once this was done, she went to her computer and transferred it to her desktop, now she could print several copies off. She would place one in the downstairs lobby and one in the corner shop and one in her own shop. She would also leave one at the police station and report the cat found, leaving her phone number on the poster so writing underneath its picture *found one cat please ring 866352 or 865950*, which was her shop number. That way she would not have strangers knocking at her door.

Getting her keys and bag she picked the cat up and her three posters, shutting the door behind her she went downstairs and fixed one on the poster board in the lobby whilst keeping a tight hold on the cat to ensure it did not roam again. Going down to her van she placed the cat on the passenger seat hoping that it would not move.

'Now stay,' will that do the trick she thought and low and behold it curled up beside her. Locking the van door, she popped into the corner store and asked if they would display the poster for her, and they kindly popped one onto the window noticeboard, that done she made her way to work. Once there she placed the cat in the work-room, making a note that she must get a litter tray and some cat food before she went home just in case no one claimed it tonight. Now she had opened the shop she went to the small table at the side and began to make the brides bouquet, once this was completed, she then made the bridesmaids posies. The bride's bouquet was made of red roses cascading down amongst greenery, the posies contained a mixture of pink and red carnations and red roses in the middle. Olivia eyed the clock, she had plenty of time to do the button holes in white and red, then it would only take a short time to complete two flower displays for the mothers of the bride and groom. Popping the invoice on the boxes they were then ready for delivery. She then set too and completed the next lot of wedding flowers, she suddenly remembered the poster she was going to display in the shop. Popping it up on a piece of trellis in the window where it was on display to anyone passing. The girl that helped in the shop would be in at ten o'clock, that would leave her free to deliver the flowers along with a couple of wreaths that she made the day before. Looking over the door in the workroom she checked that the cat was okay, it had climbed onto a windowsill in the sun and appeared to be quite happy. The door went and a man purchased two dozen yellow roses with some greenery and white small flowers. Going back to the bench she started to make a few mixed bunches of flowers to place in the window at that moment her assistant Nicole walked in.

'Hi Olivia'.

'Good morning,' she replied, 'just so you know we have an uninvited guest I have a cat that appeared from nowhere in my flat last night so I've put it into the workroom. Make sure when you go in there you don't let it out, hopefully someone will claim it before the day is out'.

'I'll just finish the orders and deliver the wedding flowers, if you could make a cup of coffee before I go, and make sure you keep your eye on it. Look,' she said walking to the door of the back room, 'it's there on the windowsill, make sure it stays in there we don't want it to escape. I'll call for a couple of cat litter trays and some cat food'.

'Will do Olivia,' Nicole said with a smile. She was dressed the same as Olivia in black jeans and the black polo top with the shop logo on, she was a pretty girl with dark curls and brown eyes, and when she smiled dimples appeared in her cheeks and her face lit up into a generous wide smile. Picking up the bucket that Olivia had filled with bunches of flowers she placed it on the shelf where an assortment of different blooms had been placed. Olivia had an eye for colour and the perfume of the blooms filled the shop.

'Right I need my coffee Nicole,' she said. 'I'll just put the flowers into the van, have my coffee and leave you to hold the fort', smiling at Nicole her face lit up as she surveyed her little domain pleased that her business had taken off and was doing quite well.

Nicole placed her coffee beside her and they both enjoyed a quick break. Taking some money out of her purse she said, 'I'll just nip and do the deliveries I might be about a couple of hours, you'll be okay?

'Yes, the delivery man won't be here until this afternoon and you'll be back by then'.

'Well I'll go now so I'm sure to be back for your lunch,' flashing Nicole a wide smile she left the shop to complete her tasks.

Standing in the queue at the pet shop as she waited to pay for her purchases she thought she must be going mad she had picked a dozen tins of cat food, some cat treats, a rubber mouse, a ball with a bell in, the litter trays and a small cat basket. She realised she had gone over the top a little but she needed to make sure if he wasn't claimed quickly, she had enough to keep it happy. Making her way back to her shop she parked the van and went in, Nicole had made a collar of ribbon and threaded another piece through it and had the cat on this make do lead to let it out so it wouldn't run off.

Nicole's mum Sadie, was in and watching the counter for her daughter and when the shop had a lot of orders to be completed Sadie would do a few hours for Olivia to help out.

'Hi! Sadie how are you keeping?' Olivia asked smiling.

'I'm quite well, I just called to drop off Nicole's lunch, she has a head like a sieve she left her lunch behind on the work surface'.

At that moment a tall man came into the shop, he had piercing blue eyes, dark wavy hair and his clothes looked quite expensive. He was browsing the flowers but every time Olivia looked in his direction' he was looking at her. Nicole came back in smiling at Olivia she said, 'I've seen to that little monster for you, we didn't want any little presents left for you, did we?'

'I'm starving, do you mind me having my lunch now?'

'Of course not, perhaps your mum would like to have a cup of coffee with you'.

'Thanks, I'd love that,' Sadie answered, 'shall I make you one Olivia?'

'Yes, that would be great Sadie'.

Turning her attention to the man she asked, 'are you looking for anything in particular today?'

'I thought I'd buy some flowers for my mum,' he answered holding her gaze.

'What colours does she like and does she have a favourite flower?'

'What colour is your hair?'

'It's Titian'.

'She likes that colour and green the same as your eyes and she likes roses'.

'Do you like roses?' he asked?

'Yes, I like all flowers', Olivia wished he didn't keep looking at her, he was unnerving her. She had butterflies in her stomach. 'Well how about these dark orange coloured roses and some yellow along with some greenery?'

'I see you've found a cat is it okay?'

'Yes, it's fine, someone will see my notice and claim it, I have it in the back room, I didn't want to leave it at home on its own, mainly so it didn't leave me any little surprise's in my absence'.

At that moment Sadie came through with Olivia's coffee, 'thank you Sadie'.

'Will you be leaving him here overnight?' he asked giving her a slow smile

'No why do you ask?'

'I thought he would be lonely for your company.' he said. 'I know I would be'.

Olivia did not know what to say to that, it was a good job that Sadie broke into their conversation.

'I'll be going now Olivia take care'.

'I will, goodbye Sadie'.

'Are these all you want sir?

'For now. Olivia that's a very pretty name'.

Not smiling she said, 'thank you,' and advised him that it would be twenty pounds ninety-nine pence, that he owed her. Wrapping them in her signature paper and adding a bow of yellow ribbon. She took his money and put it into the till.

'Perhaps I'll see you again,' he said looking directly into her eyes'.

'Yes, next time you need more flowers,' she replied.

Nodding his head, he left the shop. Nicole came back and both were soon busy putting up the next day's order's, once this was done Nicole went home, she always finished at four o'clock. The last hour was always quiet, once five came Olivia placed her shopping into her car and tidied around so all was shipshape for the morning. Going into the back room she picked up the cat, set the alarm and locked the door. Placing the cat on the seat she made her way back to the flat. Letting herself into the lobby she thought great the lift has been mended, although she was not as tired today as she was last night.

Opening the door to her flat she kept a tight hold of the cat, shutting the door behind her she placed him safely on the floor.

'Now cat, the first thing we will do is put you a litter tray in the bathroom and one on the roof garden, that way you'll have your toilets and then you can have your tea'.

The cat looked up and green eyes met green eyes, meowing as it did.

'Yes, I'm hungry as well, give me time and it will be ready. Going into the bathroom, she placed a litter tray down calling the cat to her she said, 'that's yours,' and taking the other one to the roof garden she once more pointed to it and let the cat out.

She watching it and it used the litter tray. That pleased Olivia, at least it knew what it was for. Once the cat came back in, she washed her hands and popped a fillet of salmon into the oven. Preparing herself a salad on a plate she placed it on the table. Going and picking up the clean bowl's she had allotted to the cat, placing cat food in one and some milk in the other she put them on the floor. Washing her hands again she took the salmon out of the oven and placed it on the plate, with some mayonnaise. Popping the kettle on she sat down to enjoy her meal.

Sitting on the settee with a cup of tea her mind wandered to the tall attractive man who had been in the shop today, he was really handsome and the way he had looked at her was making her heart beat faster as she thought of him. Oh well lots of people came through the shop's door, she more than likely would not see him again. The cat jumped up onto her knee, rubbing its head on her chest making his strange baby cries, moving around in a circle it curled up on her knee. Stroking its soft cream fur, she thought I could take to this cat, and as soon as she thought about it someone would be missing it and would be unhappy.

Moving the cat from her knee she made her way to the shower. Once finished she picked up her book and invited the cat back onto her knee and she sat reading for a couple of hours before she decided it was time for bed. Picking up the new cat bed she said, 'come on, you can have it in my room but you can go out for a few minutes first'.

Taking it to the roof garden she waited patiently for it to come back. Putting the bed on the floor and placing the cat into it she climbed into bed and turned the light off. The cat jumped onto the bed and lay at the side of her, 'oh all right, you win, it probably won't be for long, your owner will soon be banging my door down after you I hope'.

Chapter Three

The next day was much the same feeding the cat break-fast and taking it to work with her, giving it the ball and toy mouse to play with whilst she completed the days orders. She liked this time of the day as she went in early to get the orders ready, she could get quite a bit done in the three and half hours before Nicole came in as you only got a stray customer before ten o'clock, telephone orders would start around the same time and her order book was quite full. Nicole was becoming quite good at completing orders as well now, so once she came in, she would do a complete order herself. Today she had three orders for flower displays, two for restaurants and one for a reception area, they were all around the same area located near to each other so she would deliver them around two thirty.

'Coffee Olivia?' Nicole asked.

'Yes, please. I think I need my caffeine'.

Just then the shop door opened and who should walk in but the tall man from yesterday.

'Back so soon,' did your mum like her flowers? Olivia asked to be sociable.

'Flowers, oh yes,' he said once more gazing into her eyes.

'Have you come for more flowers?

'I might have come to see if the cat is all right'.

'Why do you like cats?' Olivia asked.

'They're okay, but they are a woman thing, if I cared enough about someone, I suppose I would'.

'Do you like cats Olivia?

'I can't say I do and I can't say I don't, it's not something that I've ever thought about,' she replied.

'But you will look after him, won't you?'

'Coffee,' came Nicole's voice, 'Thanks Nicole'.

'I've watered the cat by the way,' she said'.

'Watered the cat?' the man said with a smile on his face.

'I mean taken him out the back to you know…'

'Oh yes I know'.

'Now what can we do for you today?' Olivia asked. She couldn't quite work this man out it was as if the cat was important to him and it wasn't even his.

'I need some more flowers they are for a friend'.

'I see,' Olivia said, 'a lady friend?

'Yes'.

'What are your favourite flowers?'

'I 've told you I like all flower's'.

'Oh yes, I remember now'.

'Is this person special to you sir?'

'No, but I hope a certain person will become special to me in the future. Do you know you have lovely eyes?' he said holding her gaze.

'I thought the question was what flowers do you think your friend might like,' she said. Her cheeks becoming pink with embarrassment. 'Now how about these? There is a lovely display of carnations mixed with pink and white roses and a little foliage'.

'Yes, I'll take them'.

'Do you think you would like to have a coffee with me after work?' he said, once again holding her gaze and seeing the look of amazement in her eyes. He added, 'you could tell me how the cat is getting on'.

'I don't mix business with pleasure sir'.

'Well we could make it business I have been thinking of ordering flowers for my reception area on a weekly basis'.

'You could go for coffee with me and show me some displays and prices and if it was agreeable, we could set up a contract'.

'Please,' he said giving her a slow smile. 'Are you sure you are not buying flowers for the sake of buying them?'

'Could be,' he replied with a serious look on his face, 'but how will you know if you don't have a coffee with me, it could be that I'm just interested in the cat, either way I'm very trustworthy'.

'I'm too busy to have coffee with anyone. I will need to take the cat home again and I don't intend to leave it in my flat on its own until it goes, I don't want it to leave me any little presents'.

'Okay how about me having coffee with you at your flat?' Looking at him her stomach felt as if she had butterflies in it, 'but I don't know you, you can come back at four and have a coffee here if that will get you to only buy flowers when it's necessary and not as an excuse to ask about a cat'.

'Well that will have to do for now. I'll be back at four o'clock and I take my coffee black'.

His blue eyes seem to flash electric shocks to her, making her heart beat faster. For some reason Olivia could not stop thinking about him, suddenly realising that she didn't know his name however she liked him but she needed to be sure she could trust him.

'Nicole do you have to go home early as normal or could you perhaps stay until I lock up? I know he seems very nice but I don't know him'.

'Yes, I can stay and I can get on with the wreaths for the two funerals tomorrow, that will save some time, but if it was me, I wouldn't mind being on my own with him, he's dishy'.

'Yes, he is but you can't be too careful, thank you I'll do the same for you sometime if you need a chaperone'.

True to his word he came in at ten past four, flashing Olivia a ready smile.

'Will you be okay on your own for a while Nicole, I'll bring you a coffee? 'I'll be fine and if I wasn't, I would give you a shout, so enjoy'.

'Right come this way, we'll have it in the kitchen'.

As they walked through the back room the cat jumped down meowing loudly and running to the man.

'He seems to like you,' said Olivia bending to pick it up before taking hold of the kettle and making sure there was enough water in it to make the coffee. 'It's only instant is that okay?'

'Its fine, here,' he said, 'let me have creampuff while you make the coffee'.

'Creampuff where did that come from?'

He looked a little sheepish, 'oh he just reminds me of a cream puff.' once in his hands the cat was purring with satisfaction and snuggled down on his knee as if it belonged there.

Quickly making the coffee and reaching for some biscuits that she placed by his coffee. 'Look we are here having coffee, you know my name but I don't know your name,' she said at the same time as reaching for some cat treats from the cupboard. Rattling the bag, she was amazed when the cat ignored her, normally it would run straight to her, but today it stayed put.

'That's a first, it must like you, it never says no to food or treats.

'Now your name is?' Olivia enquired her green eyes looking into his.

'It's Richard Gregson, I own the opticians on the opposite side.

'Yes, there and a couple more shops, but that's enough about me, tell me do you have a boyfriend?'

'No why?'

'No reason other than I'm glad'.

'Why?' Olivia asked.

'It means that I can come for coffee again and perhaps we can go out for a meal sometime, when the cat has gone back home. But it could be a couple of weeks before he gets his owners back so perhaps, I could come to you and have a meal please'. Richard asked, giving her that slow smile, 'what do you think of that creampuff?' he asked addressing the cat?

Meow, meow, the cat seemed to be talking to him and all the time Richard was fondling his ears.

'I can't believe it,' Olivia said, 'it's just as if he knows you'.

'No cats are just friendly, anybody's lap will do,' he said looking a little uncomfortable.

'Now I'll just take Nicole her coffee and I'll be back and give you my decision then,' she answered with a smile.

He seemed very nice, what harm could it do give him a chance? Besides I like him, his eyes seemed to say volumes.

'Here's your coffee Nicole are you still okay?'

'Yes, I'm fine,' Nicole said. 'If you don't want him, tell him I wouldn't mind, even if he is a little older'.

'Nicole your, a cheeky pup,' Olivia smiled back at her, 'we won't be too long and when we close, I'll run you home'.

Returning to Richard in the back she smiled and sat down opposite him picking up her coffee. Giving her that slow smile he said, 'well do you think you can trust me enough to have me over for a meal? What do you think creampuff?' he asked looking down at the cat sitting contented on his knee, 'can she trust me, I was a boy scout you know'.

'All right I'll have you over, but not tonight'.

'When then? he asked leaning over and taking her hand with his free one and rubbing his thumb up the side of her hand creating waves of tingling through her body.

'Tomorrow,' she whispered just to take her mind off the strange feelings she was having she was almost sure he would see in her face that he was disturbing her in a nice way.

'What time?' he asked not taking his eyes off her?

'Seven thirty'.

'your address?'

'I live in the block of flats on Fir Tree Court, number fifteen'. Letting go of her hand he reached into his pocket and took out a small card and pen, writing the address down he said, 'I will look forward to that and I've really enjoyed this coffee and I'm sure we will enjoy time together in the future'.

Taking her hand again he laced his fingers in hers making her blush at the way he looked at her. Turning his wrist to look at his watch he said, 'I'll have to go and ensure the shop is closed on time. I don't want to leave you, but I'm afraid I'll have to, but creampuff will look after you for me. Can I come for coffee tomorrow same time?'

Smiling at him she said, 'yes, if you feel the need to buy some more flower's'.

'I might just do that'.

Looking into his eyes she said, 'you can come even if you don't buy flowers'.

Standing up he quickly kissed her on her lips, smiling at her he took her elbow so that she walked in front of him at the same time placing the complaining cat onto the floor meowing loudly. Opening the door, he said, 'until tomorrow bye'.

Chapter Four

Over the next two weeks Richard and Olivia spent every spare bit of time together, he would slip over at lunchtime and again for coffee. Richard would pop into the back to make the coffee while Olivia watched the shop and he always spent time cuddling creampuff on his way through and the cat appeared to want to go with him, they seemed to have an infinity with one another. This puzzled Olivia however they just might have taken to each other.

Sitting on the settee together after their meal Richard pulled her into his arms kissing her eyes and trailing down to her lips, 'you must know how I feel about you now sweet?'

'It's not just creampuff that you come over to see then?'

'No, I will always see him. I have a confession to make in a couple of days. but I'm sure you will forgive me my love'.

'I'd forgive you anything she said cuddling up to him'.

'That's good because you probably will have to. People can do stupid things when they want something badly enough'.

'Now it's getting late and I haven't got long before I have to go home, so kiss me now it will have to last me all night and I would prefer to stay here with you and hold you through the night'.

'It would take a little bit of paper to do that. I'm not that easy'.

'I'm glad that you aren't, if that's what it takes, I'll make sure that it will happen because I want you so much, I can't wait too long sweetheart'.

'I'll be able to take you out for a meal next week. I'm sure creampuff will be claimed'.

'I don't know about that I've got a feeling that he might become part of the family,' she said.

'I'm sure he will,' he said, 'trust me I'm sure he will'.

'Now come here and kiss me,' he said pulling her into his arms.

The next day Richard was playing with a piece of wire that she used for making bouquets, he was wrapping a piece around her finger and he said, 'I have a feeling that creampuff knows where his litter tray is now, in your bathroom and he's left you no little surprises, so how about you and me going out tomorrow for a meal, please?' he asked looking into her eyes.

Olivia looked into his blue eyes and her heart did somersaults, 'yes he seems to be well-trained now, I think I can trust him'.

'That's my girl,' he said kissing her gently on the lips, at the same time slipping the wire off her finger and putting it in his pocket.

'Put something pretty on and I'll try to book a table at Futon's restaurant, a nice secluded table'.

'I have other things other than my black trousers and polo shirt,' she laughed.

'I know but I want to make this special, just you and me, I'm sure creampuff can do without us for one night'.

'I know you're right, it's just that I worry about him, there you are you have me calling it him and it could be a lady cat'.

'Trust me it's a male, can we close up for five minutes I think I need to tell you something?'

At that moment the phone rang and Olivia started to take a telephone order at which point two customers entered the shop and Richard said, 'it will keep I've got a three o'clock eye test to do so I'll see you at home tonight, do you want me to bring anything?'

'Just yourself, that's all I want,' she said smiling at him. Leaning over he quickly kissed her and whispered, 'I love you sweetheart'.

The rest of the day was quite busy taking orders and completing some of the orders for the next day. Olivia sighed with contentment, her order book was full, her business was doing well and she was in love. She felt as if she was walking on air, she might have to take on another member of staff. She had been toying with offering Sadie a few hours a week instead of casual as Nicole was quite efficient at dealing with the orders, making up the arrangements and completing the orders. In fact, she would speak to Sadie tonight and see if she would come in for a few hours tomorrow and then she could have her hair done and perhaps buy herself a new outfit.

After traipsing up and down the High Street Olivia managed to get a black dress with a round neck and three-quarter sleeves and a black stole edged in silver, a small silver clutch bag and silver sandals. The weather was reasonably warm so the outfit she had purchased would be smart, but not overstated. Her titian curly hair the hairdresser had dressed in a pile of curls at the back of her head. Pleased with the result she made her way back to the shop. Richard was already there he said, 'wow your hair looks great but I can't guarantee that it will stay up tonight gingerly touching it'.

'Can we have coffee now because I need to get back to the shop, I have a few eyes to tests this afternoon, however I'll pick you up around seven'.

'Are you and Sadie okay?' Nicole Olivia asked.

'Yes, we're okay, but if you are making coffee Mum and I won't say no to a cup'.

'Okay coming up two coffee's'.

As soon as they entered the backroom creampuff ran to Richard who picked him up, and shutting the door to the kitchen he pulled Olivia against his lean frame kissing her and still holding the cat who seemed quite happy to lie against his shoulder. Letting go of her he sat at the table and watched Olivia make all of them coffee, placing his coffee on the table by him she couldn't resist giving him a quick kiss. 'I won't be long I'll just take the girls their coffee'.

'Hurry back sweetheart,' he said with a smile. 'I just want to hold you for five minutes before I go back to the shop'.

Coming back after taking the coffee to the girls she went to Richard as he held his arms out, sitting on his knee as he kissed her she realised he wanted her and she wanted him, she wondered how long she could hold out before they both gave in to their feelings, because she felt the ache inside her would only be satisfied by him lying with her, and she could not wait for it to happen. Inside she trusted him with her life, she felt as if he would always look after her. Feathering kisses along her cheek and down to her neck his hands began to explore her body, cupping her small breasts and kneading them softly.

'I love you,' he whispered, 'do you love me?'

'For the rest of my life and beyond'.

Hugging her to him he said, 'I don't want to go, but I'll have to. My next appointment is in thirty minutes, be ready I'll pick you up promptly at seven'.

Hugging her and kissing her once more, 'until later my love'.

Stooping to give creampuff a last fondle he said, 'it won't be long now puss you'll soon be home'.

Olivia followed him through to the shop with a puzzled expression in her green eyes, however he just smiled and blew her a kiss and left. The rest of the afternoon passed quickly as it was quite busy so she soon forgot about his remark. Closing the shop and making her way home she let creampuff out onto the roof garden as soon as they were in, she put his food in his dishes. Quickly taking a shower she stood admiring herself in the mirror the new dress emphasised her slim figure. She had used a little green eyeshadow and some lipstick, that was enough, her skin was flawless and she didn't need any more makeup. The only jewellery she wore was the emerald earrings and bracelet that her parents had given her when she was twenty-one.

At that moment her doorbell rang, quickly going to answer it, as she opened the door the look on Richards face could not be mistaken.

'Olivia you look stunning. I'll be the most envied man out tonight you look good enough to eat. I want to hold you so much but I'll be frightened of ruffling you up'.

I don't mind if you ruffle me', she answered putting her arms around his neck. We can always repair any damage'.

'Put it that way, who could resist,' he said crushing her to him. 'We had better go now before we get held up and don't make it out,' he said breathing heavily. 'Has creampuff been watered and fed?'

'Yes,' she answered breathlessly not taking her eyes off him.

'Right we had better go, now have you got everything?'

'Yes!' She answered. Closing the door behind them they walked out of the building holding hands Olivia was soon helped into his grey Mercedes car, it was so comfortable compared to her van, she sank back onto the leather seats. They were soon pulling up outside Futon's, walking and opening the door for her he leant against the car door pulling her body against his he said, 'I need and love you so much, you're driving me crazy. Are you aware of that?'

'I think I am, you see I feel the same'.

'Come on we better go in before I change my mind and take you home to make love to you,' holding her gaze with his blue eyes she could see the raw desire in his eyes, reaching up she gently kissed his lips, then reaching down for her hand they turned and went into the restaurant. The waiter conducted them to a secluded alcove table for two. Looking at the menu they ordered a selection of dishes and a bottle of wine. The waiter placed the wine on the table pouring Richard a small amount to try.

'That's fine thank's'.

Once the waiter had left Richard took Olivia's hand in his and said, 'will you marry me Olivia? 'Please say yes'.

'Tears appeared in Olivia's eyes,' she filled up with emotion, 'yes I can't think of anything I would like more, yes please' she reiterated.

Putting his hand into his pocket he drew out a blue box, taking out of it a square emerald and diamond ring that he slipped onto her finger, 'this is to match your eyes'.

'How did you know my size?' she asked, 'It's perfect'

Taking out the piece of wire he had been playing with he said, 'I'll keep this for the wedding ring'. 'Let's eat and go back, I just want to hold you in my arms I love you so much its hurts,' he said once more holding her gaze.

'That's what I want too,' she whispered. In her mind she knew what would happen but she ached for him too, she was going to marry him so it was in the lap of the Gods. She knew she could not deny him, what would be would be.

Arriving back at the flat after eating they had hardly got through the door before Olivia was in Richards arms.

'I can't help it,' he said as he cupped her small breast in his strong hand, 'I want you sweetheart"

Looking into her green sparkling eyes he couldn't believe it when she said, 'me too'.

Groaning he kissed her for once ignoring creampuff's plaintive cry for attention, he swept her up into his arms and carried her into the bedroom placing her on the bed he held her gaze asking, 'are you sure?'

Suddenly she pulled him to her, 'I love you, it can't be wrong to love you back'.

Standing her back on her feet he gently unzipped her dress, it fell to the floor leaving her standing in her underwear. She then began to undo his tie and shirt buttons as he unclipped her bra. Slipping out of the rest of his clothes, they stood close together until he lowered her to the bed holding her close until she turned restlessly towards him pushing her body against his. Quickly parting her legs, he held her until they became one, he realised that he was the first man she had lain with and his love making was gentle and caring.

Afterwards he asked, 'can I stay with you tonight?'

Her answer was, 'I never want you to leave'.

Groaning he turned and made love to her once more, 'we won't wait long to get married, we'll have to arrange it as soon as possible. I want you by my side every night'.

Reaching for his mobile phone he set the alarm so that they would be up to go to their shops on time. Pulling her close beside him he covered them up with the duvet. Just as he was winding his legs around her; thump! Creampuff jumped on the bed to snuggle down beside them, and they both fell into a contented sleep.

CHAPTER FIVE

Olivia opened her eyes to a gentle shake Richard, had already had a shower, kissing her gently he said, 'here's your coffee sweetheart, have that and then you need to get up and have your shower while I make you some breakfast'.

Smiling up at him she was so happy, 'if I get coffee in bed and my breakfast got ready in the morning you can stay tonight as well'.

'I've news for you I intended to stay,' he said with a smile, 'now chop, chop! if we don't get our skates on, we will be late for work'.

Sitting across the table from each other in the kitchen eating toast and looking into each other's eyes she couldn't believe that soon they would be together like this every morning. She would be Mrs Gregson it had a nice ring. Getting up and picking the plates up she said, 'I'll wash and you can wipe we'll start as we mean to go on,' she said smiling into his eyes.

Standing up and walking behind her he placed his arms around her and nibbled her ear saying, 'I could think of something more interesting to do'.

'No, dishes now and perhaps something interesting tonight,' she answered.

'That sounds promising. I can't wait for tonight he answered. Now will you need your van today or are you travelling to work with me?'

'I'm afraid I have a few deliveries today, but we can tweak that in the future as I can leave the van in the yard at the back, the gates lock so I would have it there for work'.

'Well that's what we will do,' he said pulling her into his arms once more and kissing her. 'I just don't want to let you go, it feels so right you being in my arms'.

'Never mind, we can snuggle this afternoon when we have coffee'.

'Now I'll have to make tracks and get that shop open.'

Picking her hand up and looking at his ring he kissed her fingers, 'love you sweetheart, now where's my creampuff'.

Hearing his name mentioned the cat ran meowing to him, bending and giving him a stroke, he said, 'do as you're told for Olivia creampuff and remember she appears to be like me and loves you too'. Giving her a last quick kiss, 'I'll see you later my love,' he said and left to open his shop.

Olivia arrived at her shop and opened up on time, putting creampuff into the back room he was getting quite used to that as his domain and appeared to enjoy the fuss from Nichole, Sadie, and herself, not to mention Richard who seemed to be his favourite, which still intrigued Olivia. Making a start of her orders she had a couple of early customers who were buying flowers for their girlfriends so ten o'clock soon came around and Nicole and Sadie arrived. Sadie's first question was 'shall I make coffee Olivia?'

'Please Sadie,' she replied.

'Now what needs doing?' Nicole asked.

Passing an invoice Olivia said, 'if you start on this one as they need to be delivered at three'.

Nicole face stretched into a huge smile, 'what's that?' she asked, her eyes sparkling, 'you're a sly puss'.

Olivia blushed, 'Richard asked me to marry him last night and I said yes'.

'Here's me', Nicole said. 'I've been waiting to see if he got fed up with you and then I could have consoled him. You've spoilt my dream, now but honestly I'm really pleased for both of you and don't forget I would make a great bridesmaid'.

'I'll definitely keep you in mind'.

At that point Sadie returned with their coffee, 'what's all the fuss going on?'

'Mum its only Olivia and Richard, he has proposed to her and I've put a bid in to be bridesmaid'.

'I saw that coming, you could tell he had it bad, but I didn't think it would be this quick you've known him less than a month,' Sadie said.

'I know, but we both know it's so right for us. I think it was love at first sight and I'm not a dizzy teenager I'm quite sensible Sadie'.

'Take no notice of me I'm really pleased for you and I hope you will be really happy you have always been so good to both me and Nicole so I tend to worry about nothing'.

Walking over and hugging Olivia she said, 'be happy, that's all I want for you'.

'Thank you Sadie I know we will be, he's all I'll ever want, I really love him'.

The rest of the day passed quickly Sadie did the delivery's leaving Olivia and Nicole free to complete the order's and man the phone. The shop was quite busy too with lots of people walking in and buying flowers. Ten past four on the dot Richard walked in and even Sadie had to admit you could see the love shining in his eyes as he looked at Olivia. Both Nicole and her mum wished them the best however Nicole told him he had broken her heart, 'I thought she might have got fed up with you and I could have consoled you'.

'Sorry Nicole, If Olivia turned me down, I would have died of a broken heart so no one would have been able to console me, she's the only woman for me. And creampuff loves her too'.

'Now how about our coffee sweetheart,' he asked Olivia, 'shall we retire to the back room?'

'Are you girl's okay?' she asked.

'Yes, we'll go when you come back'.

Olivia nodded her thanks to them and followed Richard to the back room. They had no sooner got there when an excited Nicole came in and said, 'there's a lady and gentleman that want to speak to you in the shop Olivia'. Nicole picked creampuff up in her arms motioning Richard to follow them. Walking into the shop she saw a woman and man both were well dressed. both had grey hair. The man was tall and reminded her of someone.

Olivia asked, 'can I help you?

Richard had stopped long enough in the back to put the kettle on and coffee in the cups. As he walked in the shop the woman had her back to Richard and was saying, 'we were passing when we saw your advert and I'm sure that's my creampuff'.

'Creampuff,' Olivia said astounded. 'Did you tell the lady we had christened the cat creampuff?'

'No, his name is really creampuff, my son was looking after him while we were on a cruise'.

The cat was now in her arms purring and you could tell he really loved her. At this point the woman's husband said, 'Richard what are you doing here?'

'It's a long story Dad. can I tell you and mum later? Could you just take creampuff home and I'll call and explain then, I have some serious grovelling to do to Olivia you see,' he said turning to Olivia who was staring open mouthed at him. 'I did say I had a confession to make to you'. 'And mum creampuff has really been looked after well'.

'I don't know what's going on Richard, but did you say the young lady was named Olivia, well thank you for looking after him dear, I'll come back some other time to thank you properly. When my son has explained properly to me just what he's up too. Come along Edward let's take creampuff home and give him some space, and thank you again for keeping him safe'.

Olivia watched them go through the door, turning to Sadie and Nicole she said, 'perhaps you would like to go home now, we won't have time for coffee because Richard has some explaining to do. Haven't you Richard?'

He gave a half smile and said, 'yes, but remember you said you would forgive me anything, remember'.

'Goodnight girl's'.

'Yes goodnight,' Richard said not taking his eyes off her. Walking to the door he turned the catch and put the closed sign on. 'What can I say, I saw your notice I was out looking for creampuff after I had taken him to the vets and he sprang himself out of the cat basket. I saw your notice in the window, I came into the shop and fell in love the moment I walked in, I knew he was safe with you and I needed to get to know you and I knew I would persevere if he was still here and I could tell that you would look after him. I like to think he was matchmaking and he knew I would love you the moment I saw you. A person could drown in your eyes; I know I'm an idiot but I needed to spend as much time as I could with you. Say something you're beginning to worry me, please say that you forgive me. I did tell you he would be part of the family'.

Olivia looked at him and burst out laughing, 'you did all that to get to know me?'

'Yes, and I would do it again, you're wearing my ring, aren't you?'

They both moved towards each other at the same time, she was soon in his arms. 'You forgot to tell your mum and dad I'm your fiancée'.

'Well they will be going to visit my aunt tomorrow for a week so as soon as they come back, I will introduce you to the family, but for the next week I'll have you all to myself I won't even have to share you with creampuff'.

'Yes, creampuff, I'll miss him, he had become part of my life', she said looking up at him with her green eyes.

'Yes, but he will be part of our family still, when we get married and think about it, won't I be better company than creampuff? I can do things for you that he can't'.

'You'll just have to prove it tonight, won't you?'

'I could prove it now if you wanted,' he said, 'we are closed'.

'I'm sorry I like my creature comforts, it's a little chilly in the back so we will put it on hold until tonight. Now do you have to lock up?'

'Yes, but if you wait here for ten minutes, we'll put your van around the back and I'll drive you home, we could pick a take away up and spend the rest of the night in bed. How does that sound?'

'Like heaven,' she replied smiling into his eyes, 'I love you Richard so hurry up'.

Richard was soon back and they both locked up and put the van around the back and then walked the short distance to where his car was parked, helping her in and getting into the driver's seat he leant over and kissed her, 'just to last me until we get home'.

'Do you want me to call to pick up a take away?'

'No,' she answered, 'I have salad and we could make an omelette and for afters we can have fresh fruit salad with frozen yogurt'.

'That sounds good,' he replied'.

'Don't you miss not taking creampuff home with us?'

'You will see him once mum comes back again besides I don't like the idea that he sits on the bed when I'm making love to you. For a while I just want you to myself, I'll have to share you when we have children'.

'I hadn't thought that far ahead,' she said. 'You do want children Olivia?' he said looking at her quickly.

'Yes, I do, I'd like a son that looks exactly like you with your blue eyes, that's the first thing I noticed about you when you walked in'.

'And it was your green eyes as well as every inch of you that I looked at. I couldn't take my eyes off you'.

Driving into the court yard at the back of the flats he was quickly out of the car and opening the passenger door to help her out. 'We will have to get married as soon as we can arrange it, I don't want to make babies until we have tied the knot'.

'Does that mean we have to abstain?' she asked.

'I wouldn't go as far as that, we will just have to be careful for a while. Because now I've tasted honey, I want the whole pot'.

Letting themselves into the flat he said, 'I will do the omelettes, if you do the salad'.

'Okay but I'll lay the table first'.

The two of them soon had a meal on the table, afterwards they washed up and made a pot of tea and took it into the lounge to sit together and watch the news.

'Right I'm going to take a shower, then you can have the bathroom after'. Giving him a quick kiss, she went to shower. When she came back in her nightie she said, 'your turn now. I don't want to leave you even for five minutes'.

'Well you'll have to while you have a shower and a shave, I'll hoover in here and dust then we can get in bed, it could be more interesting'.

'I'll soon be back,' he said with a smile.

Once in bed he said, 'this is what I've waited for all day. I'm sorry I didn't manage to tell you before mum and dad saw the notice in the window'.

'Well it explains why creampuff seemed to like you best'.

'We'll sort that out with mum and dad when they come back, but now all I want is you'. Anything else was smothered by his mouth as he kissed her and explored the outline of her pert breasts.

The rest of the week passed quite pleasantly with Richard coming to the shop for coffee in the afternoon and returning to his shop to lock up, and afterwards he would pick her up to drive to her flat. Once they had their evening meal and sat and watched the news they would shower and retire to bed to make love. Friday arrived and Olivia mentioned his mum and dad, 'what will they say when you tell them we are engaged? 'I'm sure they will love you as much as I do, however when I tell them is not important, just the fact that you love me is what counts. But I will tell them this weekend'.

Chapter Six

As normal Richard dropped her off outside her shop and she opened on time, nine o'clock sharp. The door opened and a petite blond walked in, she had blue eyes and a slim figure. Walking over and giving her a pleasant smile, she asked, 'are you Olivia?

'Yes, I am,' answered Olivia, 'how can I help you'.

'My mother-in-law is creampuff's owner and has asked me to invite you to dinner on Sunday evening this is my husband's card he's the optician at Gregson's on the other side of the road. I have written his mum and dad's address on the back for you. I'd love to stay and chat to you for a while however I'm having a baby and I have a doctor's appointment in fifteen minutes, so I'll have to go, but I'm looking forward to getting to know you. I'll see you on Sunday goodbye,' and with a quick wave she was gone.

As Olivia looked down at the card the smile left her face, it read Mr R L Gregson. Optician. The rest was a blur, he was married, what a fool she had been, married and his wife was to have child, how could he. Quickly getting an envelope and a pad she wrote him a note. It read:

Richard your wife called in today to invite me to your mum and dad's for Sunday evening. How you must have laughed at the way you took me in, making love to me, yes you were economical with the truth as you were over creampuff you certainly had me fooled. Was the ring to pay for my favours? However, I was being genuine. I love you but I will in no way have an affair with you, or treat your wife as you have. I will not get my happiness by spoiling someone else's life I can't believe you have sunk so low, stay with your wife and be a good father. And don't try and contact, me I never want to see you ever again. I'm leaving your ring here, you perhaps will get a refund on it unless you give it to the next unsuspecting fool, for this time I could in no way forgive you. Olivia. P.S. To prove I know your wife she gave me this card.

Taking the van keys off her key ring and putting them in the drawer she gathered the days orders and checked that there wasn't, any orders to be put up today and that Nicole and Sadie could both work, full-time for her until further notice. She needed to get away and get her head together, she would ask the agency to send someone in to do the deliveries for them there was a nice young man named Ron that had been sent before. She would adjust their wages accordingly and they were paid directly into their bank.

Olivia had made up her mind that she would go to her mum's, she only lived a bus ride away and she would make sure that they did not give Richard any information to where she was. Hopefully, when she had got her mind together and was able to be strong minded, she would go back. By the time he realised she meant what she said he would be looking elsewhere for his entertainment. But for now, she needed to lick her wounds. Once the girls arrived, she explained what she was doing and they insisted they would be fine but they would miss her being with them, and hoped she would be back soon. They also promised to give Richard the envelope and would not let him know where she was. She also couldn't tell them what had happened because she would end up crying and she didn't want that. Olivia realised that this was why he had not introduced her as his fiancée to his mum and dad when they were in the shop. Sadie looked at her and realised something had really upset her for Olivia was white as a sheet.

'We've got everything,' if we need to know any details, we can ring you to get them, we've got your phone number so you needn't worry about anything just come back soon'.

'I will, I just need to get my head together; would you ring for a taxi for me please Sadie. I don't feel like using the bus. Once Sadie rang it only took a few minutes for it to arrive right.

'I'll keep in touch I just need to get away. I'll get mum to pop in now and again,' giving both of them a hug she said, 'you both are the best friends that anyone could have'.

As she got into the taxi, she asked the driver to take her to her flat and wait for her, she would not be long. Going up she quickly packed a few clothes, checked everything was secure and made her way back down and climbed back into the taxi.

Once she arrived at home, she broke down in her mother's arms, crying for what seemed hours to her. Her mother soothed her fears, 'it might seem the end of the world now, but in years to come you will look back and laugh at this because you are lovely and someone, one day, will love you and they will be a far better person, you have done the right thing. It's his wife I feel sorry for'.

'Thanks mum, I know I will get over him it's just that he has hurt me so much. I know I'm strong I just need to be somewhere where I know I'm loved and cared about and that's here'.

CHAPTER SEVEN

At four o'clock Richard walked in as usual for his coffee, 'hello girls. Where is Olivia, in the back?' he said with a broad smile.

'No,' Sadie said as Nicole looked on, 'she's not here, she left you this envelope'.

'Is she not well?

'She's fine, just taking some time off.' Sadie replied giving him a measured look.

Sensing there was something wrong he slit the envelope open, the first thing he saw was his ring, the smile left his face, it felt as if someone had hit him in the stomach. Pulling the note out the small card that she had given to her from the blonde young woman fell out. Stooping to retrieve it he noticed it was his brothers Robert's business card, reading the note his face changed, 'the stupid girl I could put her over my knee if she was here. Where has she gone, home?'

'No, it was Sadie who once more who took control, there's no way you would be able to contact her, she's staying elsewhere'.

'What do you mean',' she staying at her Mother's" have you her address?'

'No!'

'You must be able to contact her'.

'No, she has arranged everything to run smoothly, the internet is a wonderful thing to bank and do wages and order stock. Besides her mother will call periodically to check everything is running smoothly'.

Taking out his business card he gave it to Sadie, 'would you give this to Olivia's mother and tell her it's vital that she rings me on this number and despite what you are thinking I in no way would hurt Olivia. She unfortunately has got her facts wrong and if I can't contact her it will cause both of us great deal of unnecessary pain that we could avoid and both do without. If you do speak to Olivia tell her she will need to apologise and grovel to me big time'. With that he turned and left the shop with a grim look on his face.

Three weeks had passed and Richard was no further forward in finding out where Olivia was, he was beginning to think she really believed that he had no morals, when all he wanted to do was for him to have her back in his arms. She had hurt him because she could have waited and asked for an explanation and it would have not reached this point. Now he didn't know if he would ever be able to point out she was wrong. He knew he had fibbed about creampuff, but that had been a white lie, he had just wanted something in common to talk about as he had fallen in love with her the moment, he set eyes on her.

Looking down at the papers on his desk he just couldn't concentrate on the task in hand, he was trying to compare the figures for his other three shops. At that moment there was a knock on the door.

'Come in he said,' the door opened and his receptionist said, 'you have a lady to see you'.

'I don't recall having any appointments this afternoon, are you sure it's not one of Robert's clients?'

'No, she asked for Richard Gregson'.

'Okay Denise show her in'.

'Clearing the papers on his desk he stood to greet the woman as she walked in'.

'He was amazed when the woman who walked in was an older version of Olivia, the same coloured hair although a little faded and the same almond shaped green eyes, she would have been as beautiful as Olivia at one time but now she was still lovely, just a little like a faded flower'. However, she still had a determined look on her face.

'You must be Olivia's mum I'm so glad that you are here'.

'You might not be when I have finished with you Mr Gregson, do you think I will believe your lies? How could you treat your wife in the fashion that you have, let alone broken my daughter's heart, I'm sure you wouldn't be married for long if we informed your wife about the affair that Olivia unwittingly was having with you'.

Could you please sit-down Mrs Bancroft, this is getting us nowhere fast?'

Picking up the phone he said, 'Denise if Barbara is free could you please ask her to come into my office and then could you get me coffee for three in case Barbara would like a cup'.

'Now I understand why you are like a tiger protecting its cub. I would be the same if I had any children, but it's not my fault if Olivia has got her facts wrong'.

'I fail to understand how she would have them wrong Mr Gregson'.

At that point a young blonde woman walked in, 'did you want me Richard?'

'Barbara did you or did you not take my mother's invitation for Sunday lunch to Olivia?'

'Yes of course I did'.

'Well this is Olivia's mother, could you tell her who you are married to?'

'Well you could have told her yourself. I'm married to your brother Robert, what a strange question to ask'.

'Did you tell her you were married to me? Married to you no! I 'just gave her Roberts card and issued the invitation I was in a hurry or I would have loved to chat to the woman who could take Robert's big brother's mind off work and was looking forward to her asking me to be a bridesmaid, hopefully before junior shows too much. 'Now I need to go and finish the eye test and hopefully I'll be seeing Olivia's mother again cheerio Mrs Bancroft'.

'It seems as if I owe you an apology Mr Gregson'.

'You don't need to apologise and my name is Richard and I'll be happy to call you Mum as I intend to marry Olivia even if she did think badly of me. I love her and hope you will allow me to go to her as soon as possible to put things right. I will forgive her anything, I can't say it hasn't hurt me, but it would hurt me more being without her. So, if you would tell me where she is, I will pick creampuff up and we will go and put things right'.

'Creampuff!'

'Yes, it was through Creampuff that I met her, so I know he loves her as well and it's been a whole month since he's seen her. And if you have time, I will take you to my mum's for coffee so you can get to know her before the wedding while I go to sort things out with Olivia'.

'Well Richard, my husband John has gone to London on business and I'm sure you and Olivia have lots to talk about and I'll only be in the way so yes I'd love to'.

'I'll give you my key in case she sees you arrive and has a mind not too let you in, you know what women are like'.

'I can't say I did, but I certainly do now. Many more situations like this and I'll be old before my time. That's why the sooner I get my ring on her finger the sooner I shall have peace of mind'.

Picking his phone up he rang Denise his receptionist to tell her he would be out for the rest of the day and to ask Robert to lock up for him and that he wouldn't be in for a couple of days, could she rearrange his appointments possibly between Robert, Barbara and Theo please'.

'Right let's get you to my mum's. I can pick creampuff up, and get around to your house and I promise things will be fine when we pick you up. Perhaps mum will do tea for us after or I could take us out for a meal'.

'We'll see about that, because John could be in around nine o'clock and I like to be in when he arrives home. And I'm sure that if our only daughter is to be married, he would like to be involved'.

'Well there's nothing wrong with you and mum throwing some idea's around while you are chatting this afternoon is there? Come on let's make tracks the sooner I get to Olivia the sooner this mess will be cleared up'.

Bringing the car to a halt on the drive of a large mock Tudor style house he was quickly out of the car and helping her out of the passenger side, holding her arm he led her to the front door and was soon ushering her to the lounge where his mum and dad were sitting and reading the paper's.

'Mum this is Olivia's mum,' looking at her for her first name.

'Sophie my names Sophie'.

'We are so pleased to meet you and at the same time looking towards her son and asking have you sorted the misunderstanding out?'

'No but I'm about to go now. And if Olivia's mum stays and has coffee with you while I go and see Olivia as you two ladies have quite a task arranging our wedding: the sooner the better. Now mum I'm going to take cream-puff with me, I will look after him'.

'You better do or else there will be trouble, if you lost him again there might not be another Olivia to find him'.

'Well you will have to punish me later or not at all. I think I've suffered enough already, don't you?'

Picking up creampuff he quickly made his way to his car and then to Olivia's mums house.

'Well here goes,' he said to Creampuff, 'do your best for me'.

Inserting the key in the lock and opening it up he walked in and quietly shut the door behind him fondling Creampuffs ears he said go and find Olivia. Meow, meow, Creampuff gave out his strange cry and ran with tail in the air towards a slightly open door off the hall. He suddenly heard Olivia's voice where did you came from and how did you get in. Pushing the door open he said, 'through the front door'.

'How did you get in,' she snapped not smiling? 'With a key, to be precise your mother's key. Now if you make me a coffee it will give my hands something to do because I am itching to put you across my knee'.

'Why have you come here! Does your wife know?'

'No because once and for all I don't have a wife, and I've never been married'.

'How do I know you are telling the truth?

Taking two small cards out of his pocket he placed them on the table, 'here is the one with your address written on it, can you remember the first time you had me to the flat for dinner? I wrote it on my card'.

'Here, what does it say Mr R.W. Gregson, now what does this card have on the back?'

'My mother's address, it was given to you by the woman you appear to think is my wife. Now look at the name on the card, what does it say looking at it she said Mr R. L. Gregson. Does anything strike you as different?'

Looking at the card she was about to say, 'no, oh the second initial is different'.

'Did it not occur to you there was another Mr Gregson working at the opticians, Barbara is my brother Roberts wife'.

Tears began to gather on her lower eyelid and suddenly began to fall like a tiny diamond falling on to her cheeks and running to the corner of her mouth. Quickly he was on his feet pulling her into his arms, 'don't cry sweetheart I'll never stop loving you. I can't say I wasn't hurt that you couldn't talk to me about what you thought, because it would have saved both of us a lot of heartache and hurt. That's why I intend to get a wedding ring on your finger as soon as I can'.

Bending his head, he began to gently kiss her on the lips and eyes taking out his handkerchief he dried the tears from her face, now my coffee I think Creampuff is feeling left out and needs a cuddle from you. But first is there something you want back?'

Nodding her head as tears appeared once more on her lashes Richard took her left hand and slipped her engagement ring back on her finger and in one move-ment lifted it to his lips, kissing her fingers. Pulling her tighter in his arms he said, 'you are staying at my home with me tonight. I won't have you leave my side until we are wed please,' he asked.

Nodding her head, she said, 'I can't wait'.

'Barbara wants to know if she can be a bridesmaid? I'd love her to be'.

'Richard I'm so sorry I jumped to conclusions I should have given you the benefit of doubt. I can't believe you have forgiven me'.

'I have you back that's all that matters. Now how about that coffee, we could take it into the lounge do you think, a cuddle perhaps?' he said raising his eyebrows.

'I'd love that, I still can't believe what an idiot I've been. Please you have to believe me I didn't know you had a brother'.

'I know love now let's forget it ever happened, Okay I just want a cuddle please come on. Because we will have to pick your mum up soon and we will be extremely busy for the next week and perhaps won't have much time to ourselves, we have a wedding to arrange. My mum is over the moon she had given up on me ever getting married. 'I know she'll really love you. But we will have the nights on our own because you will be staying at my house until we get married. So, come here just for half an hour,' sitting down and pulling her to him he held her close resting his cheek on her head. They were still sitting there when John, Olivia's dad arrived back home. Her mother had rung and asked if he could get back a little earlier as she would like him to come over to Richard's mums to meet them both. It was Creampuff that had most to say as he met him at the lounge door.

Eight weeks later Olivia became Mrs Richard Gregson, Barbara, Robert's wife, was Maid of Honour along with Nicole and Robert was his best man. As the vicar said you may kiss the bride, he bent to kiss his new wife and whispered this is the first day of the rest of our life.

Mountain View

Sarah split up from her boyfriend, and went on holiday to reflect on her life, going for a solitary walk on a cliff-top she took a few minutes to rest and to eat. Relaxing afterwards she fell asleep and did not realise that a dog called Dexter would introduce her to true love, okay Dexter you can have another five minutes with your lady friend but no more.

Mountain View

By Barbara Anne Machin

Chapter One

Sarah Jane stopped on the path completely out of breath, it had been a steep climb and her trainers were beginning to hurt her. Sitting down on the path she gently eased her shoe away from her foot she had a huge blister appearing on her ankle bone.

Pulling off her rucksack she rummaged around for a plaster, only to find she hadn't packed any before she came out of the small hotel that she had checked into. Taking off her trainer so that it gave her a little more relief. She decided to have her sandwiches where she was sitting and give her foot a rest.

Pouring a coffee out of her small flask she sat and ate a sandwich looking across the cliffs, she felt as if she was sitting on a mountain instead of on the cliff top path. The gulls were calling out in the blue sky, the grass at the side of the path was a velvet green, sighing she put her sandwiches back in her rucksack and decided to have a little rest before she made her way back to the hotel. Using her rucksack as a pillow she leant back and closed her eyes. The sun was hot and although she did not mean to, Sarah soon fell asleep. Suddenly she awoke to a wet tongue licking her face.

'Stop!' she cried, 'get off you,' she was still half asleep and struggling to sit up. At that moment she heard a sharp whistle and a man's voice shouted, 'heel Dexter, heel boy'.

But Dexter was not going to obey this time, he was to inquisitive and reluctant to leave his new friend, however he decided to make his master aware of where he was, giving a sharp burst of barking. Suddenly a shadow of a tall man appeared in the darkness.

'Dexter what have you got there?' Peering down in the darkness he made out the outline of Sarah, 'for goodness sake. what are you doing on the cliffs on your own in the dark, your stupid girl?'

Bending down to take a closer look, 'you've hurt your foot,' he said in a gentler voice. 'Could you not walk?' he asked as he bent to examine her foot.

Pulling her foot away she said, 'no I haven't hurt my foot and no I'm not stupid, I have a blister'.

'You have a blister, so you decided to stay here until it went dark?' he said scornfully. 'Well if that's not stupid I don't know what is?'

'Tell me,' said Sarah, 'are you rude to everyone that you meet'.

'No, not everyone, only the people that make stupid decisions and endangering themselves'.

'Now do you think you can put your shoe's back on?'

'Yes,' she replied, 'so you can go wherever you were going, to I can manage'. With that she grabbed her sock and began to pull it on but you could tell by the grimace she gave it hurt, and when it came to her trainer it was obvious that it hurt like hell.

'Here,' he said pulling her to her feet, he then reached for her haversack putting it on his back.

'What are you doing?' Sarah demanded, her cheeks red with embarrassment?

'Well you can't stay here,' he said without a smile.

'No, I can't but I can make my way back down!'

'I don't think so these cliffs are dangerous in the dark.' and with that he lifted her up in his arms.

'Where are you taking me?' she asked, beginning to struggle.

'Where you won't hurt yourself, or fall down a cliff never to be heard of again'.

'I can assure you that you are quite safe where I am taking you, we can get you back to your hotel in the morning'.

'But surely, they will miss me'.

'I'll ring them when we get home'.

'Your home not mine.'

'Yes, but that's the only option open to you. Now stop pecking my head woman'.

'Dexter heel,' he shouted, this time Dexter was happy to do as he was told and trotted contentedly by his side. He was a large red setter with big brown eyes, his tongue lolling out of his mouth as he walked. Sarah fell silent, and suddenly realized that whoever he was he had a bad limp, and she must be heavy.

'Put me down I can walk, it must be hurting your leg'.

'Do shut up,' he said, 'or else I will be wishing I had left you where you were'.

'You should have,' she exclaimed, anger getting the better of her, 'anything would be preferable to your company'.

'Likewise!' he said, suddenly there was a light ahead, walking up to a walled drive he placed her on her feet while he opened the gates. Picking her up once more and depositing her inside the gates enabling him to close them behind them.

'We are nearly there,' he said. On reaching the door he opened it and carried her to the settee and plonked her down. In the light of the room she saw that he was tall and slim with dark brown hair and grey eyes. Walking over to the phone he said, 'where are you staying?'

'At the Smuggler's Inn'.

Picking up the phone he dialled a number, 'hello Janine it's Jeremy here, you have a young lady booked in with you her name is…' at this he paused and said, 'what is your name?' he asked lifting his eyebrows.

'Sarah Jane Hamilton'.

'Sarah Hamilton.' he said, 'she's here at Whitehaven Cottage and she won't be down tonight. I'll bring her down in the morning in the land rover'. He then started a conversation between him and the person named Janine on the other end of the line, 'of course Janine we'll discuss that as planned tomorrow night, but I will be down around eleven in the morning for my meeting, goodnight love'. With that he replaced the handset on to the cradle.

'Right let me have a look at that foot'.

'No, its fine,' Sarah said, her stubborn streak coming to the fore.

So, Jeremy as he called himself walked into the kitchen, ignoring her he returned within five minutes, a towel over his arm and a bowl of water containing TCP. Taking hold of her foot he placed it into the water, and began to wash it, the TCP stung the blister where it had rubbed the skin raw, he then dried her foot and began to examine the damage. Taking a small sharp scalpel, he burst the blister cleaned it and put a dressing on with a plaster over it to keep it in place.

'There, you'll live,' he said. 'Hungry?' he asked, looking up at her for the first time, noticing her dark chestnut hair falling to the nape of her neck, one side turned under neatly and the other flicked up. The eyes he looked into were a dark chocolate brown, however she looked a little unsure of herself.

'Yes,' she nodded, 'a little'.

'Okay, I'll see what I can rustle up'.

Sarah looked around the room it was neat and tidy, the floor was polished wood with a huge Persian rug covering most of it. The settee and the armchairs were huge and comfortable in antique green leather. A book-case lined the far wall, full of books, a writing desk on the other, a side table held a phone and bowl of pink roses and in an alcove, a cross hung on the wall.

Comfortable and understated, a huge log fire was burning in the grate, she must have got quite chilly lying on the grass as the warmth was making her sleepy. It was just as well that Jeremy as he had announced himself on the phone, came back in with a bowl of hot stew on a tray with a slice of crusty bread. He placed it on the coffee table beside her, 'can you manage?' he asked her, 'or would you prefer to sit in the dining room'.

'I'm fine here,' she answered. 'Right, eat up and I'll find you something to sleep in'. He stood up and she couldn't help but notice his limp was more pronounced now, feeling very guilty he had carried her quite a distance.

Leaving the room, he was gone long enough for her to eat most of the stew, however she couldn't manage the bread. Sarah didn't dare to close her eyes for she knew that if she did, she would drift asleep, just as she had on the pathway. Until now she hadn't realized how tired she was, after splitting up with her latest boyfriend a doctor who worked at the same hospital as she did, she had burnt the candle at both ends. So, when her holiday came up, she decided to take a quiet walking holiday, thinking it would be restful. Some rest she thought she was more exhausted than if she had been clubbing. At that moment he returned carrying a large man's white shirt.

'You'll just have to roll the sleeves up, now the bathroom is to the left and the bedroom you can use is the one with the door slightly open'.

When she gazed back at him, he hastened to say, 'there is a bolt on both the bathroom door and the bedroom, feel free to lock them'.

'Thank you,' she answered.

'Take your other shoe off and leave them there, if you want a book to read help yourself,' and he nodded towards the bookcase.

'Thanks, but I think I'll go off like a light. I am quite tired'.

'Good night then,' he said with a slight smile. Making her way upstairs she located the bathroom had a quick shower and put the shirt on. She had to smile at her reflection in the mirror, she certainly didn't look sexy like the star's did in the movies it just looked miles to big, folding her clothes she opened the bathroom door and peered along the landing, she had no intention of him seeing her in his shirt. Eyes darting along the corridor she saw a door slightly open, so she quickly went in, however she paused in the doorway the sound of the five tenor's floated up the stairs. Locking the door, she looked around and saw the room was neat and tidy with a double bed, the bed covers matched the curtains in cream, the carpet a shade of coffee, the walls plain magnolia. Slipping into bed she snuggled down in between the fresh smelling sheets. Sarah fell asleep the moment she laid her head on the pillow.

Chapter Two

Sarah awoke with the sun streaming through her open window, she reached for her watch on the bedside table, looking at the time she saw that she had overslept, it was ten fifteen. What must he think of her sleeping on the pathway, going to bed as soon as she had eaten the food, he gave her and now sleeping late? She must be upsetting his routine. Thinking back to her argument with Richard her boyfriend who she worked with, it had been a little tiring and it was uncomfortable working closely together so it had prompted her to give a month's notice. Guiltily she leapt out of bed and quietly went to the bathroom, after just a quick wash and dressing herself quite quickly she realized she had no comb with her. So, she tried to pull her fingers through her hair to tame her locks. She decided to brave going downstairs.

Wrinkling her nose, she could smell bacon, Jeremy Brent was sitting at the table drinking coffee. 'Ah! Did you sleep well?'

'Yes, thank you,' she said quietly thinking she must have put him out. 'Thank you for letting me stay.' she forced out. he had been rude to her but she had been rude back, and to be fair he had allowed her to stay the night.

'No problem,' he replied, 'but next time make sure you are aware of the dangers of being on a dangerous cliff top in the dark, would you like some breakfast?'

'Just a cup of coffee and a slice of toast if I may'.

Looking at her he said, 'the toaster is there and there's coffee in the pot'.

He certainly wasn't going to get her breakfast. Looking at her he thought on reflection she was quite attractive however he found himself smiling at her unruly hair. Turning at that moment she had to ask, 'what are you laughing at?'

He just held a comb up saying, 'perhaps you would like to borrow this'.

Taking the comb, she asked, 'is there a mirror in the hall'. Walking out into the hallway and looking at her reflection her hair was standing on end. Going back into the kitchen after combing her hair, she said, 'Thank you' handing him back his comb, 'You have your breakfast and I'll get the land rover out he said and then we can get you back to your hotel'.

Sarah felt comfortable sitting in his kitchen and as he got up and walked away, she noticed again his pronounced limp, and sat wondering what he had done. Jeremy noticed the look of pity and that slight friendliness vanished. Leaving the room. It was a good thirty minutes before he reappeared. Sarah was standing at the sink washing the plate and cup she had used, she sensed that he had entered the room but she did not turn around, then she felt Dexter's tail thumping against her leg as he stood by her, bending down she ruffled his ears and snuggled up.

Then Jeremy Brent's voice broke the silence. 'you're a lucky chap Dexter I almost wish I was a dog'. Staring at him standing in the doorway Sarah locked eyes and her heart began to flutter and try as she might she couldn't look away. Feeling her cheeks go red he was the first to turn to a cabinet on the wall taking out the small bowl and antiseptic, 'let's just look at that foot, shall we?'. 'Must we,' Sarah asked? She had only just managed to get the shoe on as it still hurt her when the heel dragged against the back of her ankle.

Putting some TCP in the bowl along with some warm water, he began to cut a new dressing taking her shoe off and peeling her sock off, he placed her foot in the water and began to bathe her foot. Drying her foot on a towel he said, 'just keep your foot there a moment,' dispensing of the water and TCP he bent once more to dress the blister. It was not as sore looking as last night but it still needed the dressing. Once this was done, he picked up her trainer and left the room. A few minutes later he returned with a pair of thick socks and some more trainer's, he said, 'these will be better, they are a size larger'. Lifting her foot up and resting it on his leg he proceeded to put a pair of what appeared to be his socks on her feet disposing of hers inside the discarded trainer's. Gently placing the bigger trainers on her feet, she had to admit her foot was a lot more comfortable.

'Thank you', Sarah said, her voice sounded strange to her, he was playing havoc with her thoughts, all the time he was kneeling before her with his head bent, she wanted to lean across and feel his hair. Suddenly he looked up and caught her looking at him, at once making her blush crimson, there appeared to be a strange look in his eyes.

Picking up her trainer's he said, 'we had better go. I have a meeting in town, can you manage in them?'

Sarah whispered 'yes', she would be glad when she was back in her hotel room so that she could get back to normal, or will I! Her mind said. They had not spoken to each other very much, but the time she had spent with him she had felt comfortable and safe.

Outside he helped her into the front of the Land Rover placing her haversack and trainers on the back seat, Dexter jumped in and immediately pushed his head between the seats resting it against Sara's arm. Looking at his dog and raising his eyebrow's once more he said, 'it looks as if our Dexter is smitten', all the time looking at her face.

Driving down the cliff path Sarah stared across at the steep fall down to the sea, to her it looked more like a mountain view than a cliff top view. She could see why he didn't want her to wander down the path in the dark. Remembering how rude she had been to him she was a little ashamed of herself, he had been helpful and kind.

Pulling up outside of the inn he came around to the passenger side and helped her out, reaching for her haversack and trainer's he said, 'can you manage now?'

'Yes, thanks and I do appreciate what you have done for me, I will return the trainer's'.

'Any time will do they are an old pair my sister left when she was visiting'.

Walking into the inn Sarah made her way to her room the moment the young woman came around the bar and made her way across to Jeremy Brent. Why it bothered her, Sarah wasn't sure; but it did.

Once inside her room Sarah stripped her clothes off and found a fresh-looking blue summer dress it had a round neck, cap sleeves and a skirt, flared from the hips. Fastening a white belt around her waist she found herself a pair of white mule's that left her heels exposed so that they didn't rub her heel, the dressing on her foot was visible however she would be able to walk around the shops in comfort, she brushed her hair into submission

She tied it up into a pony tail, a touch of lipstick made her feel more human.

Going into the lounge of the inn she ordered a coffee, sitting herself at a table she watched the door that said private to the inns private rooms the door opened and the girl named Janine half opened the door speaking to someone inside, the next moment Dexter was jumping up with his paws, 'well hello my darling,' she crooned. Moving his paws and allowing Sarah to scratch his ears as he rested his head on her knee. At that moment a vicar walked out followed by Jeremy. Sarah's heart plummeted to her feet, why she didn't know, was it because he was going to marry Janine. Sarah suddenly felt like a love-struck teenager. At twenty-eight, she was far from being a teenager and had already had a string of boyfriends, and each relationship had failed. Perhaps she was too fussy, this was the first time that she had looked at someone and had these feelings and he appeared to be spoken for. Shaking hands with the vicar he had been talking too he looked around and clearly called, 'heel Dexter,' however Dexter let out a little bark and did not move from her knee.

Looking up he saw Sarah sitting and Dexter resting his head on her knee. Walking over he looked down at her and said, 'what is it about you two? Dexter boy, you are well and truly smitten. Come on now me lad'.

Dexter looked up and placed his head back. 'Okay! Okay! I get it, five more minutes'. Looking over at Janine who smiled at him.

'I'll have a coffee while he is with his lady friend for another five minutes'.

Pointing to the seat at the side of her he said, 'may I?'

Sarah nodded her head, and not moving her hand from Dexter's head the longer she kept her hand there the longer he would stay by her side, childishly she wished he would stay with her forever. Janine walked over with his coffee. 'What's wrong with Dexter he has never left you to hang around me' she said with a smile?

'He's well and truly smitten and he's not the only one,' he said looking up at Janine causing a pain where Sarah's heart was. Smiling at Sarah he said, 'we must be going after this coffee as I have some work to do for Sunday, and if Dexter refuses to come home you will have to come back with us. Well he said raising his eyebrows'.

Picking up his coffee cup he drained it. Sarah said, 'well he will have to visit me another day, won't you my darling?

'Who me? said Jeremy?

'No Dexter'.

'Now be a good boy Dexter and I might see you tomorrow, go with your master'.

'It's Jeremy you know, you can call me by my name'.

'Yes', Sarah said, her brown eye's locking with his making her heart do somersaults. Picking up her bag and sun glasses, quickly turning so that he couldn't read the confusion in her eyes. Just at that moment a voice said, 'Sarah darling at last! Your mum and dad told me where you were'.

'Richard,' she breathed staring at him. 'I had to come darling,' he said looking into her eyes, then noticing Jeremy at her side he asked, 'are you going to introduce me to your friend?'

'I'm sorry, this is Jeremy Brent', and before she could finish her sentence, he finished it for her. Dr Richard Carrington, I'm Sarah's fiancée'.

'But...' Sarah began!

'No but's darling. it was a silly argument and we need to talk and get over it'.

Sarah stared at him in amazement, 'well of all'.

'Not here darling,' looking at Jeremy who was no longer smiling, 'let's take a walk'.

'Walking along the pavement beside her he held her arm'.

'What part of we are through did you not understand Richard? I am no longer your fiancée and have no wish to become so again. What happened, did your little nurse not come up with the goods?'

'Because how I caught you, I was sure she was going to give you what I hadn't'.

'Sarah, it was a moment of madness, you know that it's you that I love'.

'No Richard, you only love yourself and always have. Now take yourself back to Warrington and accept gracefully you are not wanted, in other words go back to your little nurse'.

'Well I will be staying the night at the inn, if you change your mind after thinking about it, I will still be there in the morning'.

Walking away Sarah was inwardly fuming, now Jeremy thought she was engaged, and she thought looking into his eyes earlier she had recognized a mutual liking, now there was no chance that she would find out because he now had the wrong impression about Richard and her.

Sarah made her way along the pavement walking quickly, all the time hoping Richard would not follow. Making sure he hadn't Sarah meandered amongst the holidaymaker's window shopping. Stopping outside a book shop she looked in the window at the books display. On impulse she thought she would buy Jeremy a book as a thank you and she would post it to him from the post office she had passed further down the street .Going in she perused the books, having noticed that Jeremy appeared to be interested in theology, there had been several books on the subject in his bookcase, asking for that section she spent a good thirty minutes browsing until she found a leather bound red book on the theory of religion. Sarah wasn't sure if it would be something he would read however the thought was there. Walking out of the shop she began to look for something for her mum it was her birthday soon. Sarah only had another week of her vacation and she had to return to Southport. It was now late September there had been an Indian summer. It had been quite warm when she had walked up the cliff pathway, the sun had been so hot that was the reason she had fell asleep. Sarah stopped outside a lingerie shop, slipping in she managed to get her Mum a nightgown and a robe to match. Now just a small present for dad and her sister Gwen and she was done.

The next day Sarah came down dressed in her jeans and sweater it felt a little colder today but she intended to drive further out and see a little more of the area, she had not slept very well because she kept thinking about Jeremy Brent. Sarah had decided that she would spend today exploring and tomorrow she would make her way up the cliff path and return Jeremy's sister's trainer's. Jumping in her car she had not been aware that Dexter had spotted her and broke into a trot but too late she drove off. Looking up and whining, Jeremy fondled Dexter's head and said, 'never mind old chap I'm disappointed as well. We have another day it won't hurt for either of us to wait'.

Sarah returned from her day out quite late, going straight to her room she decided to pack to leave, having realized that her feeling's for Jeremy Brent were stronger than they ought to be, and in view if the fact that he appeared to be very close to Janine it would be wrong of her to visit him at his cottage, and of course there had been the meeting with the vicar it seemed most likely that they were to be married. So, she had decided to leave the trainers at the pub, along with the book and a thank you note she would leave early to avoid Richard.

Rising early so she could avoid some of the traffic and make sure she went before Richard came down, standing by the bar and ringing the bell she waited until a man appeared, she had not seen him before and he reminded her of someone.

'Can I pay my account please, yes of course I didn't know you were leaving today',

'No, I decided last night?'

'Have you had some breakfast?'

'No, I don't want anything to eat, but I could manage a cup of coffee'.

'Of course,' he answered going through to the back room he came back with pot of coffee on a tray with cream.

'You sit and have that and I'll make your account up'.

Five minutes later he placed the account on to the table, 'there you are.'

'Thank you.' said Sarah, 'I'll just finish my coffee and bring it to you'. So, finishing her coffee then picking the account up she extracted the money from her bag and at the same time she took the neat parcel and said, 'could you pass this on for me please, I'm sure he will be in'.

Just when he was about to answer she heard Janine's voice shout. 'Opening the door'.

He shouted, 'coming,' by which time Sarah had picked up her case and was opening the door closing it gently after herself. Turning to Janine he explained that their guest had left and she left our Jeremy a parcel.

'Did you ask her for her address?'

'Now why should I Have done that,' he asked, 'because while you have been away, I think your big brother has fallen in love'.

'Now you're kidding,' he said.

'No,' Janine replied, 'even Dexter has got it bad'. '

'And I've let her go without knowing, let's hope that he had the sense to find out where she lives. I was beginning to think it would never happen'.

When Richard came down five minutes later, he asked the man at the desk if Sarah Hamilton had got up, 'she left five minutes ago sir'.

'Can I pay for my night's stay then,' again it was the gentleman who served Richard and he had no idea that he could give them the address for Sarah, when the penny dropped Richard had left, he knew he was in big trouble.

Around ten o'clock Jeremy walked into the inn, Dexter ran around looking as if he lost something, 'has

Sarah come down yet,' he asked' its Dexter?' he said in answer to the look that Janine gave him.

'She left,' his brother said.

'left?' Jeremy breathed, 'did you get her address?' he asked.

'No, she only signed the register, she never wrote her address in the book'.

'What about a telephone number?

Looking in the book he said, 'No, why?'

'Because,' Jeremy said! 'Well what about Richard Carrington he would know?'

'Dam,' Harry said. 'He asked if she had come down. I didn't know she was your lady friend'.

'She left before he came down'.

'It's okay, it wasn't meant to be. I was too slow, you know me; she even stayed the night at the cottage and I didn't see fit to ask her where she came from'.

'Perhaps she will visit again.'

'No, you idiot I won't be here, will I? Come on Dexter boy it looks as if your lady friend was short lived'.

'I'll see you tomorrow, I have to go to visit the hospital today and I thought I would invite Sarah to lunch after'.

'So, Dexter we will be lunching alone'.

'See you later Harry, Janine'. With that he made for the door Leaving Harry and Janine wishing that they had more of an eye for detail, they had never known Jeremy to be so interested in anyone. But would it have come to anything the good Doctor had declared he was engaged to Sarah so why had she not waited for him? And Sarah hadn't seemed that happy to see him.

CHAPTER THREE

Sarah made her way on to the motorway to return to Southport, she had told her parent's that she had left her job in the hospital at Warrington and she had already applied for the position of social worker at the Southport University Hospital and had both her first and second interview, There had been quite a few applicants, so she was looking in other areas as well. Pulling of at a motorway services to have a coffee break her mind once more returned to Jeremy Brent and the time when she saw him with the vicar at the pub. She had only known him for a few days and it amazed her at how safe and comfortable she felt with him. She thought she had seen something in his eyes as he looked at her and little things he'd said. She was beginning to think he had started to like her. Now she told herself you were completely wrong, perhaps it was wishful thinking. She needed to pull herself together and get on with her life, perhaps it was yet another failed relationship that was making her feel this way.

Pulling up outside her parent's home Sarah sat for a few moments to collect her thoughts before she went in. Taking her haversack, she went in to be greeted by her sister and parents. Gwen was younger than Sarah and excitedly said, 'there's a letter for you Sarah, well two really'. Taking the letter's off Gwen she noticed one was

Richards handwriting, so she just put that down without opening it, the other was from Southport University Hospital. Ripping it open the words danced before her eyes, your application has been successful and they were offering her the position she had applied for. Well at least something has turned out well. Sarah was to start in on the twenty-first of October, this would give her a little time to adjust and get her Christmas shopping done, sitting in the chair she briefly looked at Richard's letter then ripped it up and threw it in the bin. He was saying he was sorry and wanted to get back together.

'No chance,' she said. 'He called to find out where you were, I know I told him it was all over'.

'Are you sure Sarah?' her mum asked.

'Positive Mum'.

'Well you don't look too happy dear'.

Sarah's mum was her best friend so she found herself telling her mum about what had happened on the cliff,'

'Oh! Sarah he was quite right to tell you off'.

'I know that now Mum but I think I felt such a fool because he was right and I was quite rude to him'.

'But he was so kind after and nice'.

'Carrying me all that way must have hurt his leg'.

'And I know I had only just met him, but I thought he liked me and then I realized he must be marrying the girl at the pub named Janine'.

'Did he tell you love?'

'No, but when he took me back to the pub, he went into the back room with her and when they came out, they were with a vicar and he shook hands with him'.

'So, what else would they have been discussing?'

'Well once you get back to work this fancy will pass. After all, if it was meant to be it would have happened, settle down to your job and if things are to happen what will be will be'.

'You're right as usual Mum thanks for listening to me. Is there any hot water I need a bath?

'Of course, there is love, you go up and I'll get you something to eat?'

'Thanks Mum you're a gem'.

Sarah had settled into hospital life once more and she made quite a few new friends who were trying to get her to have a night out with them, but she hadn't felt like socializing since she had been on her holiday to Cornwall. Sarah in her quiet moments still thought about Jeremy and Dexter, she knew now that she had fallen for Jeremy and there was nothing, she could do about it. She would just have to get on with life. It was just her luck the one man she felt she could love was perhaps married now. Sitting the next day filling forms in with a patient who had no support when she went home, Sarah noticed someone walk past the bed, looking up there was no mistaking the height and his limp; it was Jeremy, she was just about to speak to him when she realized that Janine was at his side, no good was to come of it if she spoke to him. So, turning her back she asked the patient to sign the form and she quietly left the ward and returned to her office, determined to stay there until visiting time was over. There and then she vowed she would do her work before visiting time so that she wouldn't bump into him again. Sarah had begun to settle down now and seeing Jeremy only made her more aware of how she felt he was forbidden fruit and she tried hard to push him into the back of her mind. She had always been quite strong minded so she was determined to put this episode behind her.

It was now one week until Christmas, Sarah and her mum were constantly in a whirl of shopping. Her mum regularly attended the local church, Gwen had always gone with her however it had been a while since Sarah had gone because the hours at the hospital weren't always compatible. Her mum was making up shoe boxes to send abroad and Sarah, along with Gwen was helping. Gwen had been prattling on about a new vicar that had taken over their church, enthusing, 'he's quite a looker you must come to midnight mass and you'll see what I mean' she chuckled.

'Gwen behave yourself, her mum said, 'you quite worry me, is nothing sacred'.

'Oh, mum I'm only trying to get misery to come out, she never goes anywhere these days, she will be old before her time'.

'Alright! Alright! I'll make sure I will come, just stop you going on about men. My feelings are your better off without them'.

'Sarah you don't mean that, you just haven't met the right one yet,' her mum said.

'Mum, I don't think there will be a right one for me'.

'Of course, there will be, there's always someone out there for everyone'.

'No, not me Mum' Sarah said smiling, 'I'll make do with my dad'.

'I heard that,' he said from under the newspaper where he was hiding, I'll always be here for all of you, now shut up and let me get some shut eye'.

This last week before Christmas passed in a whirl of activity and Gwen and her mum and dad insisted that she got herself ready and went with them to midnight mass.

'Now we'll see what you have been waffling about Gwen, he's probably sixty, bald but kind'.

'You wait and see our Sarah, he's dreamy. A little stern but dreamy'.

Sarah sat in church and suddenly she recognized someone, well two people because who should walk in holding hands at that moment but Janine and the man who she had settled her account with at the inn. How was it possible she thought? Suddenly they turned to look at her as Dexter pushed past her parents and was lodged between them. Gwen couldn't believe it as he began to lick Sarah's face in excitement.

'Dexter!' said a familiar voice. 'I'm happy too, but you know that you are not allowed this side of the altar. However, I'll make an exception today if you Sarah will swop places with this gentleman then Dexter can sit with his lady friend'.

Swopping places with her dad Gwen looked at her in amazement as Jeremy squeezed Sarah's hand. Looking into the familiar grey eyes that were full of love, Sarah could not believe that he was here and he was dressed in a dog collar. Holding Sarah's eyes for what seemed an eternity. He then patted Dexter's head that was now firmly resting on Sarah's Knees.

Walking back to the pulpit he began by saying, 'tonight I am not going to use the sermon I prepared but I'd like to share the thought that there are lots of people through the year and at Christmas that need help. We all know the story of the good Samaritan and how there was someone lying at the side of the road, two people passed and did nothing to help, however the third was a good

Samaritan'. 'As was Dexter a few months ago, he found a young lady at the side of the path in the dark, and when I called him to me, he refused to come. However, he did let me know where he was, but insisted on staying by her side. I had the pleasure of meeting that young lady who is here tonight. She went out of mine and Dexter's life as quick as she came into it and we have been searching for her ever since, now people say that God works in mysterious ways. And this is certainly one'.

'Dexter is happily sitting with his lady friend and I hope she will stay behind after the service and give me a little of her time. So, helping people who need you can bring rewards to not only the person who stops, but also people around them. Now let us remember why we are here to give thanks for the child that was born in a stable. I have cut my sermon short, however I'm sure we are all looking forward to the carols. So, open your Hymn book at Oh little town of Bethlehem'.

At the end of the service Jeremy stood by the church door shaking the hands of congregation as they left. And as Sarah and her family approached, he took hold of both of her hands just letting go of one hand to shake hands with Sarah's mum and dad, just as Janine and Harry walked towards them. Jeremy introduced them as his sister-in-law Janine and brother Harry.

'Would you mind if I escorted Sarah back home after and introduced myself?' he asked. 'I think we have things to talk about'.

At this point Sarah's father broke in, 'not at all lad it's fine by me, can you imagine what it's like three women rattling with each other, while I try to relax after a good meal? And to cap it all Sarah mooning about over you. Perhaps I'll get a bit of peace now,' he grumbled, 'and Gwen here telling her how handsome the new vicar is, you've got your hands full now lad'.

'Well alas Gwen I'm spoken for, I hope,' he added looking at Sarah.

There was still a few of the congregation to leave and it seemed an eternity to Sarah until the last person shook Jeremy's hand. He turned to Sarah and gave her a huge smile, before turning to Janine and Harry, 'could you give us five minutes?

They both nodded, 'take as long as you like big brother'

'I will he said with a grin'.

Steering Sarah to the back room, he pulled her into his arms, 'first things first.' he said. 'I'm going to do what I wanted to do the moment I met you,' he bent his head to kiss her lips, coming up for air he said, 'please tell me you aren't engaged to Richard Carrington I couldn't bear it? You love me, don't you?' he asked, holding his breath, waiting for her answer.

'No to the first and yes to the second'.

Bending his head to kiss her again, 'we had better go and tell your family we are to be married, so your father will have one less woman to peck his head'.

'But I certainly won't mind you pecking mine,' he said as he smiled down at her. 'I've loved you from the moment I set eyes on you sweetheart. Please tell me that you loved me then'.

'Yes, because I have an ulterior motive, I love Dexter and you come as a package,' she laughed, 'That makes me yours for the rest of my life'.

Holding each other close they heard Harry's voice come on, 'Jeremy if we are to have our supper at Sarah's Mum's we had better go now'.

Holding hands, they made their way to Harry's car, soon they were pulling up outside Sarah's parents. Going into the house Sarah's mum had already cut sandwiches and laid out finger food. Jeremy couldn't believe it when Sarah admitted that she thought Jeremy was going to marry Janine'.

'What happened to your leg Jeremy,' asked Sarah. 'How did you hurt it?'

'It's not important,' Jeremy answered.

'It's...' said Harry having become serious, 'it was my fault. I went into a next door's garden when I had been warned not to, and they had a bull terrier it attacked me, Jeremy rushed in and lifted me over the fence. He took the brunt of the attack himself; his leg was mauled quite badly'.

'That's enough Harry, let's get down to the wedding, because I can't marry us, we'll have to make a few arrangements if that's okay with Dad here'. Successfully he had changed the subject, he obviously didn't like to talk about it. Sarah went to the door with them, lifting her head for Jeremy's kiss.

'Tomorrow,' he said.

Two months later Sarah married Jeremy and on discussing their honeymoon she had insisted on going back to Whitehaven Cottage, and Sarah couldn't resist taking Dexter with them. Jeremy well and truly sealed their union while they were there nine and a half months later Holly arrived, Their first baby.

Lightning Source UK Ltd.
Milton Keynes UK
UKHW012244050620
364507UK00002B/439